continued . . .

HOOKED ON EWE

HANNAH REED

BERKLEY PRIME CRIME, NEW YORK

THE BERKLEY PUBLISHING GROUP
Published by the Penguin Group
Penguin Group (USA) LLC
375 Hudson Street, New York, New York 10014

USA • Canada • UK • Ireland • Australia • New Zealand • India • South Africa • China

penguin.com

A Penguin Random House Company

HOOKED ON EWE

A Berkley Prime Crime Book / published by arrangement with the author

For information, address: The Berkley Publishing Group,
a division of Penguin Group (USA) LLC,
375 Hudson Street, New York, New York 10014.

ISBN: 978-0-425-26583-3

PUBLISHING HISTORY
Berkley Prime Crime mass-market edition / July 2015

PRINTED IN THE UNITED STATES OF AMERICA

10 9 8 7 6 5 4 3 2 1

Cover illustration by Jeff Fitz-Maurice.
Cover design by Sarah Oberrender.
Interior text design by Laura K. Corless.

CHAPTER 1

"You should've asked my opinion before you went off half-cocked," Kirstine MacBride-Derry scolded her half sister Vicki from behind the counter of the wool and yarn shop they owned together on the outskirts of Glenkillen, a small village in the Scottish Highlands on the North Sea, along a protected bay called Moray Firth.

No way was Kirstine going to take her eyes off of Sheepish Expressions's cash register for a single second, or relinquish that spot to anybody else. She was in full command of the till, even though the shop wouldn't open for a few more hours.

"What do *you* think, Eden?" Vicki said, dragging me into the middle of the sisters' dispute, which served me right for walking into the shop and getting between them. Before I could think of a reply she went on, "Should I have to postpone my first yarn club skein-of-the-month deliveries just because of the charity sheep dog trial event? I mean, the club members have paid dues in advance, and I promised the yarn kits would be ready on the first of every month. Today is the first of September, in case anybody needs a reminder. When the shop opens, my members are going to start showing up. I've made a commitment to them."

Vicki's eyes pleaded for my support. I looked away as her trademark perfume wafted my way, the light fragrance of roses and jasmine mingling with the tension in the air.

I really didn't see the big deal, but I was making an effort to understand both sides.

Today the MacBride's farm was hosting the September sheep dog trials in the field next to the lane, an annual charity event sponsored by the Glenkillen Sheep Dog Association to raise funds to keep the town's hospice operating in the black. And since Kirstine and her husband, John, have been responsible for the majority of the work in preparation for the trials, it wasn't surprising that Kirstine was stressed. She was a bit grouchy even on a regular day.

The Glenkillen Hospice Center had taken quite a hit during the most recent economic downturn and needed an infusion of cash to assure its continued service to the community. The sheep dog competition was only one of many events held for that purpose throughout the year, but this one was the grand finale and the largest. Others had included 5k runs, a cycle challenge, several charity golf days, and lucky-number drawings that operated much like lotteries—tickets were purchased, winners were announced, and prizes awarded.

Spectators at the sheep dog trials could support the hospice in a number of ways. Aside from paying an entrance fee, they could buy a printed program with the dogs' running order so they could support their favorite local shepherd. Or purchase teas, sandwiches, and cakes from the massive refreshment tent that had been set up near the trial field. Or—and this one was sure to be the most popular—they could buy raffle tickets for the opportunity to win products from local businesses, including many donated by Sheepish Expressions.

"How many yarn members do you have?" I asked Vicki, glancing at a pile of beautiful and bright-red-colored skeins that my friend had hand-dyed herself. Not only was the wool from the MacBride farm's sheep, but it had all been handspun by Vicki as well.

"Thirty-five!" Vicki replied with visible pride. "Fifteen more than I expected just starting out. I even had to close membership until I can figure out how to speed up production, and already just in the last few days there's a waiting list of another fifteen or so who want to join."

"Wow!" I said, sufficiently impressed. Vicki had only recently come up with the yarn club brainstorm and had done little in the way of promoting it beyond a few handmade flyers strategically placed in hot spots around Glenkillen (and, of course, inside Sheepish Expressions). Word of mouth was a powerful tool, especially in the Highlands. News of any sort traveled dizzyingly fast around here.

Originally, I'd signed up for the skein-of-the-month club as a show of support for Vicki's new venture, even though I can't knit a stitch. But as new membership requests poured in, I'd bowed out to make room for those with actual ability.

"I'll teach you soon," Vicki had assured me, obviously

appreciating my commitment to her cause, but relieved at the same time. We both knew I needed to start out with a simpler project, like a pot holder. Besides, I was left-handed and Vicki was right-handed. She was going to need a lot of patience when that day came.

Kirstine scowled, not used to anyone else in the shop making decisions, no matter how minor or insignificant, no matter how little it might affect her personally. Forty-two years old, a few years younger than Vicki, she would be pretty if her mouth turned up more. Instead, she had deeply furrowed frown lines.

After a lengthy estrangement, Vicki's appearance after their father's death to claim her share of the MacBride estate inheritance (a sizeable fortune in land holdings and business enterprises), had been difficult for Kirstine to accept. Kirstine had been educated in England, but had spent the better part of her adult life managing this woolen shop, and her Welsh husband, John, continued to run the farm operations as he always had. Vicki and her mother, her father's first wife, had lived in London and California, and Vicki had only visited the MacBride farm on occasion as a child. Even so, she was now committed to making a go of her new life here.

"You decided this without checking with me first, I might add," Kirstine continued, with only a faint hint of a Scottish accent. She couldn't let it go. "I would have informed you that we'd be too busy with the trials to deal with your yarn club members traipsing in at the same time," she said. "Between tourist buses arriving and spectators underfoot, I'd have thought you could have waited to begin next month. Or at the very least until next week."

"Kirstine," I said, "it doesn't really seem like it would be much effort to keep the kits behind the counter and distribute them to members. Aren't those club members who come for their yarn kits going to be likely to stick around for the trials and drop more cash?"

Kirstine didn't seem to hear my voice of reason. Her lips were pressed together in a line of discontent. "Look at you, causing trouble as usual, Eden Elliott," she said, not mincing words. "Why don't you go off and make yourself useful elsewhere. Go on."

That's me. Eden Elliott. Troublemaker and major meddler, according to Kirstine. She hasn't come right out and said it aloud, but I know she wishes I'd disappear for good. And she wouldn't be too concerned about the method of my departure as long as it took me far away from the farm and shop. It's in her tone and in the snarky comments she reserves exclusively for me.

I'm an outsider in this community, having arrived here in Glenkillen from Chicago three months ago. The trip had been unexpected, courtesy of my overly pushy and well-off best friend back home, Ami Pederson, who'd decided I needed a change of scenery and had bought me a ticket to the Highlands. Generous to a fault, as they say . . . the fault in Ami's generosity being that my return ticket had been for six months down the road, which, as she explained to me, was the maximum length of time I was allowed to stay in Scotland on the standard travel visa.

In spite of my doubts and resistance, those first months had flown by. I suppose I *had* needed a change. I'd gone through some stressful personal events—a divorce and my mother's death—but now I had a small amount of cash and the freedom at thirty-eight years old to go on this adventure.

Amazingly, I'd also accomplished what I'd set out to do, which was to write a hot contemporary romance novel set in the Scottish Highlands. Glenkillen turned out to be the perfect backdrop for my inspiration to flow, and the first draft of *Falling for You* had practically written itself.

Which is a good thing, because to make it equally scary, I was already under contract to write it. I'm convinced that Ami pulled some strings with her publisher (yeah, she's *that* Ami Pederson, international mega-bestselling historical romance author), though she denies having anything to do with landing this amazing opportunity for me. But even if she had helped orchestrate the beginning, it was still up to me to make it all come together in a real-life happy ending.

The pressure, mostly created by a mind that tends to overthink things, was on. I had to perform and perform well.

Gulp.

Regardless of my current insecurities, however, the beautiful Scottish Highlands saved my sanity, restored my self-confidence, and I've made lasting friendships here. I'm planted firmly at the MacBride farm, after an invitation from Vicki. I met her on my first day of travel on a connecting flight to Inverness out of London, and we've been fast friends ever since.

And to my good fortune as well as hers, she'd commandeered the farm's main house that had been vacant after her father passed. Kirstine and John have their own home in Glenkillen near the harbor, and no intention of actually living at the farm, claiming they had devoted enough of their lives to the family enterprise without needing to live and breathe it any more than they already did. "Besides," Kirstine had sniffed, "Da should have built a bigger house, but he was as thrifty as they come. John and myself, we need more space."

The MacBride farm's lands might extend in all directions, the estate enormous with the house, shop, several cottages, barn, and numerous outbuildings, and the bank balance most likely above anything I could imagine, but no one involved was allowed to slack off. These people were hard workers. My friend included.

Vicki had brought so much to Sheepish Expressions in the short time she'd been a contributing partner. In my opinion, the current arrangement had the potential to benefit all concerned. The sisters might snipe, but they really complemented each other. Kirstine oversees stocking of the woolen wear that graces racks in one section of the shop—kilts, accessories, tartans, scarves, and much, much more. And although the MacBride farm's own Glenkillen yarn is featured, she also orders other Scottish yarns, skeins of which fill every nook and cranny in the other half of the shop.

Vicki's talent lies in dealing with customers, something sourpuss Kirstine could learn from. People skills go a long way in selling gifts to tourists. Tour buses stop at intervals throughout each day of the week, either on the way to or returning from several attractions, whether hoping for glimpses of minke whales, harbor porpoises, and bottlenose dolphins off Moray Firth, or following the whisky trail and visiting the numerous distilleries in the Highlands.

A bright and cheery welcome from the person behind the counter could sell more stock than the surly one who usually greeted them.

Vicki had also started knitting classes, and she's hoping to add spinning lessons if there's enough demand. The woman is amazing with fibers, from the moment the wool is shorn from the sheep all the way through the spinning and dying process.

Kirstine's husband, John, has his own niche, too, tending to the fields and animals. Anyone who meets the gruff Welshman can tell how much he cares about his sheep and working dogs. He'd rather be with them than with people, which is exactly how I feel some days.

Vicki, with my help, had taken on the task of restoring one of the two cottages on the property that had fallen into disrepair. The other one had been past fixing, its stonework crumbled, the interior little more than a shell. But we'd managed to salvage the other. Last week I'd suggested that I move out of the main farmhouse and into the cottage. Vicki hadn't put up much of an argument, knowing I needed my personal space.

The cottage consists of a small kitchen and sitting room on one end of the rectangular building, and a bedroom and bath on the other end. The furnishings are simple—a scarred dresser in the bedroom and an iron bedframe with squeaky springs, yellowing wallpaper in the sitting room, and two armchairs before a small wood-burning stove set in a corner. The kitchen is nothing more than a wooden table, two chairs, sink, stove, a tiny counter, and a hodge-podge of cookware. But it's adequate for my needs, especially if I'm only going to be in the country for a few short months more. The most important features are indoor plumbing that actually works as it should, along with an electrical system John updated after being coerced into repairing the rodent-chewed wiring.

Right this minute, I missed the coziness of the little cottage, and the solitude it provides.

Vicki had turned her attention back to her skein-of-the-month kits, which were beautifully packaged in a paper satchel with a fancy label that read *A Sheepish Expressions Exclusive: Poppy Sox Knitting Kit*. Each kit contained an exclusive pattern for cable-knit stockings along with a special knitting needle, and the yarn that Vicki called Poppy Red, because of its rich red poppies-in-the-field hue.

I glanced up and out one of the shop's windows, noting the dawning day. September in the States would mean shortening days, but in Scotland we were blessed with close to fourteen hours of daylight. I smiled at my good fortune—to be here in this rural setting, at this beautiful time of the year. Since Kirstine suggested I make myself useful, I went outside and stood on the shop's porch to admire the view, trying to decide what to do next.

My scenic view was partially hidden due to the arrival of the sheep dog competitors, which had been going on since well before dawn. The day was shaping up to be another unusually sunny one. We'd been having a rare run on sun since Thursday, and it was expected to continue through today. Perfect weather for a fund-raising event. I'd give anything to duck out of the responsibilities I'd agree to early on. Vicki and I had both volunteered our services for the sheep dog trials, and Kirstine had decided that Vicki would be giving spectators tractor rides out to the far fields for the competitions (a role assigned, I suspect but can't prove, to keep Vicki away from the shop), while my assignment was to help at the welcome table right outside Sheepish Expressions. I, along with several other volunteers who worked for the hospice, would disburse information, sell programs, and in general, handle any minor problems.

I shuddered at the thought of a full day wasted at the welcome table. I'd much prefer to spend that time out in the field, watching the working dogs round up sheep. A few stragglers driving vans and trucks, some hauling trailers, were still pulling off the main road and parking up and down the lane wherever they could find space. I could see them starting to double-park as spots became scarce.

The parking lot before me was empty though, due to a large sign Kirstine had erected warning that the area was strictly for Sheepish Expressions customers and carried an accompanying threat of prosecution. *Ignore at your own risk.*

A familiar white van pulled up close by. I recognized the vehicle mainly because of the heavily tinted windows that made it impossible to see inside.

The welcoming committee for the big event was converging.

I sighed heavily and stepped down from the porch.

CHAPTER 2

The arriving van belonged to Oliver Wallace, who I'd met at the first of our organizational meetings. Oliver stepped out first, followed by his two passengers.

Down the lane, Isla Lindsey, the leader of the pack, scurried toward us from her parked camper van, and came to a halt next to the van. Isla wore a lightweight calf-length burgundy tartan skirt wrapped around her ample girth, thick cream-colored knee-high stockings, and a clunky pair of hiking boots—not to mention several metaphorical hats on her inflated head. She was the volunteer service coordinator, using whatever coercing and bullying tactics necessary to get locals involved whether they wanted to be or not. She also acted as treasurer, keeping the financial aspects of the many fund-raisers in order.

"Where should we set up?" I asked.

"Next to the shop," Isla said to me, sharp and commanding. "And if you'd been at the last meeting, you would have been informed as such. Stop dawdling and help us unload. And you"—Isla's head swung toward Oliver—"are late, as usual."

I'd watched Isla seize control of the welcoming committee from the start, and almost immediately regretted having signed on. Because her husband, Bryan, was president of the Glenkillen Sheep Dog Association, Isla presided over every single aspect of this fund-raiser as though she were queen of the kingdom, wielding her special brand of obnoxiousness the minute she had us all in her clutches. She was the main reason I'd stopped attending the meetings. Really, how much advanced planning was required to set up a little tent and produce a stack of programs to sell? We were volunteers, for goodness' sake. Her job should have encompassed coordinating each of the volunteer areas, not micromanaging the four of us who had been unlucky enough to be on the one committee she'd decided to rule with an especially iron fist.

To be fair (from my limited experience with volunteerism), finding someone to head such a project as this must be a major feat. Maybe it takes a control freak like Isla to pull off a successful fund-raiser.

A scary thought.

Oliver Wallace, the only male in our bunch, was Isla's designated gofer due to the fact that he was the only one of us who owned a vehicle with toting capabilities. Oliver claims to be a direct descendent of Scottish freedom-fighter William Wallace, and usually puts on airs as though this were the fourteenth century and his lineage actually mattered. He'd been an active volunteer throughout the fund-raising year (he seemed to be on every committee

and board associated with the hospice), and didn't seem
to mind taking orders like an indentured servant. Although
he annoyed *Isla* plenty, so maybe he wasn't quite the fol-
lower he appeared to be. Now he opened the back of the
van, with some effort involved as the latch resisted, and
pulled out a stack of poles.

Oliver's passengers were the other two welcoming committee members—Lily Young, who worked housekeeping
at the hospice, and Andrea Lindsey, a nurse in clinical services who also happened to be Isla's husband's younger sister.
Between them they carried the blue-and-white welcome tent
and a bag of stakes.

I noticed that most of the welcoming committee members looked sunburned. Sun in the Highlands is an anom-
aly, especially when the clouds go "on holiday" and it
manages to shine for three days straight, as it had recently.
That means lots of burnt skin for these fair-haired Scots.
Isla's cheeks were rosy, the skin of her nose starting to
peel; and Oliver's face and neck above his golf shirt were
burnt red, a shade altogether different from his cropped
red hair.

I'd also inherited fair Scottish skin and ginger tones in
my hair from my paternal side, but I'm careful of the sun's
rays. I'd rubbed on plenty of sunscreen this morning, hoping to escape unscathed.

"Step lively," Isla called out in military fashion.

Lily, even more sunburnt than Oliver and Isla, wore no
makeup whatsoever, and her fine, straight brown hair hung
limply to chin length. She had a pear-shaped body, lots of
hips with narrow shoulders. Lily had made an unsuccessful
attempt to take control of the welcoming committee at the

beginning, and—as she'd confided in me one evening at the pub when she'd had a pint or two too many—was hoping to break out of housekeeping and into a paid fund-raising position. She still hadn't gotten over her defeat to Isla, judging by the occasional dagger glares she cast Isla's way.

Rumor had it that the two of them had been on opposite sides of the ring since childhood, with Isla always coming out on top, pounding her opponent into the ropes with perfectly executed sucker punches.

Andrea, Isla's sister-in-law, is a mouse of a woman, nondescript in physical characteristics as well as conversationally, with hardly an opinion to call her own. That must suit her sister-in-law just fine, giving Isla one more person to walk all over. Andrea, I've heard, is a competent nurse under that passive exterior, making up for her lack of interesting qualities with a superb bedside manner. And displaying a good deal of common sense, in my opinion, since she was the only one on the committee besides me who wasn't toasty crisp from too much sun.

The little group marched over to a grassy area beside the woolen shop, led by Oliver, who was wearing a pair of gray wellies made colorful by bright yellow soles. Isla attempted to outpace him, but despite her effort, came in second.

I reluctantly followed last.

By the time I arrived, Isla had already started complaining.

"This isn't the tent I told you to order," she said to Oliver as though noticing the blue-and-white tent for the first time. "I specifically asked for bright yellow."

"No yellow to be had," Oliver mumbled. I knew for a

fact that he hadn't placed the order until the last minute. Possibly his lapse was an intentional act of defiance.

"And the size is all wrong!" she continued to gripe.

"It's the exact size you requested." Oliver began assembling the poles.

"'Tis not. This won't do at all. Ye'll just have to find the proper tent, is all there is to it."

Lily and Andrea ignored the exchange, making busy rather than getting involved. I'd learned my lesson moments earlier inside the shop, so took a page from them and kept quiet, too.

Isla, realizing that Oliver was hopeless, turned on the women. "Couldn't one of you have managed this bloke?" Then her gaze found me. "And you! A fat lot of good you've been. Useless Americans."

"Let's get on with it," Lily said, while I stood dumbstruck by Isla's audacity. "Save yer breath to cool yer broth."

Which was one of the few Scottish phrases I was actually familiar with, having heard Kirstine use it on occasion, prompting me to seek a definition from Vicki. Lily had just told Isla to quit complaining and get to work. Good for her.

It was bad enough trying to referee Vicki and Kirstine, but having to withstand Isla's bickering with the welcoming committee members over every little detail was going to do me in. I had to find a way out.

But just when I thought all was lost, and I had no choice but to suffer through the day next to the parking lot, two welcome additions arrived (separately but almost simultaneously):

Detective Inspector Kevin Jamieson and Special Constable Sean Stevens.

To the inspector's continuing chagrin, the local powers that be had decided to incorporate volunteer cops into the main corps of professionally trained police officers. Odd, but true. When I first learned of it, I thought my leg was being pulled. It wasn't.

Scotland's new volunteer police force draws citizens from all walks of life, giving them the opportunity to work side by side with experienced law enforcement officials. After a brief training course, these special constables wear similar uniforms and have the same powers as regular officers. My mind still boggled at the concept.

Anyway, Sean Stevens, a former security guard, had eagerly signed on, and since he was from the Glenkillen area he had been promptly assigned to Inspector Jamieson, bringing the inspector's long and happy history of working solo to an abrupt end.

Since that fateful day, the inspector has spent much of his time dodging Sean or, when all else fails, creating busywork to keep his "special constable" occupied elsewhere. To his credit, Sean has countered those efforts with some pretty fine tracking techniques, managing to hound the inspector pretty much wherever he goes . . . though the inspector's Honda CR-V is simple to tail once one has it in sight. Its horizontal yellow stripes framed by blue and black checkers give it away easily.

Today Sean, driving his red Renault, was hot behind the CR-V. They both parked in the restricted area, inside the parking lot designated for customers. The inspector pulled in near the shop, while the rookie headed for the far end, maneuvering and backing in for a quick dash if the inspector managed to get a few steps ahead of him.

Neither of them acknowledged Kirstine's warning sign. At least there still were a few individuals out there who she couldn't control with her threats. I smiled at that.

As they approached, I couldn't help comparing the two men. The inspector was a widower in his late fifties, graying at the temples. He wore a blue button-down shirt with the top button open, a solid tie knotted loosely, and a pair of beige trousers, his hair a little mussed. Sean, a bit younger than me in his early thirties, wore his standard police uniform—white short-sleeved shirt, black tie tight and perfect, his peaked cap with insignia perfectly aligned over his buzz cut, his carriage erect, his chin held high. He was right behind his boss, having to hurry since his shorter legs had to do double the work of the long-legged inspector.

"Vicki's inside the shop," I called to Sean, and smiled as he turned on his heels and headed for the porch leading into Sheepish Expressions. The special constable had been giving Vicki special attention. "He's a young pup," Vicki had said when I'd pointed that out.

"Age means nothing these days," I'd argued.

"Off with you!" she'd replied. But the light in her eyes and the blush on her cheeks when he was around spoke volumes.

I'd met Inspector Jamieson my very first day in the Highlands, and not exactly under the best of circumstances. But over the following months, I'd come to consider him a friend, and I hoped he felt likewise. He did seem relatively comfortable around me, possibly due to the twenty-year difference in our ages and my utter lack of romantic interest in him. Single men of the inspector's age are considered hot commodities by many of the local widows and divorcees, but I'm hardly a threat to his chosen way of life. At this point, I'm not a threat to any man's freedom. My divorce and my mother's death following her long battle with MS have left me ripe for life changes. I've learned that being by myself isn't nearly as lonely as being with the wrong person. In fact, I'm relishing it. I have no desire to jump right back into a relationship. One thing I'm definitely not looking for is romance. I have more than enough of that on the pages of *Falling for You*.

"Quite the to-do," the inspector said now as I left the welcoming committee to greet him. "I've managed tae stay away until noo." I enjoyed hearing his thick Scottish brogue; even though I heard Scottish accents spoken on a daily basis these days, I still wasn't immune to the charm.

"You don't like crowds?" I asked.

"Bloody uncomfortable, if ye ask me. The main reason I'm here is tae shake our Sean, and then I'll be gone."

"We open to the public at nine," I warned him, in case he wanted to disappear before then. With the good weather, Kirstine and John expected attendance to far exceed the projected two hundred spectators.

"At least they are clubbing together to raise funds fer a worthy cause."

"Yes, there's that to appreciate."

"I've decided to put Officer Stevens on traffic duty first thing," the inspector informed me, "and he's not tae leave until the very end o' the trials."

I nodded. "Smart of you."

The inspector and I gave each other knowing looks. Mine said he'd cleverly managed to waylay Sean once again, effectively distancing himself from the overeager officer in a manner that suited both of them. Sean would hardly complain about his post, because it would keep him close to Vicki. The instigator's expression told me he was pretty pleased with himself, too.

"Officer Stevens has put in a request fer his own beat car," Inspector Jamieson said next. "I'm considering putting him on a bicycle instead. That should slow him down sufficiently."

I pictured Sean pedaling like crazy to follow the police vehicle and grinned at the image.

Then a thought popped into my head—a glimmer of a workable plan to extricate myself from Isla's clutches. "I hate to be the bearer of bad news," I told Inspector Jamieson, "but the only problem with your plan is that Kirstine has already arranged for two young men to direct traffic into another field across the way once our visitors begin to arrive." I watched disappointment flicker across his face. "Here they come now." Sure enough, Kirstine's two volunteers had parked off to the side of the field I'd indicated, and were now in position to make use of the bright traffic flags they carried.

The inspector seemed put out, but it wouldn't be for long. I continued on with growing glee. "Isla could use him in the welcome tent," I told him. "I'm sure Sean won't mind lending a hand there."

"Brilliant!" the inspector exclaimed, getting his enthusiasm back.

It *was* brilliant on my part, if I did say so myself.

Jamieson would be rid of Sean, I'd be free from Isla's clutches, and Sean really wouldn't mind, especially since Vicki was giving tractor rides from a position right next to the welcoming committee. With a small amount of effortless reorganization, I'd just made all three of us very happy.

"The two of us need tae have a chin wag," the inspector said next, placing a hand lightly on my elbow. "A private one, if ye don't mind."

Isla, as if sensing she was about to lose one of her minions, called over, "We could use a helping hand over here with the tent, Eden. We don't have much time left. Ye cannae expect the others tae do all the work!"

"I'm afraid Ms. Elliott is occupied in a matter o' important police business," the inspector informed Isla with the proper authority in his tone. Then, lower to me as we moved farther away, "Let her stew over that fer a while. Besides, it won't hurt the nag tae work with her own hands for a change instead o' exercising her mouth muscles."

CHAPTER 3

We handed an amiable Sean over to the welcoming committee, where Isla promptly put him to work moving Oliver Wallace's van into the shade of a silver maple at the far end of the parking lot.

"Over there," she ordered, pointing to the general area of Sean's own Renault. "On the far side o' that beat-up old clunker."

Sean grimaced at the insult, but Isla didn't notice. "Oliver always leaves the keys in the ignition, so no need tae track down the slacker," she complained. "I don't know how he manages tae disappear every time I turn my back."

"And yerself," she turned to Lily Young, who'd appeared on the shop porch with Vicki, whose arms were filled with paper satchel kits containing this month's skeins of yarn. "Pull yer finger out."

Pull your finger out? I shot a questioning glance at the inspector, who clarified. "It means tae hurry up."

Instead of obeying, Lily ignored Isla. As we watched, Vicki shook her head firmly and tucked the kits protectively against her body. Lily was obviously disappointed as she walked slowly over to help erect the tent.

"What's the story there?" the inspector asked me.

I explained about Vicki's new project with the yarn club and how overly successful the venture had been (if such a thing even exists in the business world—I suppose it does; too much demand, not enough supply). "I suspect Lily didn't get in on the initial wave of members," I said as Vicki joined us, "but was still hoping to claim a kit."

"That's it exactly," Vicki agreed. "She's on the waiting list, but that one has a bit of push and shove in her makeup, I'd say. I'm going to enlist Sean to help me hand these out to the *actual* members and to guard them from the likes of Lily." And off she went, still defensively clutching her treasures.

After that, the inspector and I walked up the lane. Despite what he'd told Isla about having important business to discuss with me, whatever was on his mind didn't seem to be too pressing. Why, I wondered, was he still here?

Perhaps the inspector's official business announcement had been for Isla's benefit. Or rather mine, to get me out of there. Whichever, I appreciated the excuse to escape. If he had anything to discuss, he'd get around to it. Our conversation centered on topics such as the current sunny skies, and which of the sheep dog competitors stood the best chance of winning the trials. The inspector favored Bryan Lindsey.

"Herself has hen-pecked that man practically into an early grave," the inspector said, referring to Isla. "But he's still the best sheep dog trainer in Glenkillen. Nothing like a wife such as that tae keep a man's nose tae the grindstone."

I laughed. The inspector had found some positive in with the negative, but he was more generous than I was. In my opinion, Isla and her ilk were best appreciated from afar. Life is too short to let others drag you down.

I heard the tractor start up inside the barn, which was a honey-colored structure that fit the Highland landscape to a tee. We stood aside as Kirstine's husband, John Derry, drove it out through the open barn doors, pulling a large wagon filled with hay bales intended as seating for arriving spectators. The trial field wasn't especially far out from the parking area, but those who had difficulty walking or who were accompanied by small children would appreciate the ride. John nodded an almost imperceptible greeting as he drove past us, and slight as it had been, I decided I was making progress with him, if not with his wife. I'd take the nod as a hopeful sign.

While the inspector stayed outside to answer a call on his cell phone, I went inside the barn to collect a couple of lawn chairs to carry over to the field. Jasper, the farm's barn cat, greeted me with a soft meow from the hayloft above. Ordinarily he'd be sunning himself outside the barn doors, but he was a classic introvert who chose to disappear when too much activity was going on around him.

"Does that call mean you have to leave?" I asked when Inspector Jamieson returned the phone to his pocket.

"I have a bit o' time tae spend."

We walked past the refreshment tent and over to a spot along the perimeter of the field where another group of volunteers had just finished putting up gates in strategic places. Six sheep bleated and huddled together nervously within an enclosed pen. Since spectators were beginning to assemble, I knew it must be nine and the show was about to begin.

As the newcomer that I am to Glenkillen's community events, experiences such as this sheep dog trial have an aura of mystery and excitement about them. I could feel it in the air, an unmistakable electric energy. Vicki's next-door neighbor, Leith Cameron, and his border collie Kelly would be competing in the early afternoon. Kelly had been a superior herding dog in her youth, and was sure to take the older dog division.

As Leith had explained to me, sheep trials were an important part of Highland life. They were healthy competitions among shepherds to see which of them had the best sheep dogs. While a sheep dog could be any type of dog capable of learning the ropes, the Scots insisted that the only true herder was the border collie—based on what I'd seen of Kelly, they were highly intelligent, blazingly fast, and really loved to work.

"Trials are run over an obstacle course," Leith had told me, "and competitors are assigned points by the judges based on their performance. Each dog is scored on different aspects, including the time it takes to complete the course. The object is to move yer sheep as steadily as possible without spooking them. If that happens they run every which way. That's why ye'll see the handlers signaling to the dogs to lie down before approaching slowly."

I couldn't wait to see the trials with my own eyes.

Harry Taggart, the man responsible for spearheading these events and one of today's judges, arrived on the field, signaling the beginning of the sheep dog trials. Harry was tall and thin, well into his fifties, and had never married. Perhaps that accounted for his coltish physique, not having access to as much comfort food as the typical married man. With his round shoulders and wire spectacles, I'd easily pegged him as the financial type. A banker, perhaps. Which I'd learned he had been at one time, before accepting the position at the hospice several years back. Now he was the chief executive officer of the Glenkillen Hospice Center.

The spectators gathered, some with their own dogs—all on the required leashes. An eager young black-and-white border collie and his handler appeared on the field, the apprehensive sheep were released, and the youth division was under way.

It was fascinating to watch the dogs and handlers work together. Sharp varying whistles combined with short voice commands were all the dogs needed to herd the sheep from one end of the immense field to the other, with some pretty impressive maneuvers through a maze of gates, culminating with the remarkable feat of separating the herd into two groups of three sheep each, and finally corralling the herd inside the pen.

According to the program, twenty-five handlers and their dogs would be competing in three separate divisions based on age and ability—young dogs, older dogs, and those in top-notch condition, but most of the competitors aside from John and Leith were unknown to me.

I suspected that much like John Derry, the other handlers probably tended to prefer the company of animals to humans, and so didn't frequent the same places I did, or at least not at the same time. John had his share of pints at the Kilt & Thistle in Glenkillen, but I was done with my writing and gone from town before his day at the farm usually ended.

I've been spending a lot of my time at the Kilt & Thistle, which was where I did most of my writing. The farm doesn't have Internet access, which I need for my research as well as for communication with Ami and the rest of the outside world. So nearly every day I make the twenty-minute drive into the main thoroughfare of Glenkillen, taking my life into my hands on the Highland narrow roadways, navigating as best I can on the left side (which is the wrong side where I come from).

The other reason I leave the farm to write is that Vicki isn't very good at giving me the privacy I need to feed my creative spark. If she isn't interrupting my train of thought for one thing or the other, her two white Westie terriers, Pepper and Coco, are. The dogs are as sweet as can be, but they demand a lot of attention without any regard for my other obligations.

So I take my laptop to the pub to write. It may seem counter-intuitive, but I find it easier to concentrate when I'm at the pub surrounded by people. I easily tune out pub noise and enter my characters' world. The drone of voices actually acts as white noise.

Of course, these days, I mostly stare at the monitor, practicing deep breathing exercises to control my blood pressure, and checking for incoming e-mails of the disastrous sort. Right now, Ami Pederson, that pushy and sometimes crazy friend whom I admire so much, is reading the manuscript in spite of my resistance. I'd wanted to go right into yet another round of revisions, but she'd been adamant that I needed to step back for a few weeks and give her a chance to look it over.

Any day now I was expecting an e-mail from her telling me the storyline of *Falling for You* didn't work, and I should head back to Chicago to return to the occasional freelance editorial job or ghostwriting contract augmented by any special projects Ami could come up with for me.

To say I was a little nervous about her opinion would be an enormous understatement. My fingernails would be nibbled to stubs if I were the nail-chewing type. It's disturbing to find out just how paralyzed with fear I can become when my writing is under this kind of intense scrutiny.

I pushed all thoughts of my work in progress aside and concentrated on the trials in front of me.

The last dog in the youth division drove his sheep through a gate and back into a small pen. The pro division was next, and had the most contenders. We watched John work his dogs, then the inspector pointed out Isla Lindsey's husband, Bryan, as he took the field. Bryan was a slight, unremarkable man who I bet wouldn't have stood out on his own off the field. Here, though, he had an opportunity to shine. And he did.

From what I could tell as a layperson, both John Derry and Bryan were top-notch handlers, a cut above the others they were competing against. I couldn't imagine how the judges would be able to decide who would be the winner. It was as clear as mud to me.

I couldn't take my eyes off the action, caught up in the excitement of the moment. After several more of the working dogs had strutted their stuff, I glanced over and caught Inspector Jamieson watching me instead of the sheep. He quickly shifted his gaze away.

"I don't know about you, but I'm thirsty," I said hastily, standing up, feeling uncomfortable after having been observed without being aware of it. What had the astute inspector found of such interest?

"Then it's tae the big tent fer us," he muttered, rising with me.

We sauntered over to the tent, which was as big an attraction as the trial field. It had taken major effort to erect yesterday and had required massive manpower. Whoever had decided it needed to go up the day before knew what they were talking about. At the moment, the tent was the place to be.

I've discovered in my three months in the Highlands that the Scots love all things deep-fried. The food committee had outdone itself in that department. In addition to the basic fish and chips, there were Scotch pies and sausage rolls, bacon rolls and fried pizza (which I'd been advised was really good with a sprinkle of salt and a little vinegar), and my particular favorite—deep-fried Mars bars. Dangerously delicious.

My eyes took in those offerings, but were drawn to Senga Hill's cupcake table. Senga, who had been born Agnes but decided to spell it backward and rechristened herself Senga, was a retired bakery owner in her sixties who had sold her business but never lost interest in baking sweet, delectable treats. Today, she was selling adorable sheep-shaped cupcakes, decorated with mini marshmallows for fleece, candy eyeballs, and . . .

"What did you use to make their little heads?" I asked her after gravitating to her table while the inspector stood in conversation with one of the locals.

"Toffee," she said, wrapping one wayward strand of her gray bob behind an ear to keep it off her face. "I warmed them up a bit tae shape the heads and used a toothpick tae poke holes fer the nostrils. Do ye want one?"

"Yes, absolutely, but later," I told her.

"They're goin' fast," Senga warned.

"Save one for me. Please?"

"Aye. I can do that for ye, Eden."

Once the inspector rejoined me, I followed his lead, passing up all those *un*-heart-healthy choices—for now. We both ordered tea, which we took to the end of a long table. The other side was occupied by Dr. Keen and Paul Denoon, Glenkillen's postmaster. We sat down and exchanged pleasantries. Or at least most of us did. Denoon hadn't bothered to be friendly with me from the beginning, and he didn't start now.

Dr. Keen and Paul Denoon were in their eighties, and both refused to retire. Denoon had thick, coarse white eyebrows that jutted in every direction, and a shriveled frame that reminded me of a wiry, aging terrier. His aim was to be the longest-servicing postmaster in the Highlands and at this point he was only two years away from his goal.

"I hear the post office has mobile phone top-ups noo," the inspector said to him, then to me, "So ye know where tae go fer credits."

I nodded, having finally broken down last month and

purchased an inexpensive mobile phone. Top-ups, I assumed, were additional minutes.

"Ye should carry pet supplies," Dr. Keen said to Denoon in a teasing tone, looking dapper for his age in his tweed driving cap and patchwork sweater. His patients, I've been told, are mostly the elderly.

"That's gettin' a bit doolally," the postmaster replied, shaking his head. "Pet supplies? Hunh!"

Doolally?

"Crazy," the inspector translated for me as the two old friends rose and ambled off.

After his customary puttering over tea, the inspector spoke. "It appears that Sean Stevens has managed tae make it through the selection process and become a probationer," he said. Then added after seeing my confusion, "He's been accepted intae the Scottish Police College."

"That's wonderful news!" I exclaimed. I was excited for Sean in spite of the inspector's gloomy delivery. "Why didn't he mention it when he arrived?"

"The only thing wonderful aboot it is that he'll be gone fer ten weeks tae Kincardine in Fife fer the operational phase o' his training," the inspector grumbled. "He just found out. Mebbe he wanted tae tell Vicki first."

"And what happens after those ten weeks of training?"

"He'll be assigned tae a home station fer the next part o' the process."

"You don't seem nearly as pleased as I thought you'd be," I said. "Let me guess . . . What could possibly be the cause of your dismay? Perhaps because Glenkillen will be Officer Stevens's home station?"

"Astute as ever, ye are. If he makes it through the first ten weeks, I have the misfortune o' becoming his tutor constable, even worse than having him on as a special constable." His eyes pierced mine, searing as two hot coals. "Tell me, Eden Elliott, how did such a bloke as our Sean make it through the fitness test and all the rest tae actually gain admission tae the police college?"

"There's more to Sean than we ever guessed?" I had to look away. I certainly wasn't going to be the one to tell him that Vicki and Sean had worked hard together to prepare for the physical training part of his testing. She'd acted as his coach, firmly guiding him through a rigorous fitness routine, making him stick to it. I'd played a small part, too, prepping him for some of the more scholarly aspects of the process, like the writing portion that tested his knowledge of police procedure and law enforcement. The biggest challenge for Sean had been overcoming his dyslexia, which involved constant repetition and the tenacity to never give up.

"And even worse," the inspector went on, "he'll be trained in unarmed combat and baton and handcuff techniques, and Lord help us all, CS spray, which until now I've managed tae keep outta his reach."

While helping Sean with his studies, I'd learned that pepper spray and CS spray, commonly referred to as tear gas, are classed as firearms in Scotland. It's illegal to *own* pepper spray, let alone use it. Possession carries a steep penalty, unless you're a cop. It was a good thing my key ring pepper spray had been seized by the TSA in Chicago when I'd forgotten I had it in my purse on the way over here. In Scotland, that offense would have carried a much stiffer penalty than simply having it confiscated.

"I'm sure Sean will be trained to use weapons properly before allowed to carry them," I said with confidence. "But you aren't really worried about whether or not he passes his training. What else is bothering you?"

"I'm tae be assigned another special constable tae replace him while he's away," the inspector said with a groan.

This was one of Inspector Jamieson's worst nightmares. I felt for him, but he was a shrewd man who would survive the next volunteer as well as he had this one, and I told him so.

"I've never been much o' a team player," he admitted. "Preferring tae go it alone. I can't stand cleaning up after somebody else. When it's only me tae manage, I have nobody but myself tae blame if things go rotten. See how ye have me pegged?"

He was resorting to flattery? And why was he being candid? This was a side of him I hadn't seen before.

"I've come up with a bit o' an idea," he said a moment later. I took a sip of my tea, sensing that we were coming to the real purpose of his visit. "What d'ye think aboot taking that position yerself?"

I almost spewed tea. What? Me? A volunteer cop? I wasn't even much of a volunteer welcoming committee member, and there wasn't even any required training for that.

"It's the perfect solution tae a thorny problem," he went on. "We get on, fer one thing. Sometimes I'm amazed at how much we think alike."

I gave him a sideways look and said, "You're full of compliments today."

"It's the honest truth. Besides, ye already have a remarkable working understanding regarding our legal system."

At this, I glanced up, meeting his eyes.

"Aye," he said, "I know ye've been helping Sean prepare fer the exam. I'm not blind, ye know. And I have a knack fer the process o' deduction. It comes with the job."

So he'd known all along! Why hadn't he said a word or tried to stop us?

"So what do ye say?" he prompted.

"I'm flattered."

"So, will ye do it?"

"Let me think about it." I was a writer of romance novels, not an investigator. Accepting his offer, as intriguing as it was, would interfere with my real job, with the work I was being paid to do.

"It wouldn't have tae be many hours," he added, as though reading my mind. "A few each week, four being the official minimum, but we can negotiate that down if ye prefer. As few as ye want. As ye know, nothing much happens of the criminal sort in Glenkillen. I wouldn't put too much on yer shoulders."

"What about training requirements?"

"There's that tae deal with. And residency. Yer supposed tae be in the country fer three years beforehand, not three months as ye've been."

"Oh. Well, that's it then." Was that a sense of disappointment I was feeling?

"But I do the vetting personally, and there are ways

33

around these sort o' things. I can waive the residency requirements, and ye've already done yer own homework by helpin'
Sean."

He'd certainly given this a lot of thought.

Suddenly the dim bulb in my brain snapped on with the
intensity of a floodlight, and I knew exactly what he was
up to. "You want me to officially accept the position, but
you're really giving me the job in name only."

His expression told me I'd discovered his scheme, and
he shook his head in wonderment. "Ye're on tae me as
usual. It would be a big favor, and would entail no effort
on yer part."

I still felt oddly disappointed, but wasn't sure why.
Before we sat down, I hadn't even known about the job,
and one minute ago I wasn't sure I wanted it. Maybe it was
because he'd inflated my ego with the offer, then went on
to poke holes in it. Still, doing him this favor wasn't totally
out of the question.

"Would I have to wear a uniform?" I asked.

"Not unless ye be wanting one."

I grinned, knowing I was about to say yes. What did I
have to lose? And I had much to gain. An IOU from a friend
in law enforcement, for one thing. Helping out a friend in
need, for another. This could be a win-win situation for both
of us.

"Okay," I told him, "I'll agree. But I want that CS spray."

I should have something for my troubles, right? And in
the States, I always carried pepper spray. As a single
woman traveling alone, there was something reassuring
about having protection.

"You're a hard case, Eden Elliott. Can I convince ye

tae carry pepper spray instead? It's just as effective, maybe more so."

"That would be fine," I said with a satisfied grin.

I'd remember much later how the inspector had reassured me that after all, nothing much happened of the criminal sort in Glenkillen.

At the time, I'd actually believed him.

CHAPTER 4

After having successfully enlisted me in his ploy to stave off an unfamiliar new volunteer special constable, the inspector was on his way. I walked over for the cupcake Senga had put aside for me.

"Delicious," I declared after taking a bite out of the back end of the little sheep cupcake. "Almost too cute to eat!"

Senga smiled knowingly. "Not hardly. I made two hundred o' them and look at what's left." She had been right about the popularity of her cupcakes. They weren't going to last much longer.

After offering to assist in the refreshment tent and having my offer gratefully accepted, I poured beverages, happy to help out with less abused volunteers than the ones led by Isla Lindsey. Vicki waved from the driver's seat of the tractor every time she drove by, the wagon filled with weekenders enjoying the weather and making a day of it at the farm.

"I fancy you'll be rooting for Leith," Vicki called to me on her next pass, with a pointed glance toward the trial field, where I spotted Leith Cameron walking with his border collie, Kelly, beside him.

Kelly was competing in the upcoming event!

I ducked out of the tent and hurried to my seat near the field so I could watch her in action, returning the wave Leith gave when he spotted me. Leith's farm is much smaller than the MacBride farm, but has been passed down through his family the same way. He raises barley, the most important ingredient in Scotch whisky, and sells his harvest to one of the local distilleries, though his main source of income is through his work as a professional fishing guide.

He's also handsome, with those mesmerizing Scottish blue eyes, single, and seems unattached, although between devoting himself to his career and to his young daughter, I question how available he really is. The older dog division was new this year, added to showcase retired sheep dogs. Kelly, now in her advanced years, had been a constant award winner in her prime, and many of the border collies in the surrounding hills were from her litters. Today, she had a reputation to uphold.

When her turn came, she was in her element—streaking down the field as Leith whistled the occasional command. Kelly barely seemed to need his advice, lying down at the perimeter of the watchful sheep before crouching and coming in low, driving them through one obstacle after another and ending with a flourish after the final corralling.

I applauded enthusiastically. In my opinion, Kelly won hands down, but we'd have to wait until the very end of the trials to see if the judges agreed with me.

After they were done, Leith and Kelly came over. Leith snapped a lead on Kelly; not that she needed restraint, but rules were rules. Even for a canine as well behaved as she was. Leith slid into the chair the inspector had vacated. Once again, I couldn't help admiring the fine cut of this man—tall, lean, his sandy blond hair a bit long, red highlights in a short-trimmed beard that was a new and welcome addition since last I'd seen him.

"I should have bet all my savings on Kelly," I told him.

Leith had a twinkle in his eye. "And what about me? Would ye have bet yer last pence on me as well?"

"In a heartbeat," I told him, feeling a blush threatening.

"Any word from yer famous friend Ami Pederson regarding yer book?"

I shook my head, pleased that he remembered I'd shared my concern with him several days ago. "Not yet. But I'm going into Glenkillen tomorrow to check my e-mail."

"Vicki needs tae install Wi-Fi out here. Her da was old fashioned when it came tae modern technology, but now he's gone and she should go ahead with it."

"She's been talking about adding it, but even if she does, I'll still do most of my work in the village. It isn't healthy for my head to work where I live. I need changes of scenery."

"I don't know how ye spend so much time alone inside yer head as it is. Me, I need tae be around people."

In some ways Leith reminded me of my ex-husband's better qualities (of which I concede there were a few). Both are go-getters, people pleasers, and party lovers, active individuals who draw their energy from social interaction. Neither one of them needs the amount of personal space that I seem to require. There, though, the two men's similarities ended.

"Yer American friend is going to love it," Leith went on. "So is yer publisher. I have a feeling, and my feelings are never wrong."

I really hoped that was true.

"How's Fia been?" I asked, watching the lights in his eyes dance at the mention of his daughter's name. "I haven't seen her for a while."

"She's happy and bonny as ever, and excited about the start-up o' primary school."

I smiled at the joy that resonated from him whenever he spoke of his six-year-old daughter. Fia was the apple of his eye. He and Fia's mother shared custody; they'd never married, parting ways shortly after the birth of their daughter. I gave him a lot of credit for taking on the responsibility of fatherhood the way he has. Some men would be perfectly happy writing a monthly check and seeing their child every other weekend. But Leith had chosen to become more involved, playing a very active role in her life.

I paused to consider how wonderful that would have been, to have a participating father, but it was beyond my comprehension. I felt the old familiar stirring of loss and betrayal when I compared my own father to Leith and found mine deficient. More than deficient—he'd been totally absent. He had abandoned me and my mother when I was around Fia's age, disappearing after my mother had been diagnosed with MS. Poor timing on his part, and very telling as to his character. Or rather, lack thereof.

Conversely, Leith's decision to stay active as a parent and be an ongoing part of his daughter's life elevated him to the highest possible "good dad" ranking in my book. And I had to admit that that, plus the fact that he was so good looking, was an incredibly sexy mix. He was like a romance hero come to life—not only beautiful on the outside, he had everything going for him on the inside, too.

But in real life, his sense of familial devotion meant he didn't have much time for romance, either.

He'd explained not long ago. "Fia's mum has had a string o' boyfriends since we split up. I decided early on that my girl needed at least some continuity in her life, and I couldn't have a revolving door o' temporary women parading through her life, like her mum has men. And I've held tae that commitment."

"But what if you met the right woman?" I'd asked.

Leith had grinned. "Are ye applying for the position?" he'd teased.

I'm pretty sure I had blushed. "Just curious. I'm sorry, that was presumptuous of me. It's none of my business. Forget I asked."

"The hard part," he'd said gently, "is how do ye know who's the right one, unless ye spend time together? Maybe it would be perfect. But if it dinnae work out, there she goes on her way, possibly breaking my daughter's heart. Do ye see my concern?"

I had understood perfectly.

Now, as we sat next to each other, I thought of Ami's last e-mail, her constant refrain.

"Did you get lucky yet? You better say yes, because you've been there long enough! With all those beautiful Scottish men and their sexy kilts, and without the bother of knickers, you better be exploring underneath. Forget about all that serious overthinking stuff, about making commitments, blah, blah and just enjoy. And I want details ASAP!!!!"

While I'd realized from the very beginning that she wanted the best for me, I wasn't there yet. I was still newly single, relatively speaking, and had spent most of the preceding months adjusting to a new country. Even without a language barrier (though Scottish English takes some getting used to, that's for sure), it took time to settle in and establish a new routine, to make friends here.

Not to mention that I'd thrown myself into my work, writing seven days a week if I could, preferring to live vicariously through my characters Gillian Fraser and Jack Ross, thank you very much. But when I wrote back to Ami with these reasons, she'd accused me of making excuses for avoiding any sort of romantic involvement.

Which wasn't entirely untrue.

When my six-month tourist visa was up, I'd have to leave the country, whether I wanted to or not.

And it wasn't going to be with a broken heart.

"Ye seem deep in thought," I heard Leith say, bringing me out of my head and back into the present.

"It's been an interesting day," I muttered, standing up and stretching.

Leith rose beside me and dug his mobile phone out of a pocket to check the time. "It's half past one right now, and we have some time before the judges will be announcing

the winners. John is aboot tae begin a sheep dog demonstration, and I told him I'd assist."

"And I promised Charlotte I'd watch her shearing demo,
which is starting right now, too."

"Promise me ye'll come back after the shearing."

I grinned. "Sure."

"I'll be close by."

With that, I gave Kelly a pat and went to watch Charlotte Penn, Glenkillen's sheep shearer, demonstrate her
special skill in the barn.

Charlotte was young, energetic, strong, and lightning
fast, able to finish shearing a whole sheep with the electric
shears in a matter of minutes. The ewes weren't exactly
happy with the arrangement, bleating their disapproval,
but each of them in turn exited the demonstration area
unscathed and significantly lighter and cooler.

"In times gone past," Charlotte informed the crowd,
"when electricity wasn't found in our outbuildings, we
used hand shears, which are slower but less stressful fer
the animals." She went on to prove she could also get the
job done without the whizz of electric shears.

Afterward, when her spectators had scattered, she
greeted me holding a wicker basket she'd passed during
the demo. It was filled with donations to the charity. "Guid
day tae ye, Eden!"

"Hi, Charlotte. That was impressive. You're really good
at fleecing customers . . . I mean . . . sheep!"

We grinned at each other. "Here," she said, handing
over the basket, "I'm entrusting it tae yer care."

Charlotte had recently graduated from vet school with

a specialty in large animal veterinary services, and was assisting an experienced local vet, but still managed to shear most of the hill farmers' sheep, which was the way she had funded her education. Since those in the sheep shearing profession were few and far between, she had more work than she knew what to do with. She was a regular visitor to the MacBride farm and had quickly become a good friend.

"That looks like it takes a lot of practice," I said, referring to the hand shears she still held.

"Aye, it does," she replied while packing up her supplies. "The important point in hand shearing is tae make sure ye don't leave cuts on the sheep, while also making sure the wool is in decent lengths fer the spinner."

"In that case, you were perfect," I said as she grabbed a broom and swept bits of fleece into a pile off to the side, then plucked a piece of straw from the thick braid that ran down her back.

Charlotte beamed. "I best be off. I've a lambing to assist with at a farm between here and Inverness. No use cleaning things up yet. I'm going tae leave most of my shearing equipment here since I'll be shearing more MacBride sheep in a few days. John has a lot on his mind today, so I'll remind him later to make sure the sheep are penned and ready first thing Monday morning."

"Do you want help?"

"No, but thank ye fer the offer. I'm used tae working alone."

We walked down the lane together. John's sheep dog demonstration was still going on in the field. Vicki drove past, transporting a few elderly couples and a family with small children. Charlotte called out, "Where can I pick up my yarn kit?"

"At the welcome table!" Vicki called back.

"I didn't know you were a knitter," I said to Charlotte.

"I'm not," she replied. "It's fer my granny. Her legs don't work like they used tae but ye should see her knitting needles fly!"

As we approached Sheepish Expressions, I spotted Sean sitting alone under the blue-and-white tent.

"You've been deserted by the rest of the welcome committee?" I asked.

"It appears that way," Sean said. "I haven't seen hide nor hair o' the lot o' them in ages. Other than the big boss lady, that is, who went off tae mind more blokes' businesses. She could be back any minute, heaven help us."

I mentally applauded Oliver, Lily, and Andrea for escaping from the slave driver. I pictured Isla stomping across the field, intent on hunting them down and dragging them back with a firm grip on an ear.

I deposited the donation basket of cash on the table. "More money to add to the kitty." I explained how Charlotte had passed the hat during her demonstration.

"Or rather, I passed the basket," Charlotte said.

Sean placed it under the table out of sight and said to her, "Our battle-axe . . . I mean . . . herself will appreciate yer efforts, and so do we all."

"Thanks, Sean. I'd also like tae pick up my granny's yarn kit."

Sean riffled around under the table, producing a kit and

a short list, where he crossed off Charlotte's name. I noticed a few other names had been crossed out, too.

"How's business inside the shop?" I asked Sean.

"Booming" was the reply. Judging by the number of cars in the Sheepish Expressions parking area, Kirstine should be in a good mood. A full till *and* a successful fund-raiser. Even the distribution of yarn kits was being handled without her having to lift a finger.

After a little more small talk, I scampered off before Isla could make a reappearance. I wasn't about to give her an opportunity to turn her attention my way and make any demands of me.

I headed back, making a short detour through the refreshment tent. Senga's sheep-shaped cupcakes were all gone, but the fried delectables were still available, including the Mars bars I'd been avoiding. If I wanted to live a full and long life without clogging every single artery in my body, I needed to stay away from fried food. But I liked my life exactly as it was. I had plenty of time later to slim down.

So I ate a fried Mars bar, relishing every single bite.

"Enjoyin'?" I heard at my elbow, recognizing the playful voice as Leith's.

"Yum."

"The judges are aboot tae announce the winners," he said, taking me by the elbow then turning his attention to his dog. "This way, Kelly girl."

Lily Young passed us, and I saw her collecting the final afternoon's sales for the charity coffers. Leith and I wandered back to our chairs.

The youth division winner was announced. Handler and border collie accepted the trophy to great applause.

"Next, we haff the senior division," Harry said. "And that honor goes tae . . ."

I held my breath.

". . . Leith Cameron and his dog, Kelly!"

I let my breath out in a burst. Yes! They'd won! I knew it, knew it. My smile was a mile wide as they went up to accept the award. Leith was obvious in his pride, while Kelly accepted the applause in stride.

In my excitement, I rose and hugged Leith when he returned. "Well done!"

"It was all Kelly," he said, sitting back down and stroking her coat.

As it turned out, two competitors had tied for top dog. There would be a runoff. I guessed correctly before Harry Taggart even announced the names of the two who had tied. They were John Derry and Bryan Lindsey. Hoots and hollers rose in the air.

There were nothing but bragging rights hanging on a win—no sort of cash prize or entry to qualify them for a more prestigious sheep dog trial—but everyone carried on as though this were the most important event of the year.

I decided I really wanted John to win. Out of a sense of loyalty to the farm, but also for a purely selfish reason. Neither I, nor the rest of the community, would ever hear the end of it from Isla if her husband took the trophy. Although I felt bad for Bryan; he might need to win to keep his spirits up with a wife like he had.

I'd seen Isla off and on throughout the day, but had managed to keep my distance and avoid her sharp tongue.

The last time had been right before Leith and Kelly had competed, when she'd marched toward the refreshment tent with a satchel of some sort draped over her shoulder, its plaid pattern clashing with the tartan skirt she wore. Now, with Bryan about to compete in a final round, I searched for her, but his wife was nowhere to be seen.

Vicki and Sean stood off to the side of the empty tractor wagon.

"I'll be right back," I told Leith and headed over to the pair.

"A successful fund-raiser if I ever saw one," Sean said. "This will bring the hospice into the black fer all o' this year and intae the next."

"How many printed programs did the welcome committee sell?" I asked him.

"All o' them, and too many entrance fees tae count on the spot."

"The food's gone, too," I told them.

Vicki smiled. "An all-round success."

I addressed Sean. "Congratulations on your acceptance into police school."

"I couldn't haff done it without yerself and Vicki," he said, beaming.

"And I see you survived Isla."

"She drove me tae the end of my tether, so I wound up giving her a piece o' my mind." He puffed up like a peacock. "The uniform and the man inside it kept her in line."

"What really happened was Sean drove her away," Vicki said fondly. "She went off in a snit and we haven't seen her since. She sure can dish it out better than she can take it."

Oliver and Andrea joined us. I turned and saw Leith looking our way. I held up a be-there-in-one-minute finger. He smiled and nodded.

"Has anyone seen Isla?" I asked. "And what about all the cash? Who's handling it?"

"Lily has put it safely away," Oliver responded. "And as tae Isla? Yer guess is as good as mine."

"Good riddance, I say," Sean said.

"Did most of the other members pick up their kits?" I asked Vicki.

"Some did, and I expect the others will come by tomorrow. And look, a few are already knitting away."

I followed Vicki's line of sight over to a group of women sitting on lawn chairs, recognizing a few of the other volunteers as well as cupcake queen Senga Hill. Sure enough, they were all knitting away, needles flying, conversation brisk among them.

"It's about tae begin," Sean announced as Harry and the other judges passed on the way to the field. I hustled back to my seat beside Leith.

Isla's husband, Bryan, as president of the Glenkillen Sheep Dog Association, went first. The judges converged on the perimeter with watchful eyes as Bryan and his dog went through the run with whistles and calls. Next, John was up with his border collie. I couldn't begin to guess who would triumph, the two dogs were so evenly matched. The judges had their work cut out for them.

After consulting with the other judges for what seemed like forever, head judge Harry Taggart stepped forward and announced the winner: Bryan Lindsey had won today's sheep dog trials. He held his trophy high, and the crowd responded. I applauded, too, but inwardly I groaned. The man might be the nicest guy in the world, but his win meant one more thing for his loudmouth wife to crow over. I vowed to stay even farther away from her in the future.

Where was she anyway?

"It's over then," Leith said, rising. "I expect ye have some finishing up tae do."

"Yes, quite a bit. Several hours' worth at least."

"And I need tae do some work on my fishing equipment fer tomorrow's charter. I'll see ye again soon." With that, we parted ways for the evening.

Vicki and Sean made multiple trips back and forth with the tractor and wagon from the field to the parking lot, while Oliver and Andrea left to help direct traffic before taking down the welcome tent. Since Isla was missing in action, I began to feel a little guilty for ditching my committee even though I'd been assisting with clean up at the refreshment tent, so I went to help when I saw them gathering near the shop. Lily arrived and pitched in, too. The tent came down easily and we all worked together to bag it and clear the table.

By the time we finished, most of the vehicles parked along the lane were gone. I checked the time. Five o'clock. It had been a full day, and I looked forward to kicking off my shoes and relaxing.

I took the bag of tent stakes Oliver handed to me and followed him over to the van. He had the bagged tent in his arms, so he stepped aside to let me pass. I tried to open the back of the van. It wouldn't budge. I tried again.

"It's jammed," I told him.

"Bloody thing must be rusted. It gave me trouble earlier, the bugger. Would you be a lamb and open the side door?"

I sidled between Sean's Renault and the van. The side door was the sliding kind. Only it refused to slide more than a crack. So I dropped the bag of stakes to free both hands and tugged on the handle. The door caught at first as though the weight of something solid and heavy had lodged up against it. I tried peeking inside through the window to see what might be obstructing it, but the tinted glass prevented me. I leaned into the door hard and finally felt it give way.

As it began to fully open, I caught a flash of red and at the same time sensed movement from within. Startled, I instinctively stepped back. Then something pitched out of the van, rolling in what I would later describe as a tight summersault, and landed at my feet with a dull thud. Face up, presenting empty, vacant eyes and a slack mouth. And no mistake as to the identity.

I'd been avoiding that sunburnt face all day.

Isla Lindsey was on the ground, one arm slung over my left shoe.

I edged my foot out from beneath her, feeling light-headed.

I wouldn't have to go out of my way to avoid the woman anymore. Even in my confused state, I was able to make a judgment of my own, one much more final than any made on the trial field this day by Harry Taggart or any of the other judges.

Isla was most definitely dead and gone from this world.

CPR wasn't going to help her. Nothing on this green earth would.

At my elbow, Oliver uttered an oath.

There wasn't any doubt about it. Not only was Isla very much dead, but she'd been helped along into the afterlife. The flash of red I'd seen hadn't been blood; it had been a length of what I suspected was Poppy Red yarn, folded in cords several times to make it extremely strong.

Which someone had then drawn tightly around the dead woman's neck and tied in a neat bow.

CHAPTER 5

I swung my head wildly, searching for someone else to take control of the situation.

Most of the vehicles along the lane were gone, as were the spectators, who had left for home immediately after the winner was announced. Isla and Bryan's camper van was the only vehicle still parked on the side of the lane. I scanned the horizon for Bryan. How was he going to handle this? Not well at all, I imagined.

The shop's parking lot was also empty, leaving only three remaining vehicles—Kirstine and John's car close to Sheepish Expressions, Sean's Renault, and the welcoming committee van itself.

I glanced over at Oliver. Apparently a tragedy like this one separates the men from the boys. Or in the current case, the women from the men. Oliver Wallace, alleged kin to the fierce warrior William Wallace, didn't seem so fierce at the moment. He stumbled away, dropped the rolled-up tent, clutched his chest as though on the brink of cardiac arrest, and blanched pasty white right through his recent sun damage.

I saw Special Constable Sean Stevens at the far end of the Sheepish Expressions parking lot and frantically waved him over. He hurried over and swung into action, although hardly in the manner I expected. He took one look at Isla's contorted face and promptly announced that he thought he was going to faint. Sean braced himself with one hand against the hood of his own car and teetered. Then he bent forward and tucked his head between his knees.

If I hadn't been occupied with something far more serious and important, I would have given him a swift kick in the behind. If he couldn't take command of this present situation, it didn't bode well for his dream of following in the inspector's footsteps.

I saw Kirstine come out onto the shop's porch, keys in hand to lock up the door of Sheepish Expressions, a questioning look on her face. Her husband, John, and Vicki pulled up on the tractor, in what seemed like slow motion. The tractor ground to a halt near the porch. They both hopped down and hurried toward us, with Kirstine right behind.

I turned my attention back to the body and stared at the yarn around Isla's neck. Then I followed the strand to its conclusion, to the rest of the skein. Without a doubt, it was my friend's yarn.

Vicki, in her typical reaction to crisis, began screaming when she approached and saw what the fuss was about. With operatic vocal cords like hers, those few individuals left on the grounds came running. Harry Taggart appeared, as did Lily Young and Bryan Lindsey's sister Andrea.

"Call the emergency number," I yelled out, a little frustrated that I couldn't remember the emergency code now that there was an actual emergency. But it hardly mattered. Harry Taggart started punching numbers on his mobile phone, probably relieved to be doing something useful.

"What's going on?" I heard behind me. Turning, I saw Bryan Lindsey rushing forward. He stopped when he saw his wife on the ground and shouted, "Oh, no! Isla!" He charged forward and knelt down beside her. I suppose I should have ordered him back, but I just couldn't bring myself to do so. If her body had still been inside the van, I would have worried more about disturbing potential evidence, but she'd already rolled out and taken an altogether different position than the one in which she'd been killed.

Lily and Andrea broke through the front lines, appearing beside Bryan, squeezing in beside the body, "oh, my"– and "oh, no"–ing, hands to mouths in disbelief.

I looked down and addressed the inverted Sean with as commanding a tone as I could manage (though to my ears, the words came out as squeaks). "Pull yourself together, get up, and keep everybody back! No one is to go near the van." I glanced around, noting that there were only a few of us at the scene, including Oliver, who was still pretty much incapacitated.

To my astonishment, Sean pulled himself upright and snapped to attention. "Ye'll haff tae step away," he told the women. "Bryan as well."

I'd already realized that I was in complete charge. The special constable wasn't really as special as his title and needed to take orders, not issue them. I looked around for someone else to appoint leader, and didn't spot a single capable or willing volunteer. Even John Derry, usually so gruff and self-confident, remained in the background with his wife.

"Step back," Sean repeated when no one moved.

Isla's husband didn't seem to hear Sean. He began fumbling with the yarn in an attempt to remove it. "No, Bryan!" I said sharply, grabbing his hand, forcing him to stop, knowing that the knotted strands were too tightly tied to loosen anyway. That the act of removing the yarn wouldn't help Isla. And that the murder scene had to remain as it was no matter how difficult that might be to accept.

Lily and Andrea, both ashen, helped Bryan to his feet. The sound that came from deep inside his throat was primal and heartrending. The three of them huddled together behind the van with Oliver and Vicki. Someone handed me a plaid blanket, and I draped it carefully over Isla's entire body, thinking I might be sick any minute. "Everybody back a bit more," Sean ordered, barely in control of himself let alone anyone else. "Come on now, do as I say."

The group edged back, but only by a few steps.

Time seemed to crawl as we waited for the proper authorities to arrive and take charge. The only sounds came from Bryan, who wept uncontrollably, and the soft voices of comfort from the women.

All kinds of questions went through my head as we waited. Who would do such a thing? Granted, Isla Lindsey had been as obnoxious as they come, but she certainly didn't deserve to die in such a violent manner. Nobody did. And why had she been in Oliver's van? Why not her own camper van? I'd distinctly remembered that Isla had driven to the farm with her husband. Oliver, Lily, and Andrea had arrived together in the van after picking up the tent.

And why would anyone commit murder at a public event where chances of being seen were so great?

Granted, Oliver's van was parked in the least traveled part of the lot, in the far corner, with Sean's Renault partially blocking it from view. Was that the reason the van had been chosen? That, and how the tinted windows obscured any view of what was happening in the interior?

"Now look what you've done," Kirstine said to Vicki in a sharp, loud, carrying voice.

She'd recognized Vicki's signature yarn just as I had.

"What? You're blaming me for what's happened?!" Vicki had tears in her eyes and a tremor in her voice.

"Stop it, Kirstine," I snarled, having reached my limit with the woman. "Things are bad enough. Do you want to make people think Vicki murdered Isla?" Then I thought of a more effective way to get her to clam up. "Starting a rumor like that won't be good for business, now will it?"

Kirstine closed her open mouth and stepped away.

I heard sirens wailing in the distance, and soon Inspector Jamieson's Honda CR-V appeared in the parking lot. Sean attempted to intercept him, but the inspector held up a hand in warning and kept moving forward. Without a word, he walked past the others to come and stand beside me, taking in the scene, hands in his trouser pockets, his intelligent eyes scanning the blanket, the surroundings, and then the bystanders.

The others, sensing his concentration and not daring to interrupt, waited silently.

Jamieson approached the covered body, crouched down, threw the blanket aside, and studied the dead woman. Then he rose and gestured to Sean, who hustled over to us after warning those around him to stay where they were.

"We have ourselves a murder, Inspector," Sean said.

"I can see that," the inspector said quietly. "What happened tae you? You look like death warmed up yerself."

And so he did. Sean was functioning but he hadn't regained the erect professional attitude he normally wore along with his uniform. He looked undone, like he'd just jogged a few miles after a life of complete inactivity—drawn face, panting from overexertion, sweat beading on his forehead and trickling in a thin line down the right side of his temple that he brushed away with his hand.

"I'm perfectly fine," Sean lied. He nodded toward the body. "It's Isla Lindsey."

"I can see that." The inspector took a notebook out of his breast pocket and clicked open a pen. "Who found the body?"

"That would be me," I piped up. "Along with Oliver Wallace. We . . . I . . . opened the door to put the tent inside, and Isla . . . Isla's body . . . fell out."

The inspector swung his attention to Oliver, who stepped forward at the sound of his name. He'd gone from ghostly white to sickly green.

"This is yer vehicle, if I'm not mistaken."

"Aye," Oliver said, his voice trembling. "Ye know 'tis. But I can't imagine what she was doin' in my van. Eden can vouch fer my whereabouts, if need be."

I could? That was news to me. I could only vouch for the time it took to walk back from the trial field and dismantle the tent, but that was it. Although Oliver would hardly leave Isla's dead body in his own vehicle, if he were her killer, would he?

I gave Jamieson the slightest of headshakes after Oliver offered me up as his alibi, and the shrewd inspector picked up on it and replied with his own imperceptible nod.

"Dinnae be going far," the inspector said to Oliver, who ducked back into the group with obvious relief for the temporary reprieve.

My eyes slid to Isla's mourning husband, still being clucked over by the women, but more in control now, rubbing his eyes with the palms of his hands and blinking as though that simple act might turn back the clock to an earlier time when his wife was still alive.

More sirens had been drawing closer and now an ambulance pulled into the lot, followed by a nondescript black sedan that came to rest on the opposite side of Sean's car. Several men were inside. The driver's window slid down.

"Forensics," the inspector said to me, then called to the man in the driver's seat, "Give me some time with the body. I'll let ye know when I'm through."

The man nodded and turned off the motor while they waited. The ambulance crew gathered at the back of the ambulance, also waiting.

"The rest of ye are tae remain exactly where ye are until released," the inspector called out. Then to Sean, "Get names and contact information along with preliminary statements. And if any one of them saw anything suspicious I want tae speak with them immediately. Afterwards they are free tae go, but let them know I'll be calling on each o' them individually. All but the husband and the owner of the van. They stay." Before Sean turned to go, the inspector addressed him, "And I suppose ye have nothing o' value tae add aboot what transpired here?"

Sean jerked as though he were guilty of something and trying to hide it. "Nothing that would be o' interest, no," he said, then quickly changed the subject. "Lily Young and Andrea Lindsey arrived in the van with Oliver Wallace. I'm guessing they'll need a way tae get tae their homes."

"See if Harry Taggart can offer Lily a ride. I expect Andrea will want tae stay with her brother. I'll see tae them. The camper van stays where it is, too, while we sort this out."

When Sean went off to carry out his orders, the inspector muttered something unintelligible under his breath, whether directed at the situation or something else entirely, I wasn't sure. Until he said, "Our special constable sat at the same table as this woman, and he didn't see or hear a thing? Didn't suspect any goin' ons? Why am I not surprised?"

I sensed it was my turn. I hadn't suspected anything, either.

"What about you?" Inspector Jamieson asked, his eyes piercing and sharp as always. "What can ye add?"

"I hadn't spoken with Isla since morning when you saved me from her clutches before the trials began," I said. "And she wasn't around when Oliver and I packed up the tent. Then . . . we went to put the tent in the van . . . and"— my voice cracked; I cleared my throat—"and she rolled out when I opened the door. She must have been up against the back of the door . . . no, for sure she was, otherwise she wouldn't have fallen out like that." I realized I was babbling, so I stopped. What more could I offer?

"It must have been quite a shock."

"Yes, it was. I tried to keep everyone away, but Bryan rushed up and fell to his knees . . ." I couldn't go on without showing my distress in a less than professional way. After all, I'd been recruited for a law enforcement position that very day, and I wasn't about to behave as Oliver and Sean had. Bogus title or not, I was going to make a decent showing.

"Ye did just fine," the inspector reassured me despite the fact I hadn't been able to secure the scene. "And what was the police trainee doing during all this?"

I couldn't rat Sean out, especially after all the work he'd done preparing for his entrance exam into the police college. One critical word from his superior could have an adverse effect on his chances of success. How could I say he'd almost passed out? Besides, he'd recovered and gone on to follow my instructions. So maybe he wasn't destined to handle murder investigations. Sean might be better suited for patrolling streets and traffic direction and other duties that come with less risk of encountering violence.

The inspector gave me a hard look.

"Special Constable Stevens did a fine job," I decided to say.

The inspector snorted.

Then I remembered Sean and Vicki discussing how Sean claimed to have put Isla in her place, pulling rank with his uniform, and how Vicki said she'd disappeared after that. At the moment, Sean was as dazed and shocked as the rest of us, but it was possible that he might also be feeling guilty for his confrontation with the dead woman.

The exchange of words that drove Isla away from the welcome table could hardly be an important piece of the puzzle, but I figured Sean was already on the inspector's bad side. I'd give him until tomorrow to recount the incident on his own. If he hadn't offered up that information by then, I'd do it myself. Which would only set him up for more of the inspector's wrath.

Sean chose that moment to address those remaining at the scene. "If ye know something, if ye saw something and yer afraid to step forward, contact Inspector Jamieson or myself anonymously. Ye can be safe in the knowledge that nobody will ever know ye spoke tae us."

"See! He's doing a great job," I said, cheerleading. But only got a shake of the inspector's head in return.

After that, he used a small camera to take photographs of the crime scene from several angles, then he drew on a pair of gloves, squatted next to Isla, and examined her body. Next he rose and peered into the back of the van.

"I need a torch," he called out and someone came forward with a flashlight. After shining it inside, he seemed satisfied and turned over the crime scene to the forensics team. Then he asked to speak with Vicki privately.

"I want Eden with me," she said instantly. He granted her wish without question or comment.

"Earlier today I personally witnessed ye standing outside Sheepish Expressions with that same color yarn," he said to Vicki. "So I would appreciate yer statement regarding said yarn and whether ye can substantiate that the murder weapon is in fact from yer dyed lot."

Vicki's lip trembled, but her voice was steady as she said, "I want my solicitor present."

I glanced sharply at my friend, a bit perplexed at her request.

The inspector said, "Ye aren't under any more suspicion than the rest o' them. However, we need tae clarify what details we can and as quickly as possible."

"It's okay to cooperate with the inspector, Vicki," I reassured her. "You aren't in any trouble."

After acknowledging my words of encouragement she said, "It's the same color, but I can't tell you for sure if it's from one of the skeins I dyed for my yarn club."

"It is," I told her gently. "You didn't come close enough to identify it, but I did."

"Was the victim a member of this club o' yers?" Jamieson wanted to know.

"Isla?" Vicki shook her head. "No."

"How many o' these kits did ye make up fer distribution?"

"Thirty-five."

"Thirty-five!" He sighed then said, "I'll be speaking with ye further at a later time." Then he turned to me. "That will be all," he said. "Yer free tae go with Vicki."

And just like that, I was dismissed. I watched him walk over to the grieving husband, more than slightly confused.

I stood where I was for a moment, uncertain. Didn't Inspector Jamieson plan to hold me to the volunteer constable commitment I'd made earlier? Especially since we now had an actual crime on our hands? Hadn't I been the one to discover the body and take charge? Didn't I deserve to be included in the investigation?

More important, I had to stop and ask myself, did I really want to be involved? Part of me was relieved that the inspector didn't want or need my help. But there was another part that yearned to be included in solving the case.

I decided it was best to stay with Vicki. Silently, each of us deep in our own thoughts, we walked up the lane, back to our routines, to the two adorable Westies, and to our simple lives that would carry on. Unlike Isla Lindsey, we'd wake up tomorrow to live another day.

For the first time, I noticed the night chill. Judging by the descending darkness, I realized that it must be close to eight o'clock. The trials had run a bit later than three because of the tie between John and Bryan, but still . . . almost five hours had passed between then and now.

Vicki and I parted ways at the main house. I walked down a path that led to my cottage, unlocked the door, and flipped the switch on the wall beside it to illuminate the sitting area. All was in order. Exactly as I'd left it early this morning, which seemed so very long ago.

Tomorrow, I'd drive into Glenkillen to the pub where I'd tweak the book just a little more. And I'd force myself to check those e-mails I'd been avoiding like the plague, hopeful that Ami would decide *Falling for You* wasn't a complete disaster, that it was as salvageable as the cottage I occupied, that it had potential, and she hadn't been wrong to back me.

But thoughts of my book were completely pushed out of my mind by thoughts of the murder. I tossed and turned for most of the night, analyzing the case from every angle.

I assumed that Isla's death hadn't been planned in advance—who would intentionally choose to commit murder with so many people coming and going? So it naturally followed that something must have happened at the fundraiser to precipitate her death.

But what? Certainly it had to be more compelling than

an extreme dislike for a disagreeable woman. It had to have been big, at least in the mind of the person who decided that her death was necessary. Someone felt seriously threatened and believed she had to be stopped then and there. What could that possibly have been?

What did you say, see, or do that got you killed, Isla Lindsey? You had a sharp tongue. Did it get you in mortal trouble this time?

Passage on this earth is a short journey. We need to live it well and fully. Too bad it takes a tragedy such as this one to remind us of that. I intended to listen to the message and get on with my life, wherever it would lead me next.

Chapter 6

The following morning, dark clouds moved in and the temperature dropped significantly from the highs we'd been enjoying. After a few months in the Highlands, I was prepared for anything Mother Nature threw my way, and had learned to dress in several layers. I've often heard the Scots say, "There's nae such thing as bad weather. Only the wrong clothes!" And it was so true.

I walked toward the farmhouse to see how Vicki was doing. Her Westies, Coco and Pepper, were outside. They rushed over to greet me. Out of the corner of my eye, I saw Jasper slink into the barn.

"You two have been pestering the cat again," I said, giving each of them a few strokes before Coco spotted a red squirrel up the lane, and the two dogs tore off in hot pursuit. The first time they'd run off, I'd been beside myself with worry. But Vicki had assured me that they wouldn't go far. And she'd been right. They always came back from their escapades.

I'd slept later than usual, the events of the day before having kept me awake well into the early hours of the morning. Judging by the dark circles under Vicki's eyes, she hadn't slept much, either.

"Seven degrees outside, I'll be guessing," Vicki said as we sat at her kitchen table, eating porridge.

"Seven?" I asked.

"If that," she added.

I still wasn't used to defining weather in terms of Celsius. My mind was set on Fahrenheit.

After a moment of confusion, I did the conversion, sloppy at best, and guessed it to be about forty-five degrees. I could live with that; I was from Chicago. Cool temperatures didn't bother me.

"Sean's wishing he'd held his tongue," Vicki was saying now. "Instead of telling Isla off the way he did. Maybe she wouldn't have gone off by herself and would still be alive to see this Sunday morning."

"We both know Sean isn't to blame," I reassured her, taking a sip of the instant coffee she'd set before me. What was it with the Scots and all the instant coffee? The taste was growing on me, although it would never replace the real thing.

"Of course, I agree," she said, "but try telling that to him. And what about me? My very own handmade yarn, the instrument of her death!"

"The only one to blame is the person who did this awful thing," I insisted.

Vicki slid out of her seat, picked up our empty bowls,

and placed them in the kitchen sink. "And what if the killer turns out to be one of my yarn club members? I can hardly bear thinking about it."

"It's not necessarily one of the members," I said. "It could have been anybody, really. Maybe this person just snapped and picked up the nearest weapon."

"And it just happened to be one of my skeins of yarn?"

"It's possible," I said, sounding more confident than I felt. It would be so much better for Vicki if the murder weapon had been randomly selected rather than planned. Not that it would matter to the dead woman, but maybe it would help Vicki move past blaming herself for something she had no control over. "Isla wasn't a member of the club," I continued. "So it wasn't hers. Obviously. But someone else could have placed their kit in the van, like one of the other members of the welcome committee who rode over with Oliver."

Vicki shook her head as she took her place again at the table, looking forlorn. "Oliver isn't a member. Neither is Lily Young. If you remember she was after me to give her one but she wasn't on the list. And she didn't sway me, as you saw."

"Oh, right. Yes." My memory of the beginning of the day must have still been clouded by the terrible ending, which was all I'd been able to think about. "Andrea Lindsey, then."

"Sean *did* tell me that she picked hers up. But hers isn't missing."

Vicki sighed. Poor Vicki. Poor Isla Lindsey, and everyone else this tragedy has touched.

While I sat at the table, grasping for a different theory

to calm Vicki, trying and failing to hatch up a situation where someone other than one of the yarn club members could have been the murderer, I glanced out the rain-streaked window and saw Leith Cameron drive up in his white Land Rover with Kelly beside him.

"Come inside, the both of you," Vicki said in greeting when they came to the door. "I'll put on the kettle again."

"I can't stay long," Leith said, wiping his feet on a mat at the entryway. "And my boots are wet. I'll stay by the door." As usual, I couldn't help noticing that the man was as handsome as men come, Scottish through and through. "I'm on my way tae the harbor fer a fishing expedition. I only have a few minutes."

I glanced at the window again, seeing more streaks of rain on the pane. Since Glenkillen is on the coast of the North Sea with a beautiful harbor and is also close to several rivers including the River Spey, fishing is a popular tourist attraction. Leith guides his paying customers out to sea to catch cod, haddock, and prawns. Sometimes they prefer the river when it's running high and fast, where they wade through the rushing current, casting for salmon.

"But it's pouring rain outside," I said.

"It doesn't get much finer than this," Leith said. "And September is one o' the best weather months fer fishing in the Highlands. Only eleven other months are as good." He paused to give me a playful grin. "Right now, I have plenty o' work tae keep me busy. A day like today is perfect fishing weather. Now if I could only convince my customers tae lay off the booze." He shook his head in wonder. "It never ceases tae amaze me when they show up first thing in the morn carrying enough alcohol tae inebriate a whale.

The waves will be rollin' and the wind blowin' something fierce once we get out past the firth into the open sea. Sometimes those blokes drink a wee bit too much whisky, turn green as seaweed, and spend the rest o' the trip hanging over the edge being sick. It feels wrong to take their money."

"Sounds like a picnic," I said, my tone light and intentionally implying the exact opposite. Fishing for a living sounded idyllic on the surface, but it obviously had its less pleasant undercurrents.

"Why don't ye come along?" Leith grinned again, addressing me. "Ye'd be as safe as on dry land with me at the helm."

"Thanks, but no thanks," I replied. "I'd be perfectly safe as long as the boat didn't capsize, or some giant wave didn't come along and swallow your boat. I've seen *The Perfect Storm*, you know."

"I suppose I can hardly blame ye after I made it seem so appealing," he joked, then dropped the playfulness and said, "I heard what happened yesterday after I left and wanted tae check on the two o' ye."

"It's a shame is what it is," Vicki said, answering first. "I know I shouldn't speak poorly of the dead, but leave it to the likes of her to do damage to all around her. If the woman had to go and get herself murdered, you'd think she could have done it elsewhere and with something other than my very own yarn!"

"She *was* difficult," Leith agreed. "But didn't deserve what she got. Nobody deserves that."

"That's the truth, and I should be grateful for my own healthy breath," Vicki said, with a gentler tone.

"Her husband is devastated, from what I hear," Leith added. "He can barely function."

"I'll make a dish to drop off with him." Vicki clucked, then flashed me a conspiratorial look, playing matchmaker as usual. "Well, I have chores in the barn."

And with that, Vicki called to Kelly to come along and the two of them brushed past our visiting neighbor and disappeared out the door.

"She's more upset than she's letting on," I told Leith. "I've been trying to convince her that she isn't responsible, but she's racked with guilt at the thought that the yarn she spun and dyed herself was used to strangle Isla."

"Aye, it's aboot town."

Already? Well, of course it was. News, especially bad news, traveled with lightning speed in a village as small and close-knit as Glenkillen. And Isla may have been widely disliked, but she was still one of their own. She and her husband were very visible and active members of the community.

Leith wiped his boots on the mat several more times then slid into the chair Vicki had vacated. "It must o' been awful, seeing her like that."

"It was horrible," I agreed. "I opened the van door and she fell out, right at my feet." Isla Lindsey's vacant expression flashed through my mind. I willed it away and went on to explain about the yarn club, how popular it was and how unfortunate it was that Vicki's very first one had been marred by murder. "I wouldn't be surprised if she gave up the club altogether."

"That would be a shame."

"It would. She was so excited about it."

"Are all the members women?" Leith asked.

The question surprised me. I almost replied, "Of course." Instead I paused to consider the question more carefully before saying, "Uh . . . I think so."

"Ye don't sound very sure."

I knew there were men who knit, but I tried to recall if I'd ever actually *seen* a man knitting and came up blank. I thought back to Vicki's members and wannabees lists, and after more careful consideration I said, "Yes, all the members are women."

Leith thought for a minute then said, "Sounds like the first thing the inspector will look for is one who picked up her yarn, but doesn't have it anymore."

I nodded in agreement, although I hadn't even begun to imagine how the inspector would handle the case, or where he would begin. "Certainly a starting point," I agreed. "Whoever she is will have some explaining to do." Most of the thirty-five kits were out in circulation, and one of those avid knitters had attended the trials with ulterior motives. Or perhaps the killer was a family member, or an acquaintance of a member who just happened to pick up someone else's red yarn and thread it around her hands and pull it taut.

"I wouldn't want Inspector Jamieson's job for all the gold in the world," Leith said, and I had to agree. I was beginning to think I should consider myself lucky that the inspector had dismissed me instead of calling on me as his special constable.

Besides, Sean was still in Glenkillen, acting as special constable, and willing and able to assist. Knowing Sean, nothing would stand in the way of his role in the investigation. At least until he had to leave for training.

When Leith had walked in Vicki's door, he'd claimed he couldn't stay long, but he didn't seem in any particular hurry now. So I went on to pick his brain, since he was as local as they come and was sure to have heard all the rumors circulating. "Do you have any idea who might have killed Isla?"

"Could be anyone. She managed to put off everyone she met. But most o' us are betting on her husband. Sure, he's playing the grieving widower, but from all accounts, she wasn't an easy one tae live with."

"That's always the first person an investigator suspects—the surviving spouse. Do you think, is it possible that Bryan could've been fooling around on the side?"

"Ye've been watching the telly again," he teased, then grew more serious. "I'd leave that fer the inspector tae decide."

"Isla had her husband solidly under her thumb, didn't she?" I asked. She had everyone else. Why not Bryan?

Leith shrugged. "That's the impression she gave, but though it might look like she wore the trousers in the family, Bryan isn't what I'd call a pushover. At least when it comes tae sheepherding. He's a good organizer and a hard worker. As tae their marriage, who knows?" Leith spoke slowly, measuring his words. "Sometimes a person acts out in ways the rest of us cannae comprehend. Bryan Lindsey appears on the surface to be as dull as ditchwater, but he might have had a sea o' resentment building inside of him and the dam finally burst yesterday afternoon."

I added a few more notches to that personal-assessment book of mine and put Leith's name a little higher up. Not only was he good-looking, but he seemed to study the world and the people in it. Not self-absorbed or petty or hung up on himself.

"So are ye coming fishing with us?"

"Another time?"

"Aye, on a sunnier day, and soon."

"I look forward to it." I smiled. Yes, I would look forward to spending time on the North Sea with Leith.

"Well," he said, pushing up to his feet, "I best be collecting Kelly and heading out."

"I hope you catch a boatload of fish," I told him as I rose, too, and gathered up the teacups and teapot.

"Aye, I hope so as well. And I hope you take extra care of yerself, Eden."

"Why do you say that?" I asked, surprised.

"Ye have a way o' finding trouble," he pointed out. "Or rather it finds you."

Which was certainly true. My unfortunate knack for stumbling across crime scenes could be the reason the inspector had thought of me when he needed a new volunteer police officer. Was that his reasoning? Since he had to deal with me at the scenes anyway, he might as well have me on the side of the law, however bogus the part was that I played?

Even so, I assured Leith, "I plan on staying far away from trouble in the future."

"See that ye do."

After Leith called Kelly and they drove off, I finished cleaning and putting away the breakfast dishes, grabbed my laptop and an all-weather jacket, and settled into the driver's seat of the old Peugeot that Vicki had given me to drive during my stay in the Highlands. She'd recently bought herself a brand-new Volvo station wagon with an automatic transmission, which I lusted after. In Chicago I'd been able to take that feature for granted; here, manual transmissions were the norm. Driving on the opposite side of the road from what I was accustomed, along with a stick shift on the left side of the steering wheel instead of the right, had almost done me in more than once. It's a miracle I'm still alive to complain. But I should be grateful that the Peugeot runs and gets me where I need to go.

I pulled into the lane leading past Sheepish Expressions before the gravel lane turned onto the road leading to Glen-killen. The refreshment tent still stood out in the field. Volunteers had meant to come today and tear it down and also to clean up after the spectators. Isla had been the one who had demanded that all the Saturday volunteers return on Sunday to pick up trash and dismantle the big tent, the obstacle gates, and the holding pens. Now, with the rain, those chores would have to wait a little longer.

Oliver's van was nowhere in sight. Neither was the Lindseys' camper van.

My drive into Glenkillen was mostly uneventful despite my windshield wipers flapping against a steady downpour of rain, except for one abrupt and harrowing moment when I rounded a blind curve to discover a shaggy red-coated, long-horned Highland cow calmly strolling across the narrow road. I slammed on the brakes, practically standing the car on end. The cow didn't even acknowledge my presence.

After catching my breath and stilling my pounding heart, I drove slowly away, cautious of more than my own faulty driving abilities. The cow had been an important reminder that four-legged creatures also traveled these roads.

Soon, though, my driving concerns gave way to wonder. I never grow tired of the view, even on a rainy day like this, when Glenkillen comes into sight below as I wind down from the towering Highlands to the village situated at sea level. Or the drive along the harbor with its stunning and sweeping panorama of the North Sea. Fishing boats and sailboats bob in the harbor, many in slips along the pier, others tied to moorings, and some traveling the waves on the way in to shore or out to sea. Watching the white-caps kissing the surface of the water, I wondered if Leith's boat was one of those going out, or if he and his charges were out of sight by now.

Next, I passed the beach, empty now due to the rain, but during the summer months it had been a popular gathering place for the community and visitors.

It's always a joy, too, to turn away from the harbor and drive the few blocks on Castle Street to the town center, especially now that I'm more familiar with the businesses and the owners. I love Glenkillen's cobblestone streets, red-tiled rooftops, and whitewashed buildings. Among other assorted establishments, the town has a charming bookstore whose shelves I hope my own books will one day grace, a whisky shop where the proprietor is generous with the samples, an inn for out-of-town visitors, the most amazing bakery with Scottish delectables, and my particular favorite, the Kilt & Thistle pub, where my writing muse has decided to take up residence.

After parking and entering the pub, I greeted the

owners, Dale and his wife, Marg, and put in a request for a pot of strong black tea. I also gave a passing hello to Bill Morris, owner of the Whistling Inn next door. His veiny bulbous nose and bloodshot eyes reminded me what alcohol has the potential to do, the destruction it has the power to wield in its wake.

Bill's daughter, Jeannie, has operated the Whistling Inn ever since Bill took a dive into a bottle of Scottish rye and never crawled out. A sad story, but Bill is a regular at the pub, or rather a permanent fixture unless or until he passes out. In which case, a good-hearted soul or two helps him to his feet and sees him to his bed in one of the rooms next door. The old coot hears plenty from his perch at a dark table close to the bar, but his soggy memory tends to be unreliable. And he's been known to tell the rest of us to "bugger off" when it suits him.

Today, he ignored my greeting, making me wonder for the umpteenth time why I bothered to make the effort.

"I'll deliver the tea to yer usual spot?" Marg said, and I thought she looked tired. It was rare when either of the pub owners had time off. They seemed to live at the Kilt & Thistle. "Ye have a visitor waiting."

So even before I could steel myself to power up my laptop and force myself to take a look at my in-box, I found Inspector Jamieson sipping tea in my favorite writing nook.

"I'm going tae need yer help after all," he said in his thick Scottish brogue. "Ye best sit doon."

CHAPTER 7

In the brief time it took to set my laptop on the table and situate myself in a chair opposite Inspector Jamieson, my emotions vacillated between annoyance and elation.

Annoyance, because he hadn't wanted my assistance last evening at the scene of the crime when he was taking statements from potential witnesses. Hadn't I been the one to discover Isla's body? Wasn't Jamieson the one who'd suggested that I become a special constable? Shouldn't I have had this choice from the very beginning?

But I also felt happy that the inspector, who wore his badge, job, and emotions so close to his chest, had chosen to put his trust in me. Better late than never, as they say.

"How could I possibly be of assistance?" I asked, wondering what had caused his change of heart.

"Tae be perfectly honest, I need somebody intelligent tae bounce ideas back and forth, and that's where yerself comes in."

I smiled, pleased in spite of myself. His flattery had worked. "What about Sean?" I quipped. "Isn't he your right-hand man?"

"Aren't ye the funny lass? As ye well know, Sean tries his best, and I'm not saying he won't make a good police officer one day, but following all the leads that present themselves isn't his strong suit. He isn't much fer the sort o' forward thinking required o' detective work. And asking him to carry on with more than one task at a time is a recipe fer disaster."

"I see your point." And I did. Sean was a kind man with a keen sense of justice, but he wasn't cut from the same cloth as the inspector. But was I? Hardly.

"Besides, he's a changed man, less intense in his devotion tae extra duties, since I believe he's set his sights on Vicki MacBride." The inspector chuckled. "I just noo sent him out tae the farm, and have high hopes that I won't see him again until the sun rises on another day."

Marg arrived with my tea and more hot water for the inspector's own pot. Her two redheaded twins ran through the pub, weaving around tables, making enough noises for a classroom of boys. "Shush, you wild loons," she called after them. "Ye're making enough clatter to raise the dead. Watch yerselves, or I'll put ye to work scrubbin' pots." But her warning fell on empty space; they'd already disappeared out the door. She smiled as only a mother can and said, "Sundays are always making me wish fer Monday and a nice day o' rest."

"Today *is* the day of rest, Marg," the inspector reminded her.

"Not the way I see it. Monday is my day. The boys are

in school and 'tis my day off from working here at the pub. Monday can't arrive soon enough tae suit me. Well, I'll leave ye tae yer business."

"Have you brought my pepper spray?" I asked after Marg had gone off. "That was part of the deal we struck, if you remember." I couldn't wait to have that small canister of security.

"Ah, I knew I'd forgotten tae bring something," the inspector said with an expression that suggested he wasn't being completely honest with me after all and didn't care if I knew it. "So, now that ye've had a night o' rest to think on it, what do ye make of Isla Lindsey's murder?"

"I wouldn't exactly call it a night of rest," I groused, thinking of how much of the night I'd lain awake.

"I hope it was better than if I'd put the burden o' stayin' at the crime scene on ye. I was wanting tae spare ye that ugly task."

That was a surprise. I'd just assumed the inspector was getting rid of me—yet all along he'd been trying to be considerate?

"Our Sean had words with the victim yesterday," he went on.

I almost blurted out, "Oh, good, I was hoping he would tell you about that," but caught myself just in time. Instead I said, "Oh?"

"Aye. He came clean about that early this morning, after feeling responsible fer her death the entire night, thinking she wouldn't have gone off by herself if he hadn't provoked her. I told him after all the meanness she's directed at others, he can't blame himself fer giving her a little o' her own medicine. And I suspect she stomped off in a snit, but forgot about it the minute he was out o' her sight. She was a hard one, she was."

"Isla was a piece of work, that's for sure," I agreed wholeheartedly. "She wasn't usually one to walk away from a fight." Thinking back, I realized that Sean hadn't elaborated when he'd mentioned their altercation, and I hadn't thought to ask. "What could Sean possibly have said to her to get that sort of reaction?"

The inspector surprised me with a hardy chuckle. "Ye sure ye want to know?"

"Of course." I picked up my teacup and took a sip, leaving the cup between both of my hands, appreciating the warmth.

"She was bossing him around. 'Put the van here.' 'Sit there.' 'Say this when they ask this.' 'Do that.' Finally, in exasperation Special Constable Stevens replied . . . let's see if I've got this right . . . his exact words if I'm not mistaken were"—and then the inspector did a perfect imitation of Sean—"'Perhaps ye should accompany me tae the loo. Ye could hold me private parts so the aim is more tae yer liking.'"

I burst out laughing so hard that tea sloshed from my cup. Nothing about Isla's murder was funny, but Sean's comeback to her was priceless, and I could almost see the expression on her face when he made that off-colored suggestion.

I noticed that the inspector's composure had a slight crack in it, too, for a change. "Never a dull moment with our Sean," he added.

I wiped up the drops of tea I'd spilled on the table and

composed myself. "So we know that Isla was still alive sometime in the afternoon."

The inspector nodded. "That's been confirmed by witnesses."

"I saw her myself. She was making rounds about noontime." Then I remembered a detail that probably was insignificant, but thought I should mention it anyway. "She had a bag on her shoulder, one I hadn't seen earlier. I noticed because it was plaid and her skirt was a tartan and I recall thinking the patterns didn't go together. They clashed."

"That woulda been the messenger bag used tae collect cash periodically throughout the day tae deter would-be thieves."

"Is the bag missing?" Had it been stolen? That was a whole new possibility I hadn't considered—had the motive been theft all along?

"No, no, it was tucked away safely in the Lindseys' vehicle. Isla had picked up what was available and locked it up fer safekeeping. Bryan turned it over tae Harry Taggart fer an accounting after I made a record o' the contents."

"So we still don't know when she was murdered."

"Not precisely, but I have a witness who said tha' she was in the queue fer the loo at aboot half past one. But ye know how many people were out and about. Those I've interviewed so far didn't see anything unusual. And certainly not a one o' them can account fer every minute of their time after that, so proper alibis have been scarce tae come by. It's going tae be a tough nut tae crack." He leaned back. "Ye found her body slightly after five o'clock, and that's been confirmed by several o' the others who were still on the grounds. Meaning she was murdered in aboot a three-and-a-half-hour time frame."

"Between one thirty and five."

"That's the best we can do fer the moment."

"What about her husband, Bryan?" I asked. "How's he coping?"

"He claims he can't go on living without her, but I'm beginning tae think he's going overboard with his grief. But as tae killing his wife . . . he would have had plenty of other opportunities to get rid of her that wouldnae involved the risk this killer took. Bryan stays on the list o' suspects fer the time being, however. Nobody can be ruled out this early in the investigation. Though I really hope Isla didn't die at his hand. He's a respected member o' the community, and it would be a blow tae us all."

I agreed. I didn't know the man, but Bryan Lindsey had just been through a nightmare, and I really hoped the community would rally around him rather than condemn him without any proof whatsoever. However, I had to ask: "Is there any possibility that another woman was involved? Someone on the side?"

The inspector sighed as he was busy preparing his tea, adding milk and sugar while keeping his features neutral as usual. Watching his smooth motions, I was again reminded of one characteristic the two of us shared: we're both left-handed.

"According tae the gossipmongers, there's always another person involved," he said dully, as though he'd run into this sort of hearsay often. "Best to ignore that kind of idle talk, or at least tuck it away fer the time being unless we can prove it's more than just indulging in poppycock."

"Poppycock" reminded me of poppy socks and that in turn reminded me of Vicki's bloodred yarn. The disturbing image of my encounter with the dead Isla flashed through my head as it had many times since that shocking moment when she fell at my feet. I tried willing those memories away, but they refused to scurry far, remaining lodged at the edges of my mind.

"Who else is suspect?"

"All those on the fund-raising committees who had tae deal with the victim's sharp tongue. Isla was expert at putting people off. We also have tae include anyone who came in contact with those knitting kits, either the members themselves or anyone who mightae pinched one. Who knows besides that? Even my special constable had opportunity and as much motive as anybody else."

"You don't really suspect Sean!"

"O' course not. It's the least likely person I'm most interested in, the one careful tae remain out o' sight and off the radar."

For a short time we sipped tea in a comfortable silence while contemplating possibilities. A few minutes later I asked about Oliver Wallace. "Since Isla was murdered inside his van, what does he have to say about his own whereabouts?"

"The man is a basket case. Says that he never locks the van. The silly bloke even leaves the keys dangling in the ignition as though he's begging fer thieves tae make off with it. And he says he hadn't been out tae it since unloading the tent first thing. Sean says the keys were in the ignition when he moved the van tae the back of the parking lot and he left them there and the van unlocked just as he'd found things. I can't fault him fer that."

"Oliver claimed I could vouch for him," I said, wanting to clear up any misunderstandings on that front, "but I hardly saw him until right before we found Isla's body."

"I imagine he was a bit shook up and frightened when he said that. Understandable, considering the murder occurred in his van. Unfortunate fer us, there are so many fingerprints inside the van and out, I don't know where tae begin sorting through them. A needle in a haystack would be easy compared tae this."

"What does Oliver do for a living?" I asked. "I've heard he's very active on fund-raising boards, but that hardly pays a mortgage."

The inspector considered briefly then said, "Wallace wasn't born with a silver spoon in his mouth even if he'd like ye tae think that. He married well enough, though."

That surprised me. I hadn't noticed a wedding ring or seen him with a woman who could be his wife. "Oliver is married?"

"Was. He got a bit o' settlement out o' the dissolution back a few years ago, seeing as how she came from money. Nothing tae brag aboot, I suspect, but enough tae get by. He isn't flashy and his van is an example o' that. Noo, what's yer take on our killer?"

"I've gone over what happened, and it just doesn't make sense to murder someone at such a public event. Unless the killer felt he had no choice."

"Ye're certain it's a he?" he asked, stirring his tea.

"I think so," I said, remembering that Isla was a solidly built woman. "Someone strong enough to hold the yarn tightly with a steady grip and plenty of pressure. I'm confident that Isla would have fought back against her attacker. She wouldn't just sit there while she was being choked to death without putting up a good fight."

He seemed pleased, probably because my assessment matched his.

I went on, aware that we were going over ground he must have already considered on his own. But if he wanted a second opinion, I'd give it to him. "Perhaps Isla saw something she shouldn't have, or discovered something damaging that triggered her death. But who knows what goes through the mind of a person capable of such violence?"

In the next moment, the inspector's mobile phone rang. He checked the incoming number and rose as he answered it, moving away. Out of sight as well as earshot. Ten minutes or more must have elapsed before he returned and sat down at the table, long enough that I had begun to wonder if he was coming back at all.

"An important piece of information just came tae light," he told me, "which I'm wanting tae share with ye. It's in regards tae the autopsy performed on Isla Lindsey. The cause of death was as we would have expected. Ligature strangulation."

That was hardly surprising. My expression must have said as much because he went on, "Aye, both o' us made that assumption, but nothing is cast in stone until the coroner's examination is concluded. Now we know it fer certain."

I'm pretty sure I looked disappointed.

"But there's more tae consider," he said.

I raised an eyebrow questioningly.

"Fortunately fer the investigation, Isla Lindsey had

undigested food materials in her stomach, which have been identified. Based on that information, I rang up the baker a few minutes ago."

"Baker?" My first thought was of Taste of Scotland, which was just down the cobblestone street from the pub. "Was it shortbread?"

He shook his head just as I got a flash of insight. "Cupcake," I said with pride as he changed that shake into a nod. "She'd eaten one of Senga Hill's sheep-shaped cupcakes."

"Aye, though Senga said just now that she's positive Isla didn't buy one from her directly. But one important piece o' information as I said—some o' the ingredients were still undigested. Not semi-digested. Undigested."

The inspector was watching me carefully, as though waiting for a math student to figure out a complex equation. Digested, undigested, semi-digested, I'd have to be a coroner to hazard a guess.

I didn't know what he expected, so I shrugged instead. "I'm not following."

"That's because there's more. Trace elements of a certain compound were discovered along with those miniature marshmallows and candy eyeballs. It turns out that someone doped Isla Lindsey up on sleeping tablets prior to her death."

"Oh my goodness! Sleeping pills? Were they mixed into the cupcake somehow?"

"Aye. The coroner suggested tablets could have been crushed and sprinkled on the frosting without herself detecting anything amiss. And the quantity of the drug was such to ensure she was rendered unconscious."

"Massive quantities of sugar also could have disguised any unusual taste," I said, thinking out loud, "no matter how bitter, and those cupcakes were a sugar lover's dream."

All kinds of thoughts went through my head. None of them warm and cozy. Someone had fed our victim a loaded cupcake then somehow enticed her into Oliver's van, and once she was unconscious, had wrapped yarn around her neck and strangled her.

"Has the type of sleeping pill been identified yet?"

"Aye. 'Tis a new one on the market, just recently approved, in a certain class called Z drugs."

That didn't mean much to me, not yet anyway.

"Isla likely knew her killer," Inspector Jamieson added. "She wouldn't have climbed into a vehicle with a complete stranger."

"But we can't assume she even went to the van with another person," I pointed out. "She might have been sitting there alone." But why? Isla and her husband had driven in their own vehicle. If she'd needed a place to find a bit of solitude or rest, a place to take a nap, she'd have gone to her own camper.

Perhaps she went there specifically to meet with someone. That could have been the way it played out. Isla could have eaten the doctored cupcake a little in advance. The killer wasn't taking unnecessary chances. That person had waited for Isla to drop off into la-la land, then it was a simple maneuver to wrap yarn around the incapacitated woman's neck and strangle her.

Most important, it meant that the killer wouldn't have had to be particularly strong after all. He—or she—would've had the effects of the sleeping pills on his or her side. Isla wouldn't have struggled, or even known what was happening to her.

"At this point all our ideas are nothing but guesswork," the inspector said. "It'll take solid detective work to find the truth o' the matter. And I'm forced tae admit that we need Sean's assistance as well."

"Where do we begin to sort this out?" I asked.

"We need a list of all yarn club members and their addresses for starters. We will have tae systematically exclude those kits that are intact. We begin by working our way through the list, one name at a time, eliminating suspects as we go along, and that's only one o' the burdens facing us."

No wonder he wanted my assistance. Thirty-five members to track down and question and as many kits to inspect. Then looking into any others around them who might have had access. A daunting task.

"I can get that list of members from Vicki for you," I said, as the rational part of my brain protested. An appropriate phrase came to mind: *When you find yourself in a self-made hole, at some point you should stop digging.*

"Excellent," the inspector said before I thought to stop digging, showing rare enthusiasm. "And I'll track down those sleeping pills. They're available only by prescription. It's a good lead, a lucky break."

"Yes, lucky," I agreed. Isla hadn't been nearly as lucky. She'd eaten a cupcake containing a high dose of sedatives and then had been finished off by a vicious killer, the life literally choked out of her. I stared glumly into space.

Jamieson rose and placed a hand gently on my shoulder.

"Murder investigations take a bit o' getting used tae," he said. "But I believe you're up to the task, *Constable* Elliott."

With that, he had me stand and take an oath of allegiance. I repeated word for word after him, promising to preserve peace and prevent offenses against persons and Scotland. After the swearing in, the inspector presented me with a card that he'd already had made up with my name, the letters "SC" for Special Constable, and my new title of police officer.

"That's yer official warrant card," he told me. "Be sure tae carry it on yer person at all times."

"Can I make arrests now?" I asked.

That earned me a worried scowl. "I strongly advise against it. If ye find yerself in a difficult situation, dial 999 and request assistance. Then remain at a safe distance until help arrives."

"That's hardly the actions of a law enforcement official," I complained. "Anybody can call for help and hide until it arrives."

"Hopefully ye won't encounter any problems off on yer own." He was still scowling as though just now realizing that stumbling upon trouble was a distinct possibility considering my history. Perhaps he was having regrets already.

Too late, I thought. *For both of us.*

I gave my new boss a weak smile that probably came across as a grimace, if the way I was feeling at the moment was any indication of my outward appearance.

I stared at my new Scottish police badge.

I was now a card-bearing authority.

Constable Elliott. Writer of romances, investigator of

murders. A new title and position that twenty-four hours ago, when Inspector Jamieson had first approached me with his request, I'd taken so lightly.

I hoped he wasn't being overly optimistic with his encouragement and decision to recruit me.

So much for pretending the part.

I'd been cast in the role of special constable.

And I still didn't have that pepper spray.

CHAPTER 8

After a perfunctory handshake to seal our deal, the inspector departed to conduct more interviews with those closest to the murder victim. He gave me his solemn word that he would keep me informed every step of the way. I gave him my own verbal commitment to make myself available to assist in any way I could, starting with obtaining a list of the yarn club members.

I suddenly realized that our new working relationship had the potential to turn our casual friendship into a much more formal arrangement. I hadn't considered that and wasn't sure I liked the idea.

I issued a warning to myself. Belated, this time, but I needed to remember it for the future:

Be careful what you ask for—you might actually get your wish, Eden Elliott.

I'd been pleased as punch when Inspector Jamieson had first approached me with his offer to replace Sean as special constable. I'm sure his proposal fed my ego, as I'd already been fantasizing about the power that came with the position, conveniently forgetting that it also came with enormous responsibility.

The take-charge part of me really wanted to stay involved in a hands-on way, carry on with the duties I'd sworn to, make sure this killer was brought to justice. Once I'd managed my way through the initial discovery of the body, I felt pretty good about the actions I'd taken on Saturday. I'd risen to the occasion. Unlike Sean Stevens or Oliver Wallace.

However, the saner part of me was shouting—*Run! You don't have any experience or proper training! Quit while you're ahead,* it murmured. *What is a romance novelist doing meddling in crime solving of any sort, especially when it comes to the most evil and horrible kind of all?*

I made an effort to weigh both sides of the argument waging war in my head. But from the very beginning it was a no-brainer, which in my case meant I ignored my brain and instead chose to follow my sappy, misinformed heart, romanticizing all the way. I'd serve up justice by bringing down a killer. Maybe not single-handedly (I'm perfectly aware that I am *not* Super Woman), but as one of the lead characters, side by side with the detective assigned to the case.

So, I reasoned, *all* the inspector and I had to do was follow a series of steps. Something had happened, most likely during the morning sheep dog trials, to force Isla Lindsey's killer to take drastic action in spite of extremely high risk. At the moment, a motive wasn't apparent. It was crucial that we find one. A tall order to fill.

Just as difficult, we had to pinpoint a spectator with

plenty of opportunity. At this point, that could be pretty much anyone who was out at the farm in the afternoon. Isla went to the van sometime after one thirty in the afternoon to meet a person who chose that time and place and took that opportunity to commit murder. All within an approximately three-hour window.

As to the killer's means, we already knew it involved yarn from one of Vicki's club member kits. Add to the mix two hundred cupcakes baked by Senga Hill to track down, stir in a prescription for sleeping pills, and there was the perfect recipe for murder.

The task seemed impossible when I looked at all the pieces at once.

One thing I've learned from my career as a professional writer, whether ghostwriting, editing, or romance writing, is to become as organized as I can and methodically plot the story line. The whole picture doesn't have to be viewed from the start. Some of it evolves over time. One thing leads to another. Hopefully, that skill, to look at parts first and let the whole come naturally, would translate well into detective work and come in handy to solve this crime.

So, the first item of business was to get that list of yarn club members and start working it.

Except . . .

I hadn't navigated my way through the challenging, narrow, and winding roads of the Highlands just to brainstorm what was behind a murder plot. I could have done that from the cottage. I was here because I needed to make my book better before I could begin outlining the second book in my series. *Falling for You*, the first book in my Scottish Highlands Desire series, is set in a fictional village called

Rosehearty and tells the story of Gillian Fraser, a Scottish lass returning to her hometown to heal her broken heart, and Jack Ross, the ruggedly handsome owner of a local distillery (and also an avid fisherman, based more than loosely on Leith Cameron).

My plan after that book was to introduce a new romance for Gillian's friend Jessica Bailey and Jack's half brother, Daniel Ross. To put off worrying about Ami's response, and because tweaking the manuscript had ceased to be fun, I tossed around ideas for the second title. It had to fit with the first title, leaving no question that they were part of the same series. *Made for You*? Or *Loving You*? For sure something with the word "you" in it. Keep it simple. Sweet, easy to remember, definitely one that a reader would instantly recognize as a romance. How about *Crazy for You*? Or *Hooked on You*?

Hooked on You resonated at the moment, so I opted to use it as a working title. That decided, I powered up my laptop, brought up my e-mail, and with a great deal of trepidation peered into my in-box.

There were three recent e-mails from Ami Pederson. I began with the oldest and least intimidating, because the subject line told me enough about the content. My friend seemed to have a one-track mind when it came to Scottish men. The subject was, "Have you seen under a kilt yet?" I decided to completely ignore the contents of that one since I could probably have recited it verbatim without even opening it. I sent that same-old-subject e-mail to the trash receptacle.

The second e-mail was a status update that would have

left me ripping my hair out if I'd read it right after it came zipping through cyberspace from across the pond. Another valid reason for not being overly hasty in checking e-mail too frequently. It read simply, "I'm almost finished with *Falling for You*!!!!"

Really? That was the entire extent of it? One measly, non-descriptive sentence? Plus major overusage of exclamation marks. If I'd read this e-mail right after it had been sent, I would have had several carefully chosen, colorful adjectives to describe my best friend in Chicago. And a whole lot of hours to imagine my failure as a legitimate novelist. Not a single hint as to what she thought so far, unless the exclamation points were supposed to mean something good. Or, a much worse thought, what if she couldn't find anything good to say about the manuscript?

I talked myself down from a rocky cliff of anxiety and turned my attention to the third and final e-mail, which had been sent not long before I'd entered the pub. The subject line jumped out at me. "Finished!!" I took a deep breath and opened it . . .

. . . To find a lengthy critique of my story. I took another deep breath, and began skimming, expecting the absolute worst. Instead my eyes landed on such phrases as "amazing sexual tension" and "fully realized characterizations" and "vivid sex scenes." "I loved . . ." cropped up frequently.

I began to relax, my spirits soaring, especially after her final comments. "You might not be making much of a love life for yourself, but you have created a scorching hot one for Gillian and Jack. Way to go! If you need to abstain from sex to write like this, if you need to keep it all bottled up inside of you to put it on the page as you've done, well then you have my blessing. No more pressure from me to explore those Scottish dreamboats. Well done! I still can't believe you wrote this so fast! It's good to go. Send it off to your editor. Scotland is obviously the elixir you needed."

Followed by lots more exclamation points and a series of smiley faces.

All the tension I'd been carrying around these past few days drained away, even the stress of recent sad events. The knot in my stomach disappeared. My knitted brow straightened and my lips curled up with glee. I read Ami's last e-mail over and over. And over again. I could have been one of the smiley faces she used in overabundance to make her points. Life was good.

After I forced myself down from cloud nine, I wrote back, gushing with gratitude. What a friend she was. I even wrote, "I loved, loved, loved your use of exclamations!!!"

Thinking back to her comment about the speed with which the book came together, I realized I really had finished like a flash of lightning. But I also knew that if I wanted to make a name for myself amongst other romance writers, I had to keep up with them in both quality *and* quantity.

Which wouldn't leave me any spare time for a personal life, let alone allow me to squeeze in work as a special constable. Were romance writers living vicariously through their characters because their own lives were so bound to writing deadlines? I'd have to consider that. Although Ami Pederson had a wonderful marriage, and from the tales she'd told me, it was as hot as her bestsellers. So that gave me hope that someday I really could have my cake and eat it, too. But right now I was a rookie at this. I'd eat my cake someplace down the road.

For the moment, my focus had to be on my work.

That's what I told myself.

Myself didn't listen.

I packed up my things, and headed for the farm with murder on my mind.

CHAPTER 9

I returned to the farm to find Sean and Vicki in the barn, sitting side by side on a hay bale, watching the rainstorm through the open doors. Rain swept in curtainlike sheets across the grass driven by gusts of wind. I waited in the car a few minutes in case the deluge subsided, but impatience got the better of me and I dashed for the barn.

Jasper the barn cat had taken up temporary residence on top of a stack of hay bales, nonchalantly cleaning his black coat of fur while Vicki's terriers, Coco and Pepper, wore themselves out trying to get him to come down to their level and play with them. They circled below, ears perky, tails wagging, taking turns emitting yaps of frustration while Jasper completely ignored them except for an occasional look of abject disdain.

"These two Westies still think they can make friends with Jasper," Sean said, shaking his head at the pointlessness of their mission. I noticed a bit more space between Vicki and Sean than when I had first pulled up outside. "Even despite the wee beasts both having had plenty o' cat scratches tae show fer their efforts."

"Sean told me about the cupcake," Vicki said right away.

I leaned against the tractor and said, "The cupcake? Yes, I heard, too. I assume that information won't go any farther than the three of us?"

"Four o' us," Sean said, correcting me. "Countin' the inspector."

"It couldn't be worse," Vicki said, looking as gloomy as the weather. "Senga's cupcake. My yarn."

"And me own quick temper," Sean added.

"Enough," I said. "You two have been blaming yourselves, and that is ridiculous. Sean, Isla Lindsey got under everyone's skin. I bet she was told off plenty yesterday, and not just by you. You aren't responsible for her murder, not even one iota. The only person responsible is her killer."

Then I turned to Vicki. "It's unfortunate that yarn from one of your knitting kits was used to murder Isla, but that certainly isn't your fault. If it hadn't been your yarn, the person who did this would have found another weapon to use." I glanced around the barn. "Look around you! This barn is loaded with potential weapons—hammers, screwdrivers, lengths of rope, all kinds of vet supplies, including medications for the sheep and syringes for injections." I threw up my hands. "Maybe we should spread all this blame around even more, make sure Senga Hill gets her share for baking cupcakes. Now, wouldn't that be ridiculous? Both of you need to buck up, stop moping around with all kinds of regrets for something you didn't cause, and instead do your part to help solve this crime."

They stared at me like I had two heads.

"What?" I said, realizing that this was the longest speech I'd given in quite some time.

"Look at you, talking to us like that," Vicki replied slyly, not at all upset by my little tirade. "What's got you going all of a sudden?"

"Nothing's got me going. Except you both look so down in the dumps. Shape up! Think positive, or if you can't, at least take small baby steps in the right direction."

Sean stood up. "There's a rumor going about that you're carrying a warrant card these days. Any truth to that blather?"

Oh, no! I hadn't stopped to consider how Sean might feel about my appointment to his position. Until now, he'd been the special constable, and it meant a lot to him. I struggled to find the right words to explain in a kind and gentle way. Except, judging by the smile on his face . . .

"You don't mind, do you?" I said.

"Not a bit. I'm going off tae police college soon and somebody has tae try tae fill me shoes. Might as well be yerself. Besides, when I come back, ye'll be taking orders from yours truly."

I groaned inwardly. No way was that going to happen. Was it?

He went on, "In the meantime, I'll teach ye all that I know, so ye can handle yerself properly in difficult situations." It was all I could do to keep my expression serious and my mouth closed. Which one of us had handled yesterday's situation properly? Not Sean Stevens. He'd been ready to faint dead away.

"Congratulations," Vicki said to me, although she seemed hesitant. "But what about your books? Will you still have time to write them?"

"Absolutely," I told her with newfound confidence that somehow I would manage both. It's not as if murder was a common occurrence in Glenkillen, I reasoned. "Once this case is solved, I'll only be putting in a handful of hours each week, leaving plenty of time for my writing."

Sean nodded. "That's the truth. The inspector doesn't require much o' me in the way o' time commitment. And I hardly see him. He's going one way, I'm going another. Which reminds me, I should check in with him. Do ye know where he is at the moment, Eden?"

I shook my head. I truly didn't know . . . although if I wanted to stay on my new boss's good side, I would have denied knowledge of his whereabouts regardless. "I saw him at the Kilt & Thistle, but he left several hours ago."

"Oh . . . wait . . . I almost forgot." Sean pulled a piece of paper out of his trouser pocket and unfolded it before handing it to me. "I've made both o' us a copy of Vicki's member list and also added those on the waiting list at the bottom, though we won't be getting tae that one likely as that group didn't get their hands on kits and so aren't as likely to be our perp . . . that's perpetrator in police talk, fer yer information."

I did an internal eye roll before scanning the names on the members list. I recognized very few of them. Then I skimmed the waiting list, even though Sean was correct that the wannabe yarn club members weren't priorities.

"You mailed out some of the kits in advance," I said to Vicki as I scooped Jasper from his seat of power and stroked him. He went limp in my arms and began purring almost immediately. "When was that?"

"Last week, Wednesday," she answered. "I didn't actually post them myself. I asked Kirstine to take them to the post office on her way home from the shop that day. On second thought, make that Thursday, not Wednesday, that they went out. She left the farm too late to get there before the post office closed on Wednesday."

"So she mailed them on Thursday?" I said, thinking out loud, wondering how long it took to deliver packages in the Highlands.

Vicki answered that for me by saying, "I wanted them to be delivered by the first. I'd promised, and I'm a woman of my word."

"Those members would have had their kits by Saturday, then?"

Vicki nodded, more pleased at that prospect than I was. "Most of them live within easy driving distance, but didn't want to take the time to pick them up. Some are quite elderly and don't drive. If luck was with me, they should've all been happily knitting by Saturday. You know how I am about honoring my commitments."

That's what I'd feared. Now all those kits were going to have to be accounted for, too. I'd counted twenty-two members who had requested shipment. Twenty-two that might have been eliminated from this onerous process if only Vicki had been less diligent.

"And there wasn't any surplus yarn?" I asked. "None at all?"

"Not more than a bit or two," Vicki confirmed. "I used all of it and tossed a few leftover ends." Vicki looked sad when she went on, "I suppose this is the end of the yarn club."

"Why?" I said, sensing earlier that this had been coming. "It was and is a great idea. You should be thinking about October's kit."

But my friend didn't respond.

Then Sean piped up and said, "Out of the thirteen tae come get theirs, only six actually picked up kits during the event. Ye can see on the list. That little 'x' in front o' the name means that person picked hers up."

That perked me up a bit. "So there are seven kits in our possession?" I returned Jasper to the top of the hay bales and he went back to grooming. "Where are they?" I asked. "You didn't distribute them, did you?"

"I'm not daft, ye know," Sean said. "Or incompetent. I happen to have them right over there." He indicated an open box, and sure enough, I saw Vicki's paper satchels were inside.

"And all seven skeins are accounted for?"

"Every one," Vicki replied. "And I've gone over the list and can say with certainty that I didn't see any of the other seven knitters at the event. So they are in the clear, right?"

"That makes sense," I replied.

"Does Inspector Jamieson know you have these kits?" I asked, directing my question to Sean.

Sean nodded. "He does. I keep him appraised at all times." Then he paused and muttered under his breath, "Not that he gives me the same courtesy. I'm tae take them tae him fer safekeeping."

All right. We had seven of the thirty-five kits accounted for. We were making progress.

"What about the van and camper bus?" I asked next.

Sean puffed up a bit, pleased that he had more police business information than I had. "Both haff been impounded fer thorough inspection."

"What's your plan for the rest of the day?" Vicki asked me.

"I think I'll walk down to the shop and speak with Kirstine," I decided in the spur of the moment, not especially thrilled by the prospect, but wanting to confirm shipment of the kits.

"It's raining," Vicki said, reaching down to the side of the hay bale. She held up an umbrella. "Why don't you take my brolly?"

I gratefully accepted the offered umbrella, opened it, and began my walk down the lane, thinking about rain and the Scots and how they didn't seem to care about the weather one way or the other. Whether it was blazing sun, torrential downpours, sky-high mounds of snow (or so I've been told, rain being the only weather I've yet to experience in the Highlands), or drizzles that lasted all day under the grayest clouds I've ever seen, the Scottish people went about their business without a single word of complaint. They weren't grumblers when it came to adverse conditions.

In Chicago, we complained plenty about the cold, and the snow, and every time it rained. But whatever precipitation we had, Scotland had double or triple that amount. On the bright side, that weather was what accounted for the incredibly stunning natural beauty hereabouts.

The shop's parking lot was nearly empty, with only a

few vehicles occupying spaces, and one of them belonged to Kirstine. Lulls in customer traffic tended to come and go at Sheepish Expressions, depending on the month, day of the week, and the hour. Now in September, the crowds were thinning out, the foreign tourist business winding down, children back in school, and summer vacations fading memories. Tour buses arrived less frequently as the days became cooler and the nights chillier.

All evidence of yesterday's tragedy had been removed from the far end of the lot. Nothing remained, not the van or chalk marks, and whatever minute traces that might have collected had been washed away by now. Briefly, I wondered if any additional evidence had been found inside the van since Sean's last update, and when it would be returned to Oliver Wallace—and whether he would keep it or sell it to some unsuspecting buyer who would never know what had occurred inside.

I walked to the back of the lot, stepping over and around puddles, trying to estimate the exact location where Isla's body had come crashing out of the van. I raised my eyes to the silver maple that had shaded the vehicle, and noted how its leaves were changing colors, green tinged with a hint of yellow. Soon they would turn the color of the sunset, then wither away and fall to the earth, to be renewed in the spring.

While rain pounded down on Vicki's umbrella, running from the edges in flowing streams, and with gray clouds hanging low in the Scottish sky, I thought about a life extinguished and a murderer somewhere out there.

I shivered.

Or perhaps it really was a shudder?

Chapter 10

Leaving the umbrella on the shop's porch, I entered Sheepish Expressions and was immediately struck by the kaleidoscope of vibrant colors that always greets me. Inside, bright lights replaced gray skies, rainbows of color displaced the muted shades of the lightly fogged hills and distant mountain peaks. The shop's interior felt warm and cozy even on the dampest, chilliest day.

One side of the shop was filled with woolen wears in glorious shades, all made in Scotland, most even handcrafted. On the other side was a wealth of beautiful, luxurious yarns and a small knitting room in the back available for anyone who cared to use it. This was where Vicki had started up her knitting class, and from that small group the skein-of-the-month club had been born.

The only gloom inside here resided behind the counter, sitting on a stool, watching the money with one eye and me with the other. Kirstine MacBride-Derry. She hadn't seemed particularly pleased when she'd looked up to see who had entered. I was the interloper, the pest who wouldn't leave.

I like to think the best of people. I wanted to believe that Kirstine was a good person at heart. She certainly had the respect of the community. I'd even seen her smiling on rare occasions and socializing with some of the other locals. Kirstine didn't strike me as a people person, though, not an extrovert by any stretch of the imagination, which was too bad for someone in retail. She had her friends and longtime acquaintances, but strangers and tourists seemed to sour her disposition.

In my opinion, Kirstine would be better off hiring someone to greet customers and spend her time in the back office with accounts. There had been a few occasions in busy times when she had reluctantly accepted temporary assistance from Vicki. But suggesting that she hire more permanent help wasn't an option. Nor was asking Vicki to take a more hands-on role. Vicki was a people person, but she'd made it perfectly clear that sitting behind a counter all day was *not* her cup of tea.

"The owner of a business has to be the one to take in the money and watch over the till," I'd heard Kirstine say whenever Vicki suggested hiring more staff. "Employees will either rob you blind or give it all away."

I wasn't as cynical, but whatever the case, Kirstine could be found watching the cash register most of the time.

A sudden flash of insight told me Kirstine and I weren't much different when it came right down to it. If I had to cater to customers day in and day out, I'd probably get as snippy as she was. I hadn't even been able to stand the thought of sitting at the welcome table for a single day. Lucky for me,

I had a career that suited my personality. If I needed to get away from the human race, I just crawled into my writing cave and stayed there as long as I needed to.

"Well, if it isn't Eden Elliott," Kirstine said in typical fashion when addressing me. "And what would *you* be doing out on a day like this? I thought our lovely weather would have driven you away by now, or at least kept you indoors."

"I'm adjusting to your weather," I said.

I noticed one of yesterday's trial programs lying on the counter and picked it up.

"You can't have that," Kirstine said. "It was bought and paid for by one of my customers who couldn't make it to the event but wanted a copy, as her son competed. She'll be in soon to get it."

I paged through. "I'm only taking a peek."

"Well, don't crease the pages or you'll be the one answering for it, not me."

I flipped through until I found the events listed in the afternoon. What I was looking for were the trials and participants competing after one thirty. Isla had been very much alive up until that time.

I figured we could remove the names of any handlers and judges on the trial field between one thirty and roughly four from the main suspect list, at least initially. It would be rewarding to narrow the field from everybody who attended the event to a more select few.

Unfortunately, after finding the page I was looking for, it turned out that the only events between one thirty and two thirty were a herding dog demonstration given by Kirstine's husband, John Derry, in the far field and Charlotte's sheep shearing demo. That period of time had been filled by them while the judges conferred and selected the winners. Great. Out of an entire community, I'd only been able to cross John and Charlotte off of the persons-of-immediate-interest list, and as much as I didn't want to, I also put an imaginary pencil mark (not quite ready to use permanent ink) through Kirstine's name. She'd been tending the shop all day and knowing her, she hadn't given it up for even one second of time, let alone the time it would have taken to feed Isla a cupcake, send her to Oliver's van, wait for the pills to take effect, then trot out there and strangle her. Someone would have noticed her absence.

I glanced up from the program and caught Kirstine's eye.

I didn't know how to begin communicating with her now that we were warily examining each other over the counter. With a less hostile individual, I might have started with small talk and worked my way around to the questions I needed answered. But our relationship wasn't that comfortable or polite. As for her husband, John remained remote and barely communicative, but I still hadn't figured out whether that was because he sided with his wife, or if that was simply his nature.

"Have you heard any more about Isla Lindsey's murder?" I began.

"Only that it'll be a surprise to me if the shop survives," Kirstine answered. "It's one thing to have a murder right on our own property, but the weapon of choice used in the attack on Isla is going to hurt business and I'm not sure we will ever recover. I told Vicki not to start that club until after the event. You were there. You heard me. Now look what's happened!"

"That's a bit harsher than necessary," I said, my hackles rising to defend my friend. "Vicki is already blaming herself. She doesn't need you piling on. The victim and her family are the ones who should be in our thoughts. *They* are the ones who are truly suffering. As to the shop, Sheepish Expressions will continue as always. Tour buses will still stop as they always have. I can't imagine any of your regular customers leaving because of this. Yes, the skein-of-the-month club has had a setback, but Vicki couldn't have predicted this. We can't blame her. I certainly don't."

Kirstine should have closed her mouth after that. Instead she went after me by saying, "I don't know who you think you are, coming into my shop and treating me this way. You have no right to be inside Sheepish Expressions without my consent, and I'm asking you to leave right now."

Without giving it much thought, I whipped out my warrant card. "I'm investigating a murder," I said. "I'm a special constable, appointed by Inspector Kevin Jamieson himself, and I have questions for you regarding the murder, which you *will* answer."

Kirstine looked stunned as she squinted at proof of my appointment, but she recovered quickly. "Well, I'll be . . ."

I felt a surge of satisfaction. But it didn't last.

"Your threating attitude means nothing to me," she went on. "What are you going to do? Arrest me under false pretenses?"

Kirstine had her arms crossed and her mind set. She clamped her mouth closed. I wondered if my expression appeared as thunderous on the outside as it felt inside. I sincerely hoped so. I knew I had to act fast, before she paralyzed me with venom from her snake tongue, rendering me helpless before injecting her special brand of poison. Chances of coming out the winner would be about as likely as betting on an injured horse in the Kentucky Derby.

It was time to get down to the real reason for my visit to the shop.

"Vicki gave you the yarn kits to be shipped," I said. "Did you mail them as she asked you to?"

"What is this? I'm under suspicion?"

"No, of course not. The inspector wants all the kits accounted for. I'm merely following his instructions and inquiring." Okay, so I used his name to get what I needed. Kirstine wasn't going to cooperate with me without some sort of higher authority in the mix. "There were twenty-two of them. You took them with you. Did you or did you not mail them in a timely fashion?"

I was actually hoping that Kirstine's natural unhelpfulness meant that they hadn't gone out until Friday or even Saturday. If they'd still been in the mail on Saturday, those kits and members wouldn't be of interest to the investigation.

"Well?" I prompted when Kirstine didn't answer my question. "When were they sent?"

Something about her attitude changed in that moment. She still had dagger eyes that could wilt a whole field of sunflowers, but they weren't fixed on me as before. They were roaming the room.

She began puttering instead, straightening items on the counter before she said, "If you must know, they went out the minute the post office opened on Thursday morning."

"Obstructing an investigation is a serious offense," I told her, sensing that she wasn't telling me the entire truth.

"You and your threats! I answered your question, didn't I?"

"Anything you care to add?"

"Certainly. Here it is. Be gone with you, and next time my assistance is needed in this investigation, send the inspector. I'll be answering only to him from now on."

Well, that certainly hadn't gone well. I'd need to brush up on my interrogation skills, and either learn to deal with difficult people or learn to avoid them in the future. Although avoiding them probably wasn't an option if I planned to continue on in the capacity of a law enforcement official. We all have to deal with nasty people from time to time. Even the inspector must have to put up with disparaging remarks and unwilling subjects.

Standing outside on the porch, I decided to follow up on those cupcakes tomorrow by paying a visit to Senga Hill. She'd surely be a refreshing change after dealing with Kirstine. I expected that Senga could enlighten me regarding cupcake purchasers.

Although with two hundred of them sold, I wasn't holding out much hope.

CHAPTER 11

In the early evening, Vicki appeared at my cottage door with a covered dish in her hands.

"Barefoot broth," she told me, setting it down on my small kitchen table. "It's been such fun making some of the Scottish dishes that I remember from my childhood."

The aroma was heavenly. Vicki was an excellent cook. "Barefoot broth?"

"Potatoes, barley, cabbage, turnips, whatever is on hand. As the days cool off, I'm thinking about inky-pinky and bubblyjock."

She laughed at the expression on my face and went on to translate. "Inky-pinky is beef-and-carrot stew and bubblyjock is roast turkey. You'll get a chance to try both before . . ."

The light in her eye turned sad. She didn't finish her sentence.

We both knew what she meant. Before I had to leave Scotland.

Quickly changing the subject, she said, "I made a big batch and took some over to the Lindseys."

"How are they doing?"

Vicki shrugged. "Bryan wasn't available. Andrea seems to be screening his visitors, making sure he's left in peace as much as possible. She thanked me, though."

"You're a good person, Vicki."

"I do what I can."

"Do you want to stay and chat?"

"No, I better dash," she said.

"A hot date?"

"I'm expecting company is all," she said vaguely.

"I was hoping you could make a few phone calls to the members you sent kits to," I said, still bothered by my confrontation with Kirstine. "Make sure they arrived, let them know that we will have to pick them up. Let them know in a nice way, of course."

"A few calls! I packaged twenty-two! I'll contact them first thing tomorrow. Okay?"

What could I say? I couldn't insist. The woman was expecting company. And I was pretty sure I knew who it was.

Speaking of company—I hadn't been expecting any but soon after I'd finished the delicious barefoot broth and straightened up the kitchen, Leith Cameron and Kelly dropped by on their way home from the chartered ocean fishing excursion. It was still drizzling, fog patches had drifted lazily into our valley right before dark, and the air was heavy with the promise of more precipitation. In the yellow glow from my table lamp, Leith was sun-nipped and wind tossed. He smelled of fresh sea breeze as he sank into my armchair in the humble little cottage I now called home (however temporarily) and accepted my offer of a hot cup of tea.

"A fine fishing day. We caught plenty o' bass and a few flounder," he reported, biting into a shortbread I offered, which I had recently purchased at Taste of Scotland, hand-made by Ginny Davis. Leith went on, "And a conservation-minded bunch o' blokes they were, practicing catch and release, since they were on a business trip with no way tae keep their catch anyway. And nary a single mate hanging over the rails."

"No excessive drinking?" I asked, pleased when Kelly came and sat down next to me. Her eyes closed in content-ment as I massaged one ear then the other.

"There was some, but this lot could hold their liquor."

I smiled with pleasure at his enthusiasm for his work. What a life Leith led—raising barley for the production of whisky in fertile Highland soil, spending pleasurable days on the water of the North Sea or wading the River Spey, enjoying a local whisky or brew here and there. An active outdoorsman, rugged and capable. It gave me pause to consider what it would be like to travel in Leith's world, glamorous as it seemed on the surface. But he'd been out all day in the rain. Spending the entire day outside, rain or shine, wasn't my thing. Customers who might or might not behave themselves, rough seas, rain gear, dampness that penetrated and chilled the bones, gave me a better perspective.

I shook off my initial jealousy. My life was rich in color

as well, even though I chose to live inside my head as much as or more than I did outside of myself. I created action scenes. Leith lived them. The introverted me served tea, while the extroverted he related his adventures on the high seas. Although I hardly had anything to complain about, either. Here I was wishing for Leith's life when probably many dreamed of having one like mine. I should be happy with what I had.

Actually, I realized with a sense of contentment, I was.

I had to admit that I'd been missing something in the past, but I'd found it the minute I stepped off the plane and walked into this new country. Back home, I'd lost my way, had barely existed. These days, though, I feel alive.

Besides, after the last few days, nobody could accuse me of retreating from life. Events had been far more exciting than I preferred.

Leith helped himself to another shortbread.

The romantic side of me had chosen to loosely base my hero Jack Ross in the first of the Scottish Highlands Desire stories on this man. If only Leith knew about that little fantasy and his role in it! What would he think? He would never find out unless I told him, and that would never happen. *But what if he read the book?* I hadn't considered that until this moment. I could only hope he wouldn't recognize himself within the pages if he did.

"What have ye been up tae since morning?" he asked.

"You won't believe what I'm going to be doing," I said, going on to tell him about my new appointment as special constable.

"You'll be an asset tae the inspector, that's fer sure," he said when I finished describing the brief ceremony. "But watch yerself out there. That line o' work is as dangerous as bad weather is on the open sea. The difference being those o' us who travel these waters usually are aware from certain signs if conditions are aboot tae turn on us. You might not have that same warning when it comes tae criminal types."

"The inspector isn't going to give me anything I can't handle," I assured him. "He's so used to investigating solo and on his own terms, it's going to be difficult for him to accept my help for anything other than the most mundane tasks."

"What does Sean Stevens think o' all this?"

"He's looking forward to bossing me around once he gets his permanent badge."

"Isn't that just like him."

We laughed together.

"I have a fishing charter later tomorrow morn," Leith said. "But if ye don't mind rising early, and if ye care tae meet me at the harbor fer a short ride, I would like tae show ye something."

"What is it?" I had so much to do tomorrow as it was. None of it pleasurable, though. I'd love to chuck it all for the open sea.

"I'm hoping tae surprise ye."

"I like surprises." Oh my gosh. We were flirting. "But tomorrow is going to be busy, so I can't afford to be away for long."

"Aye, an hour or so and I'll return ye to chasin' yer villains?"

I laughed.

Leith gave me a winning, lopsided grin. "How aboot seven?"

Inwardly I groaned. Outwardly, I smiled and said, "Seven is fine."

"First light at sea is a priceless experience."

"You just ruined the surprise."

"Not a bit," he said mysteriously. "Ye'll see."

A few minutes later, he stood. "I best be goin' home tae give Kelly her supper."

After they left, I'd barely cleared away the dishes when I thought to check my mobile phone. I'd turned off the ringer in the pub so I could focus on my work, and had forgotten to turn the volume back up. The phone rang in my hand.

A familiar voice on the other end said, "It's aboot time ye answered. I was ready tae drive over and wait fer ye to show up."

"Inspector. And hello to you."

"Ye haven't set up the voice messaging, forcing me tae call repeatedly."

"I'll take care of that," I said reluctantly, with little enthusiasm to follow through. I was getting used to free-dom from devices that tracked my every movement and from long lists of those excepting immediate responses to their voice messages. "And you shouldn't have bothered. I can see the missed calls from you."

"Is it too late fer me tae come by yer cottage? I'm still in the area."

"Not at all. I'll put on the tea."

After hanging up, I wondered where he might have been when he'd made the call to me. That led to a moment of speculation over his solitary life and his home. I'd heard that he lived in a remote area well outside of Glenkillen and inland from the sea. In a hunting lodge of some sort. Sean had told me that after his wife's death, the inspector had sold their village home, preferring the woodland seclusion of a rustic cabin.

In contrast, Leith Cameron, like most gregarious individuals, never minded sharing his past, present, and future plans. We'd had long conversations about his family history, about his ancestors who worked the important small-scale food production land while sharing grazing on the poorer-quality hillsides. These early tenant farmers were called crofters, and Leith still lived in the traditional crofter farmhouse where he'd been born and raised.

Inspector Jamieson, on the other hand, rarely allowed a conversation to turn from professional to personal, and when it threatened to do just that, he rapidly brought it round to topics of a less private nature.

Ten minutes later, his knock resounded, and he swept into the room when I opened the door. "I thought we might begin by breaking down the list o' those we need tae interview first thing," he said after hanging his raincoat on a hook by the door to dry and we were situated at the table with yet another pot of tea and more shortbreads. I cradled my cup, enjoying the warmth, but had had more than enough of the beverage for one day if I expected to sleep later.

"Have you acquired any new information since we last spoke?" I asked.

"Follow-ups with the deceased's family haven't uncovered anything more as o' yet. Nor has the van. I've been wading through more paperwork than I'd like and the feeling that I'm muckin' aboot instead o' solving this thing. I have high hopes that morns mornin' will bring better results."

I must be getting used to Scottish vernaculars because I didn't miss a beat with the meaning of morns mornin', aka tomorrow morning. And a fresh start to the murder investigation.

"What would you like me to do?" I asked. "Sean told me about the seven kits that weren't picked up. That means only six were."

"If ye would be so kind as tae have words with those six as well as any who were present who ye know will cooperate with ye, I'll start with the others."

"So I shouldn't have spoken with Kirstine Derry?"

There was a significant pause before the inspector said, "Probably not. I'm fully aware of the tension between Kirstine and yerself, and it would have been best to leave her fer me. But since ye did, what transpired?"

I went on to tell him of our conversation. "She's hiding something," I said at the end. "And it has to do with those kits she mailed."

"Ye be thinking she didn't post them?"

"Possibly. But it's only a feeling, and might be tied more to our discord than any actual deception on her part. In any case, Vicki intends to call those members tomorrow and verify they were received. I thought I'd stop at the post office in the morning and confirm her story. I'll be in Glenkillen anyway, since I want to question Senga."

"Paul Denoon won't release information to just anybody."

"I'm no longer just anybody since my appointment," I said. "Besides, he's warming to me."

"And how do ye know that?"

"I believe he actually tipped his head in a brief nod when we sat down at his table under the tent."

I heard the amusement in his tone when he said, "Well that settles it, then. You take on the postmaster. But if ye learn anything of value, speak to me before ye take action."

"Of course." I had visions of search warrants for Kirstine's home and vehicle dancing in my head.

What a team we were about to become. I would track down skeins distributed at the event, the inspector would continue to search for clues to more damaging evidence, Vicki and Sean would account for the twenty-two that had been mailed, and somewhere along the way, we'd figure out who the murderer was and bring justice to the dead woman.

"We need tae move quickly," he said next. "Time is critical. Can ye put off yer writing temporarily? It's fer a good cause."

Well, when he asked like that, what could I possibly say but yes? Besides, I was here in the Highlands in pursuit of authenticity, for firsthand experiences rather than research from afar. I'd met some pretty unique characters in the three months I'd been in the Highlands. Some of them were bound to show up on the pages of my books, and I told myself that all of this would make great fodder for future scenes.

Jamieson drank his tea in silence, lost in thought. Then abruptly he set down his cup with a clatter and said, "Ye need to ask the following during yer interrogations of those at the farm Saturday afternoon: Did ye see anything suspicious? Did ye see Isla Lindsey? And if so, where was she and what was she doing? If they spoke with her, get the entire conversation down in a notebook. Was she angry or upset, that sort o' thing."

"Like a detective on a crime show."

"Aye, on the telly, if that's what works fer ye. And don't forget tae take their kits away with ye."

I nodded, expecting that. "You know, they're all going to worry that they're suspects."

"As they should. Seeing as how they are. Perhaps the real killer will get nervous and start making mistakes," the inspector said, unapologetic. Then he frowned. "Sean appears tae be missin' in action. I haven't seen hide nor hair o' him. He's usually nippin' at my heels and noo I can't even raise him on his mobile."

"Earlier you couldn't wait to get rid of him."

"Aye, but . . ." He actually stammered, unsure how to defend his changed position. So I helped him out.

"But he should be available when you need him."

"Exactly. Oh, I almost forgot. I have a few things fer ye." He rose, headed for his raincoat, and riffled through one pocket after another before finding what he was looking for.

One item was a notebook, exactly like the one he carried.

The other he presented by placing it on the table in front of me. I immediately recognized it as pepper spray, and broke out in a grin. To me it was a sign of confidence and acceptance.

"Ye know how tae use it?"

"Yes, certainly. It's legal to carry in the States, and I often carried one in my purse."

"It's not a toy tae be taken lightly."

"I'm aware of that."

He sighed as though exasperated and shook his head as though his next statement was only wishful thinking. "Let's hope ye never have a reason to use it," he said.

"Of course," I agreed, fondling my new canister.

I couldn't settle down after the inspector left—the problem with taxing my mind and increasing my adrenaline rush in the evening is that it becomes nearly impossible to quiet my thoughts enough to sleep. This was no exception, made worse by all the black tea. It might contain less than half the caffeine of a cup of coffee, but drink enough of it and the effects are the same.

I tossed and turned. Conversations from earlier in the evening played through my head over and over. The bed springs squeaked every time I turned, which happened often. In the early morning light, I gave up, not sure if I'd slept at all.

CHAPTER 12

Monday morning it was still dark when I made a cup of strong instant coffee after a hot shower, popped a piece of shortbread in my mouth, drained the cup and considered having another, but decided to hold off.

Hoping that fresh, cool air might revive me from the exhaustion I felt, I bundled up in layers and left the cottage. My breath whirled in a steamy dance before my face. The sun's first rays barely peaked over the horizon and the few clouds floating in the sky were soft and white, promising a relief from yesterday's constant rainy drizzle and dampness.

The main house was steeped in darkness. Sean's red Renault was parked in the shadows on the far side of the house, offering an explanation for his disappearance last night. My suspicions were confirmed. Vicki and Sean. I smiled at that. Good for them.

A light shone in the barn, and a familiar Jeep four-by-four was parked outside. I found Charlotte Penn already beginning to set up for a day of shearing sheep. Her penned-in customers sensed something was up, had determined that they wanted no part of it, and were loudly bleating their complaints.

Jasper the barn cat watched calmly from the hayloft as though he enjoyed the spectacle about to commence. His sharp eyes swept my way, but he didn't come down the steps to greet me as he usually did. There was too much action happening in his territory.

Charlotte wore a pair of jeans, a red top under a dark hoodie, and her standard footgear—moccasins she'd made herself and wore for shearing, with a special grip to keep her from slipping on oily wool clippings.

"I'm happy tae see that John had the good sense tae bring the sheep in before the rain began yesterday," Charlotte said after we greeted each other, "or I would have come all this way fer nothing. A wet sheep cannae be sheared."

"Why not?" I asked. "Wouldn't they be easier to hold on to?"

"'Tis not good fer the sheep, fer one thing. It causes boils on their legs. Fer another, the fleece doesn't store well if damp."

"Ah." I'd already learned something new for the day.

"Isn't John going to help?" I asked next, although if he wasn't, I couldn't offer. I was due at the harbor soon.

"I'm a one-woman show," Charlotte said, flexing a muscle. "He'd just be in the way."

The main house door slammed, and a moment later Sean appeared in the doorway to the barn, his mobile phone clutched in his hand. He was rumpled and bleary-eyed, not at all his usual tidy, uniformed, overly confident self. This morning he wore more casual trousers, a striped pullover shirt, and a befuddled expression.

"Must o' fallen asleep in front o' the telly," he muttered. "It's naught like it appears, ye can trust me on that."

"We aren't gossips," Charlotte said, plugging shears into a cord running to an electrical outlet. "Yer secret is safe with us."

Sean blushed to the very roots of the hair on his head. "Nothing secret aboot it. I dozed off is wha' happened."

"The inspector was looking for you," I said, eyeing his phone. "But you know that by now."

"Aye, he's gonna be in a snit, is wha'."

And with that, he turned and practically ran to his car to make his getaway.

Charlotte chuckled.

"He's trying to protect Vicki's reputation," I said, laughing along.

The poor guy really had been disgruntled. He and Vicki had probably assumed he'd be up and gone from the farm before anyone noticed. They hadn't expected Charlotte to appear at the crack of dawn, or me, either, and their plan hadn't exactly panned out.

Or was that the romantic in me? Perhaps Sean was telling the truth and really had fallen asleep watching television. I chose to believe otherwise. Those two would make a cute couple.

"I heard about what happened tae Isla Lindsey after I left the farm on Saturday," Charlotte said, taking off her hoodie and exposing bare arms that were trim and muscular from handling sheep. She didn't seem to mind the cool air inside the barn. "It was quite a shock."

I told Charlotte about my new role in the investigation as a special constable, which hadn't made the gossip rounds quite yet, and suddenly realized that I had a professional dilemma. How many details of the investigation could I reveal? What insider information did I have that should be kept confidential? I found myself in a quandary. The inspector had shared sensitive information with me. Discussing the sheep-shaped cupcake laced with sleeping-pill frosting was off the conversational table for certain. For the time being, I figured I'd better ask more questions than I answered.

I had a flash of empathy toward the inspector, realizing now why he was so reserved when dealing with the locals. He couldn't open his mouth without carefully choosing his words in advance, filtering them to make sure he wasn't giving away classified information. To make matters even more difficult, small talk wasn't his forte.

Charlotte dug in her backpack on the barn floor and came up with one of the yarn kits I had been charged with retrieving. "I'm thinking the inspector will want all o' Vicki's kits accounted fer. I didn't get a chance to visit Granny, which is just as well, considering."

"News is traveling fast."

"Aye, it's out and aboot that the yarn from the new club was involved. Something like that spreads faster than hill heather, especially with witnesses tae the fact."

I took the kit Charlotte offered up. "Thank you," I said, relieved that at least one knitter wasn't going to give me a hard time about relinquishing it. Charlotte didn't seem put out at all. "I'll see that it's returned once this is all over with."

"Are ye having yer sights on anyone in particular?"

"Not yet. Right now, I'm gathering kits for inspection and asking questions."

"What sort o' questions?" Charlotte asked.

"Did you see anything suspicious? Did you see Isla? How did she seem? Angry? Upset? Standard questions."

"That woman always looked a bit on the angry side. Good luck makin' anything o' her mood on Saturday. I only saw her fer a brief moment early when she was giving Sean the business about moving the van. Seems he didn't do it right on his first try."

"What do you mean?"

"He put it in the car park on the wrong side o' his own car, according tae herself. On the shop-facing side, and she made him move it tae the far back, behind his. He pulled a face, he did, not liking tae deal with her."

Sean hadn't mentioned that incident specifically, but it wasn't surprising. Isla was a woman of many complaints. I remembered her crabbing about the color of the welcome tent. One more objection wouldn't have meant much. Although . . . I wondered if she'd had a reason to want the van well hidden. Could Isla have had preexisting plans to meet someone there later?

Unaware of my thoughts, Charlotte went on, "Isla needed tae control everybody around her, and that's a fact. Some say a body that feels the need tae manage others like she did has problems in that department, and cannae manage their own lives properly."

Several sheep bleated. Charlotte directed her gaze to

the penned sheep, who were clumped in a mass toward the back of the enclosure, their pink-painted hindquarters crammed together. The MacBride sheep were marked on both hindquarters and ears, like all the sheep in the Highlands, to distinguish one farm's from another. "Which o' ye beasts wants tae go first and get it over with?" she asked, addressing them as though she expected a response. Then to me: "They act all pitiful but once they lose all that extra fleece, they are happier fer it."

I asked another question. "Did Isla have issues in her personal life?"

"Wouldn't ye, if ye had her personality?"

"What about her marriage? Was it stable?"

"Nothing but meanness is flying around with the busybodies out at the clothesline pole. I try tae avoid that kind o' talk." Charlotte turned away.

I put a hand on her arm and said, "I appreciate that you don't participate in that sort of idle gossip, but in this case, between the two of us and going no farther, I think it's warranted. Please tell me what you've heard."

"Only that Isla and her husband had quite a row in the Kilt & Thistle last week."

"What was the fight about?"

Charlotte shrugged. "Nobody really can say fer sure, and some o' the speculation is just rubbish. I'll keep my ears open, but only fer you I'd do such a thing."

She opened the pen's gate and passed through, closing it behind her, eyeing up the sheep as they eyed her back with trepidation. "Don't be shy with me, now, ye pretty ewes," she told them as they hunkered in the very back of the pen.

Before I slid into the driver's seat of the Peugeot, I opened the kit that Charlotte had returned to verify that the skein of yarn was inside. It was. I stored it in the trunk and headed for Glenkillen, toward the surprise Leith had promised me.

I arrived to find him waiting for me near the docks with a jacket draped over his arm. Kelly had been sniffing around the pier until I approached, then she ran to greet me.

"I forgot tae recommend a warm windbreaker," Leith said, "so ye can wear one o' mine. It'll be a wee bit big, but ye'll be happy tae have it."

I accepted the jacket, slipped it on, and we walked down one of the piers. I could smell the salty air and hear gulls beginning to circle above the boats.

Leith's fishing boat had a royal blue hull and a long white rear deck that housed a motor the size of an airplane engine. A small cabin to the front contained all the bells and whistles for saltwater fishing, most of which I couldn't begin to identify. The name of his boat was lettered on both sides—*Bragging Rights*.

He helped me aboard, but Kelly made an expert leap and landed effortlessly. We moved to the cabin, where Leith fired up his turbo engine. *Bragging Rights* eased out of the slip, then out of the harbor, and once clear, the front end surged out of the water and we roared through the waves.

It was a good thing I have a strong stomach.

"It's calm this morn," Leith pointed out.

This was calm?

I looked back. The harbor was a tiny dot. Scanning the shore, I realized that at some point we'd turned until we were traveling parallel to the shoreline. Leith cut the engine and the boat instantly responded.

Before us, the sun had barely risen over the horizon. The rolling hills, covered with dew, glistened, and the sky was painted with streaks of pink.

Neither of us spoke. The moment was too magnificent for words. Even Kelly stared off to the east, watching the day begin.

"It's beautiful," I finally said. "Thank you for showing it to me."

"Ah, but there's more."

He powered up and we drove on. I found myself peeking at the man at the helm. He was rugged and strong, made for the outdoors and the open sea. Leith really was perfect inspiration for a romantic hero. I took a mental picture of him and filed it away for my next writing session.

After that, I scanned the sea ahead of us, wondering what was coming next. I didn't speculate for long. Ahead, I saw the waters part and a sea creature shoot straight up into the air, twirl, and dive back down below.

"What was that?" I shouted. Which made Leith laugh.

He slowed the engine to a crawl and said, "A bottlenose dolphin. Keep watching. They travel in pods, so we're in fer a treat."

Sure enough, as we crept along, first one rose, then another shot up. At times several dolphins broke the waves simultaneously, playing.

"I'm hearing them!" I exclaimed. "Clicks and whistles."

"That's how they communicate." Leith had a huge grin on his face, enjoying my reaction as much as the scene before us. He went on to tell me that bottlenose dolphins can live for up to forty years, and that they are larger and have thicker blubber than most other breeds of dolphins. "They need that tae survive in our cold climate," he explained. "And they never really shut doon tae sleep. Half o' their brain stays active while the other side sleeps."

Too soon, we headed for the harbor. Back on the pier, when I removed and returned his jacket, Leith said, "Might ye have preferred some deep-water fishing?"

I shook my head. "This was better than anything I could have imagined."

"Isn't life grand!"

Yes, at times it really was.

CHAPTER 13

I arrived at the post office a few minutes past nine a.m., right after it opened.

Glenkillen's quaint little postal service is painted cornflower blue with white-framed windows. Flower baskets filled with trailing pansies, geraniums, and petunias hang from hooks outside the door. There is a cash machine under a sheltered awning for withdrawals and a red letterbox at the front of the walkway for outgoing mail. The post office is closed on Sundays as well as Wednesday and Saturday afternoons, and any other time that Paul Denoon chooses to flip the window sign from open to closed with no discernible rhyme or reason. If he made lunch arrangements or had a medical appointment or any number of other errands, he closed the post office, leaving a note on the door announcing his return time, which I can personally attest to as an approximation only.

Mondays, it turns out, are exceptionally heavy mailing

days. I had to stand in a line that extended out the door, as the small interior accommodates only a few people at a time.

Some customers in the queue gave me the standard "Good mornin' tae ye" greeting, though I also sensed several curious and furtive glances. Which was a bit disconcerting. Coming from a big city where nobody minded anyone else's business to a small village where everybody knew everything and then some, took getting used to. And this bunch obviously had an inside track.

I tried to figure out what they'd heard about me—that I had found Isla's body? Almost for certain. And everyone would know about the yarn, how it had been wrapped around Isla's neck and that Vicki had supplied it, however unintentionally. Perhaps they also knew about my role as the inspector's newly appointed assistant. I almost welcomed that bit of gossip. It would make my job easier if I didn't have to waste time explaining myself to every person I spoke with in regards to the murder.

As I waited in line, I could almost hear their collective minds working overtime, wondering what was true and what wasn't. It seemed like they wanted to interrogate me instead of the other way around, but none of them was quite that bold.

The line inched slowly forward. As my turn approached (holding the door open, half in, half out of the building), another postal worker appeared from the back room to assist the postmaster and began taking customers as well to speed things up a bit. Neither the incoming staffer nor Paul Denoon were in any particular hurry, neither so much as glancing up to assess the length of the line.

Same as in the States. You didn't have a choice. You waited as long as it took. And if you didn't like it, that was just too bad. And as to the employees behind the counter, I couldn't imagine dealing with never-ending lines. They had to have nerves of steel.

The interior was cramped. It encompassed a counter behind which the two postal workers assisted customers. In addition to buying stamps and mailing packages, we could exchange pounds for euros or make photocopies at a self-help machine next to the counter. I noticed the cards required to add minutes to mobile phones that Doc Keen and Paul Denoon had discussed as we shared a table at the sheep dog trials.

When my turn finally came, the postmaster was still waiting on another customer. His assistant waved me over, but instead I allowed the woman behind me to go ahead and continued to wait while I studied Paul Denoon. He seemed ancient to me, well past normal retirement age.

"What'll it be?" Paul said shortly after, eyeing me over spectacles perched on the end of his nose.

"I need to speak with you in private," I said, feeling the entire line behind me leaning forward, catching every word.

He scowled at me while I did my best to present a pleading, respectful attitude—one that hopefully announced that I would be grateful if he consented and appreciative of any amount of time he could offer me, no matter how brief. His eyes slid to those still in line behind me before he said, "In case ye didn't notice, we're a wee bit busy at the moment."

"Perhaps there is a better time to come back?"

He thought about that and must have decided now was

as good, or rather as inconvenient, a time as any, because he told his assistant he'd be right back, and directed me through a side door into another room. Rows of wooden pigeonholes ringed the room, some of the slots containing letters. A table stood in the center for initial sorting, and large postal bins were stacked in a corner.

I began explaining myself immediately. "I'm assisting Inspector Jamieson in the investigation of Isla Lindsey's murder. Would you like to see my credentials?"

He regarded me rather suspiciously over his reading glasses. "That would be proper," he said, giving no clue as to whether he had prior knowledge of my involvement, although he hadn't expressed any surprise, either.

I dug through my pockets until I found the warrant card, and presented it to him. "We have reason to believe that certain packages should have gone out last Thursday. I'm here to confirm that they did."

Paul handed back my card. "Parcels go out daily," he said with a clipped tone.

"Yes, but these would all have had the return address as Sheepish Expressions. Kirstine MacBride brought them in."

"An' why are ye askin' me and keepin' customers waiting when ye could be askin' her an' saving us this bother?"

"I'm simply following up," I muttered. This wasn't going quite as well as I'd anticipated it would when the postmaster had acquiesced to the interview.

"An' ye suppose I should be rememberin' every customer, an' what's been sent? And at me advanced age at that?"

I sighed in exasperation. Should I put more pressure on him? And if so, what kind of pressure? He didn't look as though he scared easily, and I doubted that I was any good at twisting arms.

Instead, I threw my boss's name out there. "It's very important that I find out about those packages so I can inform Inspector Jamieson. He asked me to do this for him since he's busy with other aspects of the case. There would have been twenty-two packages."

That got a reaction. "Twenty-two o' them! Why didn't ye say that at the beginning? It woulda saved us this little jig." But then he immediately squashed my excitement by shaking his head. "That number o' posted parcels, I woulda remembered."

"Do you recall Kirstine MacBride coming in on Thursday?"

"Not Thursday, nor any other day last week. Haven't seen her in the post office fer several weeks or even more."

"Well, why didn't . . ." I stopped myself. I was about to say that if he had said that at the beginning, the jig he mentioned would have been up before it began. But I let it go. In a way, this was the best news possible. Well, maybe not the absolute best, but good enough to make my day worthwhile, and it had barely just begun. I could cross off traveling around the countryside retrieving kits.

Except, if Kirstine hadn't mailed them, where were they? Their whereabouts still needed to be determined.

After thanking the postmaster, I practically flew out of the post office door, intent on racing back to the farm and confronting Kirstine. She'd clearly intended to sabotage Vicki's club before it even had a chance to get off the ground. The nerve! Talk about cutting off your nose to spite your face. Didn't Kirstine even realize that she was also hurting her own business?

I should slow down, try to get a search warrant. I'd love to watch her squirm under my scrutiny. Yes, a search warrant would be enormously satisfying. Although the inspector might think that was excessively aggressive. I could hear him telling me he'd handle her himself, implying that she would have been more forthcoming in the first place if not for the tension between us. If I involved him, he might take me out of the loop, or could even decide to remove me from the case permanently.

Maybe I should take a little time to cool off and figure out my next move without involving red tape and the inspector. I was a big girl. I could handle this.

I was already in the center of Glenkillen with the rest of the day before me, and I had other tasks to do (if only I could stop seeing raging-bull red and remember what they were). Apparently an organized mind is most effective when it isn't ticked off and wanting revenge over personal issues, which at the moment were outweighing the professional aspects two to one.

Kirstine would have plenty of explaining to do. She was a thief and a liar, and she could *so* easily become my prime suspect. Except for several logical reasons that she most likely couldn't be.

First and foremost, if Kirstine had decided to kill Isla, she would never have chosen the shop's parking lot. She'd have disposed of the body anywhere else, rather than besmirch her precious Sheepish Expressions's good name. No, if Kirstine was going to commit murder, she would have stuffed Isla's body in a back room then later dumped it somewhere else, like off a cliff on the far side of the MacBride farm where the bluffs were steep and the discovery of a body could take weeks or months or years, maybe never.

Not to mention Kirstine's complete lack of any obvious motive. No, most likely Kirstine MacBride-Derry was simply being difficult, something she excelled at. This time, though, she'd crossed a line, interfering with an ongoing investigation, withholding pertinent information. Did she even realize that? Probably not. Her ongoing hostility toward me could be clouding her better judgment. Had I ever seen her better judgment? Not yet, I hadn't.

I must have been stomping down Castle Street oblivious to the world around me, because my thoughts were interrupted by a familiar voice close behind me asking, "Where are ye going in such a snit?"

Sean Stevens appeared at my side, outfitted in a crisp, clean uniform, much different than earlier when Charlotte and I had caught him creeping away from Vicki's house.

"I'm not in a snit," I told Sean, although I really had been.

He stopped in front of Taste of Scotland. Although the shop wasn't open yet, the wonderful aroma of freshly baked sweets drifted our way on a light breeze, so I ground to a halt, too. The owner, Ginny Davis, makes all her shop's shortbread from scratch in a kitchen to the rear of the building. I've had the good fortune to sample some of her shortbread creations, including java mocha, orange chocolate chip, and almond shortbreads. Today's special was posted in the window—chocolate-dipped shortbreads.

"I was aboot tae go inside Taste of Scotland and say

hello tae me cousin Ginny, and here I find ye with an expression that could frighten a lesser man."

"I'm okay, really. Where is the inspector this morning?"

"So that's what's got ye fired up. Now he's hidin' from ye, too?"

Which hadn't crossed my mind recently, but now that Sean mentioned it . . . Jamieson *had* been sending me out on errands that assured our paths weren't likely to cross.

"I just wanted to touch base with him," I muttered, thinking that it was fine with me if I didn't run into him until after I'd followed up on Kirstine and exposed her deceptive actions. I wanted to be the one to deliver those twenty-two kits she'd stashed away. If I had the opportunity to bring Kirstine down from on high at the same time, that was an added bonus.

"Ye can get in touch with me any time ye have questions," Sean said. "That is, if the inspector isn't available. I'm willing tae answer any questions ye have."

Oh, right, yes, that's what I needed. Tutelage from the special constable *I'd* tutored. "Sure," I said, not able to imagine that ever happening. Then Charlotte's remark about an additional exchange between Isla and Sean came to mind. "I heard Isla didn't like the spot you originally picked for the van?"

"Aye, she made me move it from one side o' my car tae the other." Sean shook his head as though trying to understand her reasoning but failing. "Just showing who's in charge, she was. Well, she's in the great beyond now, givin' orders tae the angels."

She probably was.

"Oh," he went on, "I almost forgot tae mention, I picked

up two of those yarn kits that I distributed on Saturday."
He dug a piece of paper out of his trouser pocket and
showed me the names written on it, which I recognized as
two other fund-raiser volunteers.

Sean went on with a touch of self-importance. "These
are two volunteers who designed and printed up the program guides. I went tae each of their residents and interrogated them thoroughly, but unfortunately without
learnin' a bit o' new information. Neither o' them was too
happy when I confiscated their handiwork, which both had
already started to knit intae socks. One o' them even
threatened tae let the air out o' the tires o' me car if I
unraveled what she'd already accomplished. I promised
tae return it in the same condition as I found it."

"I can't believe you were threatened," I said.

"Aye. She's another cousin, she is, thinks she can bully
me around. What's a bloke tae do with the likes o' relatives
such as mine?" He sighed. "So how is yer own investigation going?"

"I'm on my way to see Senga Hill."

"What a coincidence that ye mention her name. I'm
about tae speak with Ginny regarding Senga this very
minute."

"Really?" That caught my attention. "Why?"

"Senga worked in this establishment fer my cousin."

I hadn't known that. Although there were probably a
lot of things I didn't know about the local residents.
"Maybe I'll tag along then, since we're right here," I said.

"As ye see fit, but let me do the talkin' and ye the
listenin'."

I shook my head in disbelief. Talk about putting on airs.

"Exactly when are you leaving for police training?" I asked.

"Soon enough. We need tae crack this case fast. I cannae leave in the middle o' an active investigation."

What? No! Surely his training began at a certain time, and Sean would be on his way regardless of the status of this case. Wouldn't he?

Sean continued, "I have plenty o' advice fer ye."

"Such as?"

"Such as, just because ye have police power in yer new position, it's not smart tae flaunt it. Ye might be ordered tae follow up with crime incidents, but ye have tae be subtle about it, ye do. Ye're a crime stopper now, and don't ferget it."

"Are you finished?"

"Fer the moment."

"Then let's go."

CHAPTER 14

A small sign hanging on the door told me that Taste of Scotland was scheduled to open in about fifteen minutes, at ten o'clock, but I could see Ginny Davis responding to Sean's knock through the glass bakery displays in the window. She hustled through from the back kitchen, wearing an apron around her waist and a scarf tied behind her head.

Ginny had been one of the first local business owners to treat me with hospitality and warmth. I hadn't forgotten her kindness and made a point of frequenting her shop. The fact that I loved sweets certainly didn't hurt our casual and friendly relationship, either.

"What is that wonderful aroma?" I asked her right away.

"Scottish buns," she told me. "They aren't outta the oven, though, or I'd offer ye one."

I inhaled with delight and said, "I smell cinnamon and almonds."

Ginny grinned. "Ye have the nose o' a hound, Eden

Elliott," she said, then to Sean, "Also, I put in raisins, currants, and a wee bit o' brandy."

"Brandy, now that's the secret tae the best kind o' buns," he said.

The bakery was a small slice of heaven, a welcome retreat from the harsh realities of the outside world. We made it our first order of business to sample the shortbread of the day. Sean and I agreed that the chocolate dip was delicious. Soon Sean was on his third piece and seemed to have forgotten the reason he'd come to Taste of Scotland.

But I remembered why we were here.

"We wanted to ask a few questions about one of your past employees," I said. Sean, focused on devouring shortbread, still hadn't jumped in. "Sean! You came here about . . ."

Only then did he snap to. "Oh, right then, cousin. I need information about Senga Hill."

I watched Ginny's expression go from sunny and clear to cloudy and overcast. "What about her?" she said.

"If I recall," Sean went on, "she had a position with ye fer a short time in the spring o' this year."

"Aye, she did."

"Didn't Senga have her own bakery at one time?" I asked. "Not in Glenkillen, though, if I understood correctly."

"She owned a bakery in Elgin, down the coast a ways from here," Ginny said grudgingly. "Which she sold once she turned tae pension age. I thought she'd be an asset to the business when she came in and applied fer part-time employment, but it didn't work out as I expected."

"What happened?" I asked, watching Sean bite into yet

another chocolate-dipped shortbread. If he wasn't paying attention, someone had to, so I pulled out the small notebook that Inspector Jamieson had given me. At least one of us would take notes.

"Shortly after she began," Ginny said, "this was in the spring, April I believe, all of a sudden my gluten-sensitive customers started complaining about symptoms. Since Sean and I have a dear aunt who is a celiac, I know the signs—bad reflux, cramps, brain fog, digestive issues tae name the most common."

"Who would that aunt be?" Sean asked her, back in the conversation now that the shortbread was gone.

"Aunt Hildy."

"Oh right, her."

"See, over here"—Ginny indicated a display with a large sign that read *Gluten Free*—"are the special bakery items I've added as more and more people are becoming intolerant tae gluten, so gluten-free it 'tis. Or is supposed tae be. Senga changed everything around, swapped a gluten-free batch for one with gluten! She made my customers sick, is what she did. I had no choice but tae let her go."

"Surely it was a mistake on her part," I said, but couldn't help wondering about that sleeping-pill-laced cupcake and the connection between that and this. Though there was a vast difference between a mistake in placing the wrong products on a shelf and intentionally adding drugs to baked goods.

"Senga admitted her error, said she needed new glasses, and apologized from the bottom o' her heart," Ginny said. "But tae my mind, the choice was either her staying on, or my customers staying safe. I lost trust in her judgment and ability tae accomplish the most basic tasks, and found I couldn't get it back. Which would ye have picked if ye had tae choose?"

I didn't reply. I might have handled the situation exactly as Ginny had.

"Ach, employees! Ye haff tae watch them every second," Sean said to his cousin as though he were an expert. "Nothin' worse fer a business than bad employees, if ye ask me."

"I've learned my lesson," Ginny agreed. "I always baked my own products in the past and wouldn't change that, and after what happened I'm shelving them myself, too. A business owner has tae mind the shop."

Which was exactly what Kirstine had said about Sheepish Expressions and keeping watch over the cash register. Being a small business owner had to be hard work. Even doing your absolute best wasn't good enough if an employee messed it up for you. Thankfully, I didn't have to worry about that in my line of work.

After leaving the shop, Sean asked if I needed directions to Senga's home. I told him the address I had and he added, "She's in the upper flat. Go in through the close. Ye want my assistance?"

Absolutely not, I thought, but said, "I can handle this one."

With that, he went his own way and I went mine. I'd pay a quick visit to Senga then head out to the farm for a showdown with the conniving Kirstine MacBride-Derry about the missing yarn kits.

In a small community, avoiding unpleasant people isn't as easy as it was in the city. Or maybe in a village this size it's simply easier to peel away the layers of their public personas and expose them for what they really are.

However, so many of the other locals were kind and welcoming. Despite Ginny's issues with the woman, Senga Hill struck me as one of the many who were fun to be around.

Senga lived on Oldcroft Street, which runs parallel to Castle Street two blocks north of the very center of the village. She rented a bedroom upper flat in a row of identical apartments. I stood on the sidewalk studying the building and seeing only one door, which led to the lower flat. And a walkway on the side of the building. The close? I followed the path, passing garbage receptacles, and found a gate in the back.

I opened it, walked into and through a lush communal flower garden, past a timber shed, and up a flight of stairs. Senga answered on the first buzz.

"Eden, what a lovely surprise," she said, letting me into her kitchenette. "We'll sit in the lounge. Would ye like some tea?"

Thinking of how massive amounts of caffeinated tea had been the primary reason for my sleepless night, I declined. I followed her into her living room, or the lounge as she'd called it, where she motioned me to a seat on one end of a floral sofa.

"I heard ye were helping solve the case," she told me, sitting down on the other end of the sofa. "Are ye making headway on finding Isla's killer?"

"We're still early in the investigation," I told her, which amounted to a negative. "Right now, we're asking routine questions."

"The inspector has been puttin' inquiries tae me through a series o' telephone calls." Senga appeared fairly calm, but I noticed she was wringing her hands in her lap. "And he was asking about the cupcakes, and if Isla had bought any. Lots did, but not that one. A very strange question, if ye ask me. 'Twas yarn around the neck that killed her. What would my cupcakes have tae do with anything?"

A tricky question to answer without giving away too much.

It wasn't my place to tell Senga what the coroner had discovered. She might suspect something odd, but she couldn't know for sure why we were asking. Unless, that is, she turned out to be the one who murdered Isla.

"Well?" she said, still waiting for my response regarding her cupcakes and Inspector Jamieson's suspicions. Thankfully, she went on, "What's Inspector Jamieson up tae?"

"The inspector keeps his thoughts to himself most of the time," I said, intentionally vague, but definitely true.

"Aye, he's a hard one tae read."

Tell me about it, I almost said, catching myself in time. Then to change the topic I asked for her yarn kit, explaining that we were collecting all of them.

She immediately rose, went into her bedroom, and returned with it. Like several other members, Senga had started knitting—I recalled seeing her knitting alongside a few others at the trials. She didn't complain, simply turned it over. "There ye be," she said. "I have nothing tae hide."

I placed the kit beside me on the sofa. One more, with yarn intact, accounted for.

"Did you see Isla during the day?" I asked.

"Aye, she came around with her money bag tae collect the mornin's take."

"How did she seem?" I asked, keeping to the script.

"She seemed same as always. Her usual self." I sensed something then, as though Senga had her own opinion about Isla Lindsey, but wasn't going to share it on her own.

"That was the only time you saw her?"

"Aye."

"Anything else that might help?" I prompted, not ready to end the interview yet. "Anything at all that struck you as unusual?"

"Nothing at the moment, but if I think o' anything, I'll be sure tae ring ye up."

I thought of asking her for a list of those who had purchased cupcakes, but she'd sold hundreds; she couldn't possibly list every person who'd bought them, let alone known who may have actually eaten one.

Before I could think of a last line of questioning, Senga said, "Dinnae take this the wrong way, Eden, but ye look exhausted. Ye should get some sleep. A nice nap would do ye wonders."

"I *have* been having trouble sleeping," I admitted. "The murder is preoccupying my thoughts, even at night when I should be asleep. Especially then, actually."

"If Doc Keen sees ye, he'll be on ye with a remedy. The doc's been givin' away samples o' a new type o' sleeping pill," Senga told me.

"Really?" I kept my expression as neutral as possible, but my breath took a leap and my heart began to beat faster.

Senga went on, "Some salesperson left plenty o' samples behind in Doc Keen's office and he's offering them tae some o' his patients tae try."

I hoped the doctor wasn't distributing sleeping pills like candy, especially if it was the same kind that had been given to Isla. So much for the inspector's "good lead" if he was. "Doc Keen has a lot of patients from the village, does he?"

"He's the only private-practice doctor o' medicine between the North Sea and Inverness that isn't affiliated with the hospital and therefore not charging an arm and a leg fer his service as some o' them do. Doc Keen takes care of us pensioners who don't want some young pipsqueak barely out o' nappies examining them."

Senga continued, "I wish I'd kept the sample he gave me, so ye could give it a try, but I threw the package in the rubbish. I'm not a big believer in using drugs tae get by, but each tae his own. I made the mistake o' mentioning tae Doc Keen that I'm up several times through the night and I couldn't bring myself tae tell him I don't believe in poppin' pills. So I carried them along when I left with the full intention o' throwin' them away. Now I'm sorry I did. They woulda helped ye get some shut-eye, if ye aren't against such a thing."

"When did you toss your sample?" I asked.

"Just a few days ago, as a matter o' fact. But ye can go by his office and make a request. Although he might have tae see ye first, make sure ye're fit as a fiddle before given ye a sample tae try."

"I passed a bin on the side of the walkway leading

round back to your door," I said, suddenly excited that the conversation had made a turn from routine to right-on. "Is that where you discarded the sample?"

"That's a funny question tae be askin'," she said, eyeing me with concern. "Ye don't plan on digging fer them, now do ye?"

"No, of course not."

"Ye poor dear. See how exhausted ye are. I'd dig them out meself, but they're buried but good by now. Should I phone the doctor fer ye?"

"No, no, that's quite all right. I rarely take medications myself." It was time to move away from this hot topic, so I went on, "Did you know Isla well? I get the feeling that you're holding back." There, I'd put it out there.

"Ye could tell that, could ye?"

"I had a feeling."

"I knew her too well, if ye must know," Senga said. "I learned tae steer clear o' that one. She had a way o' making a body feel small and worthless."

"You sound like you had personal experience," I prodded.

Senga nodded. "Aye, it'll come out anyway, so I might as well be the one tae tell it. I worked fer a short time in the office o' the hospice. I was helpin' keep the books fer the charity events. Data entry, it was mostly, but a little bit o' accounting as well. I had tae do all o' that when I owned my own business, and I have a certain knack fer numbers."

"Who hired you?"

"Harry Taggart himself. I'd already been making baked

goods fer some o' the other charity events and he knew I'd
been a business owner. He thought I'd be useful tae catch up
on the books. But I was forced out early in the summer."

"Forced out?"

"Aye. Isla took a dislike tae me. She challenged me
every time I turned around. After only a few weeks, she
claimed I'd made too many mistakes. She didn't give up
with complaints against me, and soon after Mr. Taggart
told me my help was no longer needed. It was herself that
was behind it, I'm sure o' it. But I didn't make any mistakes
at all, in fact I found several errors. She had it in fer me
fer some reason or another."

I murmured something comforting, but my thoughts
were elsewhere. Another mistake that Senga Hill had
made. Another mistake that had led to her termination.
Was she a vengeful woman? Had she killed Isla for accusing her of poor accounting skills? That hardly seemed
likely. I paused to recall the timeline of Senga's employment, and was certain that Senga had worked for Ginny
in the spring and for the hospice during the summer. If she
was going to kill someone over losing a job, wouldn't her
first victim have been Ginny Davis at Taste of Scotland?
Ginny, though, was a sweetheart. Isla was a whole 'nother
story.

A few minutes later, I wished her a good day, tromped
down the stairs, rounded the corner, and paused beside the
trash bin. Senga claimed that she'd thrown away a sleeping
pill sample. What if she'd lied to me? What if she used her
sample to knock out Isla before choking her to death?

Was I really considering digging through her trash?

But if I found it, that would be something. Not much,

but better than nothing. We'd have proof that her sample wasn't used as a special ingredient in a cupcake.

And if I didn't find it? What would that prove?

Someone else might have taken it. I couldn't rule that out. But not finding it would throw a very bad light on the baker.

Senga had obviously had access to those cupcakes. She'd been the one to make them, so of course she had plenty of opportunities to tamper with one. By her own admission, she'd also been given a sleeping pill sample, and had been let go from Taste of Scotland for making customers ill. Not only that, the recently murdered Isla had been the reason Senga also wasn't working at the hospice office any longer.

We only had Senga's word for it that she hadn't given Isla a cupcake. And having her yarn kit didn't exonerate her. She could have stolen someone else's and used their yarn. The important thing to do was track down every single kit until we found which one was missing. That kit's owner wouldn't necessarily be the killer, but it was the best place to begin. Not here in a garbage can.

Or so I told myself even as I placed Senga's knitting kit on the walkway and began digging in her trash. It seemed like an investigator sort of thing to follow up on.

The trash receptacles were shared by several apartments. There was way too much waste for one household, and the communal trash—dirty diapers, canned fish remains, stinky odorous food—was made worse since multiple days' worth had accumulated. Worse yet, when I didn't find any pill samples in the top layers of either bin, I was forced to delve deeper.

And deeper.

The only positive thing about this task was that there weren't many windows facing the walkway between the apartments, or I would have been exposed to any tenant looking out. I certainly didn't want to get caught by any of the tenants, but if I did, at least I had a warrant to present, which was something, but it would have been embarrassing at best.

My phone rang when I was elbow deep in garbage. I fumbled to answer it before the sound gave me away.

"How is it going on yer end?" the inspector's voice came through loud and clear after I greeted him in a whisper.

"Messy," I replied.

"I've traced those sleeping pills tae Doc Keen," he told me. If I could find any amusement in anything at the moment, it was in knowing I was several piles of garbage ahead of him. "He's been offering samples tae some o' his customers."

"How many pills in each sample?"

"Two."

Next, I asked him to describe the package and learned that the two capsules came in a two-inch-by-two-inch heavy-duty clear plastic container. "The capsules are red on the one half and gold on the other," he added.

Red and gold. Bright colors to be searching for in a heap of garbage. At least they would stand out. I was almost through with one trash can and about to move on to the second.

"Did you get a list of patients who he gave samples to?" I inquired.

The inspector sighed on the other end. "I've known Doc Keen since I was a wee lad," he said. "The doc is an intuitive physician, as good as they come, but he doesn't always abide by the proper rules as they pertain tae this modern day and age."

"He's not hiding behind patient confidentiality, then?" I said.

"That would be proper use o' the rules, but not valid as a legitimate excuse when it comes tae cooperating with a murder investigation. No, after dodging my questions, he finally came clean that he's been giving them out freely tae his patients over the last month or so without keeping any records."

"So you have no idea who received them?" I asked. I had every intention of telling him about Senga's sample, but I hoped to find it first.

"That's aboot right. Although I asked if he'd given any tae the hospice fer distribution tae the patients, and he hadn't. And he hadn't given any tae the hospital, either, due tae the fact that it has a strict policy against using samples. So his own patients are the extent o' it."

"How can he be so sure that the sample salesman didn't leave any at the hospice?"

"Doctor Keen is consultant physician fer the hospice. All changes regarding medical protocols and medications like that have tae be approved through him."

"But staff members might be able to obtain them?"

"If they are his patients *and* they saw him in the last month, aye. It would make it more difficult fer us if the physicians at Kirkwall Hospital also were disbursing samples. I've asked the doc tae make a list of patients from memory, but just tae be on the safe side, I confirmed with the hospice and hospital. He remembered that much at least. Neither has samples."

"Even if we tracked them all down, those patients might have given them to someone else," I said, fighting disappointment.

"Aye, there's that. Our job isn't any easy one, is it?"

"I'll call you back in a few minutes," I said. "I'm sort of in the middle of something."

In the thick of things, actually.

We disconnected, and I went back to work. In the end, nobody came along to ask what I was doing. But I didn't find any sleeping pill samples, either. Had Senga Hill lied to me? If so, why bring up the pills at all? Because she thought we'd find out anyway?

Afterward, with garbage aroma wafting from my clothes (which became particularly pungent in the confines of my car even with the windows open), I called the inspector and related the conversation Sean and I'd had with the owner of Taste of Scotland, my subsequent interrogation of Senga, the discovery that she'd gotten those sleeping pills from Doc Keen, and how I'd searched through the garbage without finding proof that she'd thrown them out.

"I have tae admire ye," he said when I finished. "Ye followed that lead tae its final conclusion."

That didn't sound quite as sincere as I'd hoped. I detected amusement in his tone along with a concerted effort to remain professional.

Then he was gone, but not before I heard him laughing out loud as the connection terminated.

"Very funny," I said into the phone, even though he wasn't there to hear me.

Now I didn't feel nearly as bad about keeping the information about certain unsent kits from him. That would teach him to laugh at me.

Besides, I rationalized—I deserved to handle this one by myself.

I was going to take Kirstine down single-handedly.

CHAPTER 15

When I arrived at the farm, Vicki was in what she refers to as her yarning room, a small bedroom that she'd converted for her own use. There she had created her Poppy Red yarn skeins, dying and spinning them from the farm's wool. Ordinarily, her presence in this room would be an encouraging sign. She could usually be found there wearing an apron and a pair of yellow gloves, surrounded by sponges, and brushes, and all the other tools of her trade. Today, she sat at her painting table, apronless, with her two Westies sleeping at her feet and her hands clasped together on the table as she stared listlessly into space.

Coco and Pepper perked up at my arrival and ran over, discovering plentiful odors on my pant legs to indulge their canine senses. Vicki glanced up, did a double take, and said, "What happened to you?"

"I'll explain later," I said, heading for the kitchen where I washed my hands at the sink while making a mental list of future investigation supplies to purchase. Disposable gloves were at the top of the list. Vicki followed me at a distance, but the Westies were right on my heels, loving the new me. "I need a shower and a change of clothes," I told her unnecessarily.

Wrinkling her nose in distaste, she said, "I'll agree with that." Then she slunk back to her yarn room, shoulders hunched, dragging her feet.

I trailed behind, drying my hands on a towel. Coco and Pepper were right with me.

Vicki plunked down and said, "I've decided to end the skein-of-the-month club. After what happened to Isla, I can't continue it."

My eyes traveled over her worktables, taking in the batches of wool in varying stages of completion. Vicki had a knack for turning wool into beautiful fiber, and I enjoyed watching the process, from sorting and washing to carding (which she told me means combing the wool to straighten the strands), then dying the fleece before spinning it into yarn.

"You can't give up," I told her.

"I have."

"And look how that decision has affected you. You've thrown in the towel." In my frustration, I literally threw the kitchen towel down on the table. "How does that make you feel? Pretty awful, right?"

Vicki stared at me with wide eyes, before sputtering, "It's too late anyway. I couldn't possibly be ready by October first."

"So, you regroup. Notify your members. Shoot for November."

Vicki shook her head. "I can't."

But I wasn't about to give up yet. "I have an idea! This month's kits will be released for distribution at some point, after the murder is solved. We'll send them once that happens, or not at all if you think that's best. And we'll notify the members that the club will resume in November. Or even December. That gives you time to make enough skeins for all the knitters on your waiting list, too."

"I don't know."

Well, at least that wasn't a no.

"How about mittens? Holiday mittens. And . . ."

"No red yarn!" Vicki was listening.

"No red," I agreed. "Blue? Green? Silver? All three?"

I could see the beginning of renewed interest in her eyes. They weren't dull anymore.

"Apple green, lime, and a sunshine yellow," she said. "That would be a great combination."

"Perfect."

"And I'll call them Merry Mittens!"

"That's the spirit."

"I need to get to work."

Vicki had her groove back.

"I made some calls," she said as she draped plastic over her painting table, already inspired to begin. It took me a few seconds to realize we were back on the subject of this month's yarn kits. "No one has received them yet." She paused and frowned in thought. "It seems odd. They should have arrived by now."

"They'll turn up," I assured her. Now that I'd put a smile back on her face, I wasn't going to turn around and wipe it off. Besides, Vicki would find out soon enough that Kirstine hadn't mailed the kits. Knowing Vicki and her tumultuous relationship with her half sister, I didn't want her to blow her stack and interfere with my own takedown of Kirstine.

I left my friend to begin her new project, showered at my cottage (much to the chagrin of Coco and Pepper, who'd insisted on accompanying me to my tiny home), and then I walked down the lane toward the shop.

Why Kirstine had done what she'd done—or rather, not done—was easy to figure out. She'd obviously wanted to sabotage Vicki's efforts to get the yarn club off the ground. Kirstine didn't want her half sister to succeed. Her actions had been vindictive and petty and she was about to pay for being so mean-spirited.

Where would she have stashed those packages? I'd bet anything they were still in the back of the shop or in the trunk of her car. In the boot, as the Scots call it. What foreign words the people of this country use, or at least they're strange to an American like me—boot instead of trunk, bonnet instead of hood, petrol instead of gas, and that's only the car terms.

Anyway, I'd have to get into the back room of the shop, because I was positive I wasn't going to get that search warrant, in spite of my wishful thinking. If the unmailed kits weren't there, then I'd have to figure out how to search her trunk.

For a fleeting moment, I considered stepping aside and handing this over to the inspector. That would be the most practical choice. But the conflict with Kirstine had turned personal for me. Kirstine had been nasty to my friend. I wanted to see justice served in my own way. So, I headed toward Sheepish Expressions for a showdown.

I saw volunteers out in the fields, dismantling the large refreshment tent, disassembling gates and pens, and picking up litter. If the event had gone off as planned, without the tragedy of murder, I would've been out there with them. But things had gone more than a little awry. Instead, I was about to have a confrontation over the willful withholding of information pertinent to the investigation.

Life takes strange turns sometimes.

A compact car pulled up next to me on the side of the lane, and Lily Young climbed out of the driver's seat of an aqua blue Mazda, while Oliver Wallace unfolded from the passenger side. He was wearing the same gray Wellies with yellow soles that he'd worn for the trials, but he had a deflated air about him today, far from the self-assurance he'd displayed Saturday morning.

I wasn't exactly pleased to see them. After all, I was on a personal vendetta mission, and they were about to slow me down.

"Oliver's been whining about helping today," Lily informed me, and I couldn't help noticing that she was glowing, in spite of her lack of any sort of makeup. Her nose was in the process of peeling, but the glow radiating from her didn't have anything to do with too many rays. I'd seen the same shine on Sean recently. Interesting.

The sun above wasn't nearly as bright as the light from this woman, despite her less-than-sunny words. "Oliver is coming up with all kinds o' reasons tae avoid manual labor," she continued with a flirt in her voice, "but I told him the only people with valid excuses are Bryan and Andrea, who has her hands full caring fer her brother. She's always been there fer him, more like a mum than a sister. And she's putting her nursing skills tae good use these days, having takin' time off from her duties at the hospice."

"It's not helping out that has me bothered," Oliver told her. "It's having tae sit in the passenger seat o' yer cracker box. I've never been good at shrinkin' back down tae the size o' a peanut, or ant, or some such thing."

Lily giggled. "Yes, I noticed. And ye're a horrible back-seat driver."

"When will the police release your van?" I asked Oliver, noting that his sunburn had already faded away completely and been replaced by the kind of tan that Leith had, an outdoorsy one. Lucky Oliver. Most Scots just burned and peeled, and never really tanned.

"If the coppers know when they'll part with my van, they aren't informing me," he replied. "Until then I'm at the mercy o' this mad driver."

Lily beamed. Did she have something for Oliver? If so, how had I missed that during the fund-raiser? Probably because I had been more interested in ditching the welcoming committee than being part of it, I admitted. But if Lily did have romantic feelings for Oliver, I wasn't sure he'd noticed. My initial frustration with Lily and Oliver disappeared. Kirstine wasn't going any place until the shop closed and that was hours away. I had time for these two.

"I'm thinking I will have tae trade in the van after what happened," he said to me. "I get a sick sensation in the pit o' my stomach every time I think o' you opening the side door and Isla . . ."

He couldn't go on at that point, pausing to compose himself. Lily placed a hand on his shoulder. Oliver reached up and put a hand over hers and said, "You're a good hen, Lily." Then he moved away a few steps, straightened his back, and said to me, "Have ye seen Harry Taggart?"

I glanced out into the field. "He could be in the field with the others. I haven't been out there yet myself."

"He should be around here someplace." Lily scanned the field. "That looks like his truck on the far side." She pointed to a vehicle I recognized. I'd seen Harry driving it around the village. Then she went on, "Harry isn't too pleased with our fund-raising efforts. He's disheartened by the returns."

"But everything sold out!" I said, stunned. "Programs, food, drinks, the raffles were successful, we had more spectators than we originally anticipated. I thought it was a huge success."

"I agree," she said. "It appeared tae be the best fund-raiser o' the lot; I don't know what more he expected."

"I believe Harry was speaking about prior events," Oliver said. "He couldn't possibly have a financial report on this one so soon."

Lilly scowled. "Well, instead o' complaining, he should count himself lucky fer his hospice that Isla's body dinnae turn up until late in the event," she said, "or he'd've been unhappier still."

Oliver's face registered shock. "Lily! What a thing tae say!"

"Well, it's true. If we'd found her in the morning, our fund-raising efforts woulda ended before they even began."

Oliver looked concerned. "Well, ye shouldn't say things like that out loud, fer goodness' sake. The inspector will turn his sights on ye and ye'll have some answering tae do. Or Eden here will get the wrong idea. She's workin' with the inspector, ye know."

"I never made it a secret that I couldn't stand her." Lily sniffed.

"But ye don't have tae announce it tae the world, either."

Lily looked as though she may have gone too far. "I only meant . . ." She didn't finish.

"Why didn't you like her?" I asked.

"You knew her. Did you like her?"

Good point.

"We simply had a clash o' personality," Lily explained. "Ever since we were wee children. Surely, ye can understand that, Oliver."

As a new law enforcement recruit, it was fascinating to watch the interplay between Lily and Oliver. Working from a professional point of view was turning out to be enlightening. Common sense dictated that I shouldn't indulge in idle gossip. However, I had free rein to encourage locals to inform on one another, and I wasn't beyond instigating conflict amongst them. I considered this as Oliver gave Lily a conciliatory hug. She practically dove into his arms. He remained expressionless.

Hoping to dredge up more of that lively conflict and possibly learn something of value, I addressed Oliver. "Who do *you* think murdered Isla?" I asked him.

"The husband," Oliver said without any hesitation. He'd already decided. "Bryan Lindsey."

Poor Bryan was the default suspect. I was curious if there was a particular reason for Oliver's certainty. "And why do you think that?" I asked.

"Isla and himself were at the Kilt & Thistle Friday night," Oliver said. "Havin' quite the row in one of the back corners. They weren't lovey-dovey and smiling at each other, that's fer sure."

That was the same thing Charlotte had mentioned this morning as having made the gossip rounds.

"Isla Lindsey never smiled once in her whole life," Lily pointed out. "Looking angry was standard fer her."

"You actually *saw* them together at the pub?" I asked Oliver. An actual witness to the scene rather than a secondhand informant would be helpful. "Or did you hear about it from somebody else?"

"I saw them with my very own twenty-twenty-vision eyes. I couldn't hear what they were speaking about, but if looks could kill . . . Bryan woulda done her in right there on the spot. I've never seen him look so angry."

"Have you shared this with the inspector?" I asked, thinking I needed to follow up with Dale and Marg, the pub owners. One of them might be able to give me more detailed information.

"Course I told him. Right after we found Isla, when the inspector was questioning the lot o' us. You'd already gone up the lane, Eden, so ye weren't privy tae that."

Ah, yes, after I'd been dismissed. What else had I missed? "How about you, Lily? Do you think Bryan killed his wife?"

"Not a bit." She shook her head, adamant that Isla's husband wasn't an option. I had to give her credit. Even if she'd set her sights on Oliver, it wasn't preventing her from speaking her mind and disagreeing with him. "Bryan never woulda done such a thing. He is kind and gentle with his sister, and goes tae visit his mum in the nursing home every Sunday, and a man like that, well, he cannae be the same man who killed Isla."

"You're assuming the murder was committed by a man?" I asked, wondering if the news about the sleeping pill had gotten out yet.

Oliver answered for her. "Aye. A woman doesn't have that kind o' strength."

I studied Lily and Oliver while they discussed the merits of his belief that only a man could have strangled Isla. So far it seemed the inspector had been successful in withholding certain details from the general public. The cupcake sprinkled with crushed sleeping pills was still a secret known only to a few of us investigating the case. And, of course, to the killer.

My thoughts turned to the sort of person who felt the need to offer the victim that cupcake as a prelude to murder. That act, more than anything, made me suspect a female killer now that more information was available. It just didn't seem like the sort of thing that would occur to a man. Men are so much stronger than women, especially in their upper bodies; a man probably wouldn't have worried about Isla Lindsey putting up a fight. Plus, sexist though it might seem, between the cupcakes, frosting sprinkles, and the Poppy Red yarn, this murder seemed to have a woman's touch. At least I thought it did.

Let go of preconceived ideas, Eden, I chastised myself. Men didn't always choose violence, shooting or stabbing their adversaries through the heart, or slicing open throats. And women didn't always avoid bloodshed by concocting poisons or pressing pillows over faces.

"We'd best get some work done," Lily said, "before it's all over." She grinned at Oliver. "Come along now."

"As long as I don't have tae get back in that vehicle," Oliver quipped. "I'll agree tae anything."

After leaving Lily and Oliver, I was just about to finally storm Sheepish Expressions, when my cell phone rang.

It was Sean. "I thought we should coordinate our efforts," he said. "What are ye up tae?"

"Interviewing some people," I said, intentionally keeping my movements vague, as I realized I was behaving exactly like the inspector would. "What are you doing?"

"I'm startin' tae drive the countryside gatherin' yarn kits that had been posted."

"Hold off a bit," I told him, planning to save him wasted time and petrol. "I'll get back to you shortly. Very shortly."

"Wha' are you? Me new boss?"

"Fine. Have at it." And I disconnected.

At least it would keep him out of my way for a while.

CHAPTER 16

Monday tends to be the slowest day of the week at Sheepish Expressions. Saturdays and Sundays are busiest, with tour buses arriving one after the other; then comes a lull during the first days of the week with a slow buildup again as the week progresses. With summer winding down, business had fallen off substantially.

So it wasn't surprising to find the parking lot practically empty.

Before entering the shop, I tested the doors of Kirstine's car. Alas, they were locked, as I'd expected. Peering through the windows didn't produce anything of interest, either.

I considered my options. There weren't many. So I took a deep breath, reminded myself to stay cool, calm, and collected, opened the door to Sheepish Expressions, and ventured inside to do a little snooping.

"Not you again!" Kirstine said when she looked up from a pile of knitting needles she was organizing by size. Her dismissive attitude almost sent me into a fit of anger before I'd even begun.

I forced a smile. "Thought I'd pick out some yarn," I said, heading for the opposite side of the room where barrels, baskets, and nooks and crannies were brimming with soft, colorful skeins of yarn. Several customers were browsing at a table filled with folded scarves. Another was sifting through a stack of tartan skirts.

"Since when do you knit?" Kirstine asked.

"Since . . . um . . . Vicki offered to teach me."

Just like that, Kirstine lost interest and went back to what she'd been doing with the knitting supplies when I walked in. A fly, or as the Scots called the most annoying insects, a wee midgie, would have gotten more attention than she was paying to me.

Wonderful.

I casually wandered into the knitting room, turning a few pages in a pattern book. Next, I ran my fingers over some of the skeins of yarn, enjoying the sensations of the different textures as I waited for the perfect moment.

Soon, I heard Kirstine speaking with someone, a customer at the front counter asking questions about tartans and clans. I knew that would give me at least a few minutes to complete the first stage of a rather haphazard plan of action.

I slithered into the back room where Kirstine kept her personal belongings amid a small supply of inventory. I quickly scanned the shelves for twenty-two packages of the same size, prepped for mailing. After making certain they weren't there, I scooted over to a large desk covered with stacks of paperwork, and began opening drawers, searching for her purse so I could swipe the keys to her car. Of course I didn't locate her purse until I'd opened every single drawer. Then I fumbled through it for the keys, which of course were buried at the very bottom.

A sound directly outside of the room startled me. I froze, my heart pounding so loud I thought it would be heard through the door. If someone entered the room, they'd see me right away. It would be tough to explain what I was doing, rifling through Kirstine's belongings.

But the knob didn't turn, and the sound that had caused my blood pressure to spike didn't come again. The breath I hadn't realized I was holding rushed out.

Quickly, I palmed a key fob and chain with several keys attached, which I assumed were shop and house keys. Then I slowly opened the door to the storage room, peered out, saw that the coast was clear, and ducked back into the knitting room.

Just in time. I'd barely made it before I heard her voice.

"What are *you* still doing here?" Kirstine said from the doorway. She was suspicious now rather than disinterested.

"I can't decide what to knit first," I said, slipping her keys into my pocket with one hand while turning the pages of the same pattern book with the other. "A scarf or a shawl. Which should I start with?"

"You don't need a pattern for a simple beginner's scarf," she said, eyeing me with disapproval. "Anybody should be able to handle that."

"Perfect." I closed the book and edged around her, heading for the door. "So no pattern necessary. And Vicki is sure to have some extra yarn."

She followed me through the store as though she

thought I might lift something on my way out. As if! I've never stolen anything in my life. I didn't even consider the pilfered keys in my pocket stolen. "Borrowed" was a better term. I was only borrowing her keys, and certainly had no intention of stealing her vehicle, either.

If I couldn't have a search warrant, I'd operate under the guise of reasonable grounds. I'd helped Sean with his homework to apply for police training, and it was paying off. I remembered clearly that the police have the right to search if they suspect drugs or weapons, or a variety of other conditions, including stolen property. Still, the inspector would have hardly condoned my actions. He was a by-the-book investigator as he'd been trained. Jamieson was intelligent and thorough, but he was also proper. He followed the rules, didn't bend them.

But I knew that Kirstine had lied about mailing out the kits, and those skeins of yarn were important to the investigation of a murder. Further, she'd lied to me, a law enforcement agent, which I hoped carried some sort of punishment. I wouldn't have to sneak around searching for the truth if she hadn't gone out of her way to deceive me from the beginning and obstruct justice. If she'd just admitted her wrongdoing and given up the kits, I wouldn't have had to stand in line at the post office and then grill the postmaster. I wouldn't have had to search her office for her keys and be going on a hunt for those kits this very minute.

Kirstine deserved jail time for wasting precious time and resources.

With that pleasant thought in my mind, visualizing her

behind bars, I stepped outside and away from the shop, made sure no one was observing my movements, and pressed a button on the fob. Kirstine's trunk popped open.

I peered inside the car boot. It was filled with brown cardboard mailing packages.

Kirstine was *so* b-u-s-t-e-d!

I didn't bother counting them right away, but I did open up one mailing box, just to make absolutely sure that these were the kits we'd been looking for. There was no mistaking the contents Vicki had packed, or the label *A Sheepish Expression Exclusive: Poppy Sox Knitting Kit*.

I smiled with sheer delight. Then I used my cell phone to contact the inspector and request his presence at the shop.

"Can ye tell me the reason?" he pressed.

"It's complicated. I'd rather you see it for yourself."

"In that case, I'm on my way."

Only then did I count them. Twenty-two. No more. No less. Just as I'd expected.

This discovery meant almost all the kits Vicki had assembled for the yarn club members were accounted for. Only a few still remained out there. I did a mental appraisal. Thirty-five at the beginning minus twenty-two right here was thirteen, minus the other seven that hadn't been picked up on Saturday left six. Of those six, we'd obtained the ones from Senga, Charlotte, and the two belonging to the volunteers who had designed the programs. That meant only two were still out there—Andrea Lindsey's and the kit Harry Taggart had picked up for his sister in Glasgow.

I couldn't help feeling a sense of pride in my accomplishment. Yet a cloud fell over my sunny outlook. So . . . we were making some progress. Thanks in part to . . .

Well . . . now that I really gave it some thought . . . to Kirstine . . . but only because of her obstinate behavior. If she hadn't been trying to stick it to Vicki by neglecting to mail out the kits, our work would be more difficult than it turned out to be. So in a way she'd helped rather than hurt us.

Not intentionally, that was for sure, but still . . . in spite of her efforts otherwise, she had.

I didn't want either Harry or Andrea to be involved in Isla's murder. How could they be? Harry was committed to the hospice, and by all accounts, had done a superb job of securing its future. Isla took orders from him, but if he didn't want her around, he could have gotten rid of her easily enough without resorting to violence. *Shove off*, he could have told her, in a nicer way of course.

And Andrea Lindsey? Andrea never made waves, didn't have strong opinions, and definitely wasn't the murdering type. Was she? Besides, why would she kill her own sister-in-law? Although the use of the crushed sleeping pill did give me pause, as did the fact that Andrea *was* a nurse. . . .

I had to remind myself that neither of them had to be the killer. If I was going to murder someone, I wouldn't use my own weapon if I could steal someone else's.

I considered ringing up Sean and announcing my successful score to relieve him of a wasted day of traveling around to collect them. But he'd been climbing up on a high horse and since he'd expressed his reluctance to take my advice when I'd tried to offer it, he was on his own. He could continue on the snipe hunt until the inspector called him home.

Which, knowing the relationship between the inspector and Sean, wasn't going to happen too quickly.

While I waited impatiently for Inspector Jamieson to arrive, I leaned against Kirstine's car, still feeling the satisfaction of a job well done.

My smugness faded soon after.

"What are you bloody doing?" I heard from the direction of the shop, a familiar voice filled with a roiling, boiling combination of surprise and rage.

Turning, I saw Kirstine charging my way, snorting fire, shooting me with eye-glare daggers, a ruddy, splotchy red flush on her contorted face. She was also clutching one of the knitting needles she'd been working with, one of those enormous needles with a wickedly pointed tip.

My impending death flashed before my eyes. For a brief moment, my mind went numb and my limbs locked in place. Then I took in what was about to happen. If I didn't get moving, my innards might end up spilled on the ground.

So I ran around to the far side of her car, making sure to stay on the balls of my feet in case quick direction changes were required.

Kirstine was at the open trunk. She slowed down. Her eyes slid from me to the contents of the trunk and back to me again.

Perhaps if I'd been wearing a police uniform, she might have remembered that I deserved a little respect as part of the inspector's team. She certainly wouldn't have reacted with such open hostility if Inspector Jamieson were here instead of me. She would have shown the proper decorum and behaved rationally.

Although on second thought, the inspector might not have allowed himself to be caught in this predicament. But that's where I was at the moment—in a difficult situation with no way out.

She rounded the car, coming straight at me.

"Stop right there!" I shouted a warning, trying to figure out whether I should keep running around the car or make a stand. She hadn't raised the knitting needle in a threatening manner, but was I prepared to take the chance that she would? This wasn't going to become Eden's Last Stand. "Stop! Right there," I repeated, still moving away from her.

Kirstine didn't acknowledge the warning.

So I did exactly what the inspector had hoped I'd never have to resort to. Although he couldn't have anticipated the precarious position I now found myself in, with a crazy woman attacking me wielding a needle sharp enough to do serious damage to the body I highly valued.

Not able to come up with a better option in the spur of the moment, I whipped out the pepper spray and hit the button, giving Kirstine a healthy blast. Healthy for me. Not so much for her.

It did the trick.

Kirstine came to an abrupt halt, stopping dead in her tracks. She dropped the knitting needle to the ground. Her eyes slammed shut, her hands shot to her face, and she started screeching.

Pepper spray isn't life threatening, it doesn't even result in raised blood pressure, so I wasn't a bit worried that she was really injured, even though to listen you'd think she was in her death throes. Temporarily blind, maybe, but that would pass.

What *did* concern me were the volunteers out in the field. I looked out and saw all heads turned our way. I waved and shouted as loud as I possibly could, "Everything's fine."

Several waved in return and all of them went back to what they were doing prior to Kirstine's screams.

She began coughing, a sign she'd inhaled some of the fumes.

If sprayed, according to prior research, the best bet was to move away to fresh air. I really wanted to leave her to suffer but instead I led the blind woman away from the area.

"It's only temporary," I told her.

"You attacked me!"

"Blink," I ordered. "And keep blinking. That will help wash the spray out."

Milk would also help. I could call up to the house and tell Vicki to bring some over to the shop. And we needed access to soap and water so Kirstine could wash her face.

"I'm filing charges!" Kirstine said.

"I acted in self-defense," I replied.

"My arse, you did. Pepper spray is against the law. You'll be shipped out of Scotland for good, and the sooner, the better, if you ask me."

I changed my mind about helping her. An hour or so of pepper pain might do her a world of good.

Right then, the inspector arrived.

"What happened here?" he said, taking in the scene.

"She attacked me with pepper spray," Kirstine said, still blind as a bat, but her tongue wagged away as sharp as ever. "I want her arrested!"

"Did ye have cause tae use the spray?" the inspector said to me, his face unreadable, his expression neutral.

"I have a warrant card," I told him as though that explained everything.

"That's not enough. Ye have tae have cause."

"And I have cause. She tried to attack me with that." I gestured toward the knitting needle on the ground.

"I did not," Kirstine said.

"She most certainly might have."

"That's preposterous."

We went back and forth that way for a few minutes, talking over each other, accusing, denying, until the inspector had had enough and ordered us to be quiet.

I got in a final word or two. "Look inside her trunk . . . uh . . . I mean boot," I said.

With a questioning expression, the inspector did as I asked.

"Packages addressed fer posting," he announced, instantly on the alert.

"Yarn club member kits," I informed him. "The ones Kirstine claimed she'd mailed."

"Is what Special Constable Elliott says true?" Jamieson practically roared, almost losing his normal reserve.

"I'm in pain," she whined. "Please do something. Help me."

"I'll be helpin' ye when ye answer my question."

So the truth finally came out.

"I didn't send them out because Vicki interfered with

the trials when she should have been holding off," Kirstine admitted. "I was going to post them eventually, once the event was behind us."

"Ye must have had some idea that they were important tae the investigation?"

"I didn't know! And what about her, using excessive force?"

I managed not to roll my eyeballs. "Can I have a word with Kirstine in private?" I asked, realizing that she and I could go at each other forever without either of us winning. In the end, we both could lose.

"If ye can manage tae be civil tae each other," he said. "I'll count the shipping boxes in the meantime, and I'll keep an eye on ye."

"Listen to me," I hissed at Kirstine while he investigated, "those kits you've been hiding here caused us a whole lot of extra trouble. I could push to have *you* arrested. But we both made mistakes. Let's try to learn from them. Nobody needs to go to jail."

Kirstine looked beaten down. That might not last long, but for now, she was considering my olive branch. Finally she said, "You'll see that nothing happens to me?"

"I'll try, but only if you overlook the fact that I pepper sprayed you. Remember, you attacked first."

Kirstine opened her mouth to argue, thought better of it, and nodded. "See what you can do."

So I went over and had words with the inspector.

"I wasn't going tae cite her anyhow," he said, happy to agree. But he still gave her a verbal reprimand and a caution regarding her cooperation in the future. Whether it happened to be he, himself, asking the questions or one of his special constables, he said we all needed to, as he put it, "pull together."

Then he took Kirstine's car keys from me and led her into the shop. I saw John coming from the direction of one of the far fields. He hardly glanced my way before disappearing inside.

Several minutes later, the inspector came out and started in on me, as I'd anticipated, "Another situation like this one, and I'll have tae take away the pepper spray."

I nodded my understanding, trying to hold my tongue and take the dressing down like a professional.

"Ye're tae use it in life-threatening situations only," he continued. "And this dinnae qualify, at least not in my mind."

I picked up the knitting needle and held it out, unable to keep quiet any longer. "If an enraged woman clutching this and refusing to back off after multiple verbal warnings doesn't warrant pepper spray, who does? Should I have stood there without defending myself while she stabbed me?"

He pondered that, and wasn't nearly as gruff when he answered. "She wouldnae used it. Most likely."

"That's certainly reassuring."

"Cannae ye see it from her point o' view?"

I saw a point, all right. One that could have been jabbed into my body. Or my eye. Or in my ear to puncture my brain like I'd seen on television. Or . . . the possibilities were endless and grotesque, and not one of them was to my liking.

"Ye were snooping through her auto," he said. "Without the proper documents, without any legally binding cause, and ye stole her keys from inside her personal belongings besides. You woulda reacted the same as she did if the situation were reversed. What ye should have done was ring me in advance."

He was right, of course. I'd overstepped. But it had felt *so good* at the time.

"Ye're a wee bit on the straightforward side, I can't help noticing that."

"Beating around the bush isn't my style," I admitted.

"It's yer American upbringing," he said, not quite as stern as before, blaming my impetuousness on my nationality. Did I even detect a bit of playfulness in his tone? "Ye're direct. It takes some getting used tae."

"I'll take that as a compliment." I smiled before saying, "Should I call off Sean? He's searching for these kits all across the countryside. Should we let him know we found them?"

"Ha! And spoil my day? Are ye mad, woman? Or was that a threat?"

But he already had his mobile phone to his ear, informing Sean of the newest development and giving him his next order. "Go over tae Senga Hill's home and see if ye can find a sample o' those sleeping pills the doc's been givin' his patients. Senga claims she threw them in the rubbish outside her apartment. See if she's tellin' the truth."

When he returned the phone to his pocket, he addressed me. "That'll keep him busy fer a time."

"I already went through her garbage and didn't find them," I reminded him.

"Oh well," he said, chuckling. "Best tae double-check, don't ye agree?"

CHAPTER 17

Vicki stared at the mound of shipping boxes in the back of the inspector's police car, her face clouding over as the truth dawned. "Kirstine never sent them?" she said. Vicki's feelings were hurt, and not for the first time, either. And probably not for the last.

"I found them in the trunk of her car," I said, placing a hand on Vicki's shoulder, a small token of my understanding of the tense situation between the two half siblings.

The inspector stood to the side and said gently, "There's good that came out o' this. Our Sean won't have tae drive far and wide tae recover them."

She nodded, and I could tell that she was doing her best to shake off her emotional upset, realizing that Kirstine's treachery was actually a valuable shortcut in our hunt for the murder weapon. And it didn't hurt that the inspector mentioned the benefit to Sean as well.

"Well, I doubt that we'll find any skeins missing from

this lot," he said, indicating the recent arrivals. "But we best be as thorough as we can and make a good showing o' it."

Together the three of us opened each package and examined the contents. We didn't expect to find anything out of place, but it was a necessary task.

"All accounted fer," the inspector said when we finished.

I placed Charlotte and Senga's kits in with the others.

"Ye have handled yerself as a right professional," Jamieson said to me. Was that a hint of a smile? "Don't look so surprised, Eden. Ye've collected the majority o' the kits in record time. With these, we've accounted fer nearly all the kits. Whose are still missing?"

"Only Andrea Lindsey's and Harry Taggart's sister's," I told him.

I heard Vicki gasp beside me. "Don't tell me one of them murdered Isla!"

"That's a bit premature," the inspector reassured her. "Finding the source o' the yarn will be only one o' the missin' links in this case. We cannae assume anything."

I was in full agreement with Jamieson.

"However," he warned. "We proceed with caution from this point forward. We are dealing with a desperate and violent individual."

That, too. This murder hadn't been hatched up long before Vicki had made up her yarn club kits. This was most likely a desperation killing. Otherwise the killer would have chosen a more convenient time and place. That same desperation might cause the killer to strike out again.

"Once I get the last kits, then what?" I asked, thinking

of cupcakes and sleeping pills, and a motive so compelling it seemed worth killing another human being over.

"Ye mean the last *kit*," the inspector corrected me. "One of those two has tae be missing a skein o' yarn." Then he addressed Vicki. "We've gone over this, and ye say there isn't any spare yarn. Not an extra skein tucked away?" .

"No!" Vicki shook her head. "I used all of it to finish up the kits. That's why I didn't have any extras for the people asking."

"So one o' those two it 'tis," he said, glancing at me. "Do ye want me tae take it from here? Finish up the collecting?"

"I can handle it," I told him, not exactly sure what he'd been working on, but confident that it was at least as important as this task, most likely more so. And I wanted to see this through.

He nodded, pleased, and said, "I've been working on a plausible motive. I'll send Sean to poke around a bit, speak with as many o' the spectators as possible. We have a tough nut tae crack. But with each o' us doing our part, we'll soon have the proper suspect in custody and charged with homicide."

The inspector seemed confident in the end result as he bade us farewell and we watched him drive away down the lane.

"Sometimes, the man is unreadable," I muttered.

"He keeps too much to himself," Vicki said, heading for the house. "But he has a difficult position and this is the way he's learned to cope. And at least he has you and Sean to lean on."

I followed her in and gave her a detailed accounting of my confrontation with Kirstine.

Vicki gasped in shock when I related the confrontation over the contents of the trunk, how Kirstine had chased me around the car. But after I described how Kirstine had been on the receiving end of a hefty blast of pepper spray, she was laughing out loud.

"You really let her have it?" Vicki squealed. "Oh, I wish I could have been there!"

I was feeling pretty satisfied with myself. It wasn't too often that I got the best of Kirstine in our occasional skirmishes. But this time she'd really gotten what was coming to her. Maybe in the future, she'd think twice about crossing me. We were never going to be BFFs, but some plain old common courtesy would have been appreciated.

"You're a loyal friend," Vicki said after hearing every single detail of the pepper-spray scene and enjoying every minute of it. "Now I better get back to dying yarn, and you need to catch Harry before he finishes up and drives away."

"He's still out there?"

"He was not too long ago, and he had quite a lot of equipment to load," Vicki informed me.

Good. That made him the obvious next person to contact. Besides, he would be the easiest of the last two to approach. Andrea would be with her grieving brother. I was going to feel like an intruder when I showed up, asking about her yarn kit.

And, according to Lily, Harry had been disappointed in the hospice fund-raising efforts. This was the perfect opportunity to follow up on that as well.

Leaving Vicki, I walked outside and found Coco and Pepper running toward me from up the lane. They followed me to the side of the barn, and I took the time to pet each of them and give a little cuddling to Jasper, all while keeping one eye on the lane in case Harry drove past.

I sat down on the hay bale with Jasper in my arms, and while he purred my thoughts drifted.

Bryan and his wife had argued the night before she died. Why? Had she done something unforgivable, given her husband a reason so powerful that he'd lost control? Could he have really been so unaffected as to have killed his wife and then gone out to the field to compete—and win?

But Isla Lindsey seemed to have a knack for arousing strong emotions in just about everybody. Didn't normal people have controls, switches that flicked on when their tempers flared? Instincts that warned them in advance when they started seeing red? But maybe somebody had finally snapped. It was possible.

Except the sleeping-pill-laced cupcake indicated that her murder wasn't quite as spontaneous as all that. Someone had planned ahead far enough to make sure Isla was incapacitated before attacking her, which weren't the actions of a person who had lost control. Same with the presumed rendezvous at Oliver's van—if Isla went there on her own, it must have been prearranged.

The person responsible probably had to act quickly, yet execute with perfect precision and keep his (or her) wits about him all day long.

I smiled at Jasper and said, "Look at me. Pretending like I have experience dealing with a cold-blooded murderer." He continued to purr, unconcerned with human issues.

I was certainly out of my element. There wasn't exactly a huge need for researching homicides in the romance genre. I dealt in very different chemical reactions, mixing male and female attractions and watching the results. Exploring life, not death.

I needed to keep this case in perspective, not let it get under my skin, not allow it to affect me on a personal level. Keeping emotions out of it wasn't going to be easy. No wonder the inspector had an aura of sadness about him. I couldn't imagine dealing with violence and the most perverse sides of humanity on a daily basis without being changed by it.

As Vicki had pointed out, at least the inspector had Sean and me. He could complain all he wanted about the volunteer, but Sean was eager to please. And now he also had me, for what that was worth. Maybe, eventually, he would learn to put more trust in my ability to shoulder at least a little of his responsibilities. A part of me really wanted that to happen. In fact, I told myself, he *did* act as though he valued my opinions. That was a start. If only he'd confide more, allow me a glimpse into his inner thoughts. What *was* the mysterious man thinking? Most of the time, I didn't have any idea.

Sitting on the hay bale it occurred to me for the first time that I'd never picked up the lawn chairs I'd borrowed from the barn to watch the dog trials. I hoped they were still in the field.

I left Jasper, walked up the lane, and cut into the field, heading toward Harry's truck parked in the general vicinity of the huge refreshment tent, which had been taken down and hauled away. The props—gates, pens, fences—had also been disassembled and removed, and any accumulated litter had been picked up and disposed of.

There was no sign of two lawn chairs.

Actually the grazing field had been restored to its original condition, leaving not a single sign of our human interruption other than a few tire tracks I noticed here and there where volunteers had driven through with their loads. A few more Highland rains and those would disappear, too.

A flock of sheep watched my progress from a hillside nearby. I saw two border collies higher still, lying on the shady side of that same hill, resting but alert to the possibility of wayward action on the part of his sheep. John wasn't in view, but from past performance, the dogs knew their jobs inside and out and didn't need anyone managing them on that front. Don't let sheep stray, that was their mission.

Oliver and Lily, who'd arrived late in the cleanup process, had stayed until the end, and now I saw them walking away together in the direction of the lower lane where Lily had parked her car. They both waved and continued on.

For me, the only lasting reminder of the fund-raiser would be the memory of Isla Lindsey's dead body and that awful moment when I'd opened the van door. Those few minutes would stay with me forever.

I veered toward where Harry's truck was still parked, the cab pointed away from the lane, the bed filled with metal parts. And were those the lawn chairs on top of the pile? I saw Harry on the far side of the vehicle. He opened the driver's door, then grabbed an overhead handgrip for leverage and pulled himself into the seat. I heard the motor start up, so I hurried around the back of his truck.

I was about to call out to him to get his attention, but his name lodged in my throat when I realized the truck's taillights were glowing and the vehicle had begun to move backward, not forward as I'd expected. I was right in its path.

He gave the gas a blast, and the truck lurched directly at me. I had seconds to react. With my survival instincts in full gear, I realized there wouldn't be time to sidestep clear.

I did the only thing that came to mind—I lunged to meet the gate at the back of the truck and anchored one foot on the bumper, then pulled myself up.

"Harry! Stop!" I managed to shout, clinging to the truck.

He must have heard me because he whipped his head around, and if the look on his face was any indication, he was just as startled as I was. He slammed on the brakes, threw the gears in park, hopped out, and ran around to help me down.

"Wha' the blooming heck! Oh, my dear God! I didn't see ye there!"

To say I was a bit rattled would be an understatement. It had been a close call.

"Are ye hurt?" he asked, helping me down.

"Shook up a little, that's all." The fear I'd been feeling subsided and turned to annoyance. Why had he backed up instead of driving forward and circling around? And didn't an experienced driver automatically check the rearview mirror before backing up, even in an abandoned field?

"I never even saw ye back there!" he went on. "Ye coulda been kilt."

CHAPTER 18

"Let me give ye a ride," Harry offered, his voice still a little shaky. "That way I'll know exactly where ye are."

Hadn't I warned myself to tread lightly around those involved in this case? And here I'd almost been run over by a potential suspect. Yet Harry really did look shocked, almost taking the incident harder than I was. I managed to smile and accept the ride. So I got into the truck beside him, and we drove the short distance back to the farmhouse.

"I have a few questions for you anyway," I told him when he stopped. "Do you have time to stay for tea?"

"I could use it, that's fer sure."

"By the way, those are Vicki's lawn chairs in the back of your truck," I said.

"That saves me asking around fer the owner."

After Harry carried the chairs into the barn and placed them where I directed, we paused beside Vicki's door. I most definitely intended to let her know that he was with me, so I stuck my head in. "Harry and I will be having tea in the cottage," I called out to her.

I heard her muffled reply from the direction of her yarn workroom.

Then I led him back and put on the kettle while we practiced the fine art of small talk. Then, with cups of tea and a few scones, we settled at my small kitchen table to discuss important issues, especially those concerning his disappointment in the proceeds from the earlier events.

"Lily told me this morning," I said when he asked how I'd found out about his financial concerns.

"I thought the inspector might have been the one tae inform ye, seeing as how ye're assisting him with his investigation."

So it seemed that Harry, along with most of the village, already knew about my new appointment as special constable. I refrained from telling him that the inspector hadn't mentioned it. For a moment, I felt exasperated, but what did I expect? A few days with a new title didn't instantly make me an equal partner.

Harry went on. "It's no secret, anyhow, about the lack o' funds. All those at the last o' the fund-raiser's organizational meetings heard me say our past efforts were most likely goin' tae be short o' expectations."

I pulled out my notepad, clicked open a pen, and politely asked if he objected to me taking notes.

"Ye do whatever is best," he answered.

"All right. Where and when was the meeting held?" I asked, starting with what I already knew.

"Friday, the day before the fund-raiser, at the Kilt & Thistle."

"Who attended the meeting?"

He named several individuals, including Isla, Oliver, Lily, and Andrea. Briefly I wondered why everyone from the welcoming committee had been included except me. Then I realized that I might have been, but since I'd stopped attending the earlier meetings, how would I have known about this one?

"I spoke with the group that evening," Harry said, "about certain concerns."

"Regarding their efforts on behalf of the hospice?"

"Aye." Harry wasn't exactly evading with his responses, but he wasn't elaborating, either, and that bothered me. Was I going to have to drag every bit of information out of him, piece by piece?

"I'm a special constable, as you are aware," I ventured. "Inspector Jamieson requested my assistance with the murder investigation. So you can feel free to speak with me the same as you would with the inspector. Everything you say will remain confidential."

"I already went over all this with the inspector."

"Once more time, please. You might remember something now that you didn't earlier."

Harry nodded, but still didn't speak.

"Why don't you start at the beginning," I nudged.

"I don't like tae speak ill o' the dead, is all."

Interesting. "I understand and sympathize."

"I was hoping it wouldn't have tae come tae light."

"It's going to have to. Come to light, that is. But all of us involved in the investigation will be as discreet as possible." To say I was intrigued would be understating my growing enthusiasm.

Harry sighed, took several sips of tea, and gazed out the window while I waited for him to elaborate.

After he must have realized that I wasn't going to give up, I learned that he'd been concerned about the financial records pertaining to the fund-raising events throughout the summer. Collected funds seemed to be off from what had been thought were realistic projections. High hopes and crowded events had been offset with disappointingly low returns.

"As treasurer, Isla Lindsey was responsible fer keepin' the books," he said. "She seemed tae be havin' trouble getting caught up with financial reporting and hadn't made much headway by early in the summer, so I went ahead and hired help fer her."

"Senga Hill?" That was consistent with what the baker had told me.

"Aye, but she didn't work out. I had reports that Senga didn't have the required knowledge and that she was makin' mistakes and causing even more setbacks in getting current with financials. I had tae let her go."

"On Isla's advice?"

"Aye."

I sipped my tea while Harry admitted that at some point after Senga left he'd begun to suspect a thief inside the office.

"By last month, my suspicions were mounting. Something wasnae adding up. So I hired an outside firm tae do an audit without alerting the staff. The auditors came in after hours tae go through the books. Last week, I was given the results o' the audit. Somebody was embezzling, that was fer certain. Most likely skimmin' cash during the actual events, but far worse—unauthorized checks had been written against the account as well.

"I dinnae know what tae do. The only one with that much control was Isla, and sure if it wasnae her handwriting on the checks. I'd considered her a valuable asset. Bryan Lindsey has been a longtime friend. How could I make this public and ruin their lives?"

Harry's story was credible. It would only take a quick phone call to the firm he'd hired to verify his claim. I had no reason to doubt him.

I thought about how Isla had been instrumental in Senga's dismissal from the hospice office. In Senga's own words, she'd been accused of making mistakes. My mind went back to the conversation with Ginny Davis about the importance of a business owner being involved in all aspects of the business. I even considered Kirstine and her tight grip on the cash register.

Isla must have been extremely nervous having someone around who knew a little about debits and credits and reconciling accounts. No wonder she'd been anxious to get rid of Senga.

"Why would Isla steal?" I wondered out loud.

"That's what I can't understand. She dinnae have any financial problems that I knew aboot. No major medical expenses. She coulda asked fer help if she needed it. Although it's no secret that hospice wages are low. And she *did* complain from time tae time."

"How much money are we talking about?" I asked.

"There'd be no way o' knowing about all o' it," he told me. "Because part of the loss is in cash we bring in from the events. It'd be easy tae pinch some o' that with no one ever the wiser."

"But a few pounds wouldn't have made you suspicious," I pressed.

"Projections fer last month's charity golf day were off by twenty percent. Goin' back through each one o' the events, I found the same thing—each o' them off by about the same, twenty percent. Between an estimate o' cash skimmin' at the time and checks payable tae cash in her handwriting that the auditors found . . ."

Harry seemed reluctant to go on, still trying to protect the reputation of a dead woman, who herself hadn't apparently given a second thought to stealing from the sick and dying in the hospice. "It amounts tae quite a lot," was his final remark on that subject.

"What did you decide to do?" I asked him, taking notes as quickly as possible.

"I thought I'd give her a way out. If she'd come tae me with a confession and return the funds, I wouldn't bring up charges against her. So I decided if I told the group about my suspicions, and that I was considerin' an outside audit, she'd come tae me. I even directed a good deal o' my comments in her direction at the meeting, hopin' she'd pick up on my concern."

"You pretended as though the audit hadn't been already conducted, and that you were already aware of the results?" I really needed to speak with Dale and Marg about that evening. The pub owners may have noticed some of this interaction.

"Aye, it was fer Isla's benefit, tae give her a chance tae come clean."

"And this occurred at that last meeting the night before

the event, on Friday, early in the evening at the Kilt & Thistle," I said, being very specific.

Harry nodded. "I asked her tae stay behind when the others left and put it tae her that whoever had done such a thing could make amends without involvin' the police. That there'd be no reason tae put a body's dirty linen on public display, that it would all be hushed up."

"What was her response?"

"All huffy, saying she was only the bookkeeper, merely recording in the ledger what was given and if I had an issue, I should speak with some o' the other volunteers who'd helped collect the funds after each event. She was in such a snit, I told her we'd discuss it again under different conditions that didnae involve alcohol."

"Had she been drinking?" I asked.

"Aye, we all had a pint or two, but Isla'd downed more than her fair share."

"And did you bring it up with her again later?"

"No, I never had another chance."

Later, when Harry went out to his truck, I realized with a start that I'd forgotten to ask him about the yarn kit he'd picked up for his sister. Luckily, I remembered just in the knick of time and managed to catch Harry before he drove away. (More carefully this time, staying out of the way of his truck.)

He told me that, unfortunately, his sister had already taken the kit home with her to Glasgow. After discussing its recovery with him I went back inside and sat for a time considering all that I'd just learned. Isla Lindsey, with her superiority complex and holier-than-thou attitude, had been a common thief. Worse than common. She stole from the very group of people she was supposed to be helping. No wonder she had to be in control of every situation, every second of the time!

I went over the notes I'd taken, adding a few, rehashing, wondering if Isla's stealing had anything to do with her murder. It seemed possible. But it would be wise to find out if her husband knew about his wife's sticky fingers and where the money had been stashed. Finding out that Isla Lindsey had been embezzling from the hospice fundraising events was overwhelming.

Part of me longed to go back to my romance writing, to escape into my make-believe world where love conquers all, where things like this didn't happen.

With a sigh, I left the cottage and walked to the main house.

CHAPTER 19

I found Vicki at the stove (or rather at the cooker, as the Scots call it), standing over an enamel canning pot, wearing her apron, protective gloves, and a masklike contraption. The door had been thrown open and the windows were raised for cross-ventilation. She saw me and motioned me to stay outside.

"I'm setting the dye in batches," she said when she joined me, tugging off the mask. She picked up one of her latest creations and presented it with pride. "The hand painting went well. Now it's steaming time."

I'd watched this process when she dyed the Poppy Red yarn. She'd inserted a steamer basket into the pot then added the wool. After simmering it for an hour, making sure there was plenty of steam, she'd rinsed the fleece and hung it to dry.

The next step would be spinning it into yarn.

Vicki's Merry Mitten yarn was going to be gorgeous.

The fleece was multicolored with the colors running in sequence—apple green, lime, and then sunshine yellow.

"But how in the world will two mittens match?" I asked, perplexed as only a non-knitter could be. "Won't each one be completely different?"

"You simply start knitting both mittens in the same place in the color run."

"Color run?"

"The color run is the pattern. See? You'd begin both at the beginning of the length of apple green or one of the other colors. As long as you start both mittens at the same place, you will have matching mittens."

"Ah," I said, sort of understanding the concept.

"How did it go with Harry?" Vicki asked.

I related my "near miss" experience in the field. "Near hit" was more like it. But I was no worse for wear. An adrenaline rush was pretty much the extent of the damage.

After Vicki made the appropriate sounds of concern, she asked, "And his sister's yarn?"

"Unfortunately, it's in Glasgow. His sister was passing through on her way home from a vacation on the Isle of Skye, and took the yarn kit home with her. Harry said he'll have her send it back."

"It's one of only two still out there. Hers and Andrea's." Vicki shook her head sadly.

"He promised to contact her today and will stress the importance of shipping it before the end of the day. Maybe I should have offered to drive there and pick it up."

"The drive to Glasgow would take you over three hours," Vicki announced. "More like four or five, the way you drive."

"If I even made it." Seven to eight hours of driving, counting there and back? Forget it. I'd only recently started to get over my fear of driving between the farm and Glenkillen. Inverness, a forty-mile drive away that felt like four hundred when traversing all the curves, hills, and dips, was another accomplishment. But I wasn't eager to repeat even that one unless I absolutely had to.

"Okay, we'll have to wait then," Vicki said. "I have a hard time believing that Harry's sister or Andrea might have murdered Isla."

"As the inspector said, we can't jump to conclusions."

"Andrea Lindsey is a mouse of a woman. There's no way she could've done it."

I shrugged, noncommittal. "Who knows what goes through a disturbed person's mind?"

"And when it came to Isla, a person didn't need much of a disturbed mind to consider doing her in."

"That's the truth. I've been trying to reach Andrea, but no one is answering at her house or at Bryan's."

"You'll be able to find her tonight at the Kilt & Thistle. The Lindseys can't hold the funeral yet, since Isla's remains won't be released until who knows when. But some of us have arranged to meet and have a dram or two in her honor at the pub."

Mention of the pub reminded me that I hadn't checked my e-mail recently, so I decided to drive into Glenkillen to do that and maybe jot down some of my ideas for the next book.

"I think I'll drive to the pub now," I told Vicki.

"Get a table near the fire," Vicki suggested. "It's going to turn cold tonight and a fire will be a comfort. By late afternoon, all the tables will fill up, and we don't want to be buried way in the back where you usually like to perch. Tonight, we want to be where the action is. So it's on your shoulders to get us a good table."

As I drove to Glenkillen, I thought about the community's favorite meeting place. The Kilt & Thistle had been one of the last places Isla visited before her death. First to meet with the organizers of the fund-raiser for one last time before the big event, followed by a conversation with the head of the hospice regarding financial concerns. After that she'd been seen with her husband, and from several accounts, they'd quarreled.

But about what? That was the question I wanted answered.

I was able to park close to the front of the pub. When I stepped onto the cobblestone walkway, carrying my laptop in a tote, I spotted Sean coming from the direction of Senga's apartment and called out. We walked to meet each other.

He still wore his uniform, but it had suffered some serious wear and tear. His shirtfront was stained, the cuffs streaked and dirty, and overall he looked worse for wear than ever before. Dumpster diving will do that to a person.

He also had an unsavory aroma about him that reminded me of my own dip into the contents of the rubbish bins.

"Did you find that sleeping pill sample?" I asked, though I had a pretty good idea he hadn't been any luckier than I'd been. Sean tends to wear his emotions on his sleeve, and his expression was as grim as the grime he'd collected.

"Not a sign o' it," he confirmed. "I informed the inspector o' such, and fer now the powers that be order us tae keep the facts tae ourselves. And no further questioning o' that suspect until advised tae do so."

"I wonder why."

Sean leaned against a lamppost and said, "He wants tae go after her himself now that we've done the legwork. Senga Hill worked at the hospice financial office with Isla Lindsey. Did ye know that?"

"I did. And Isla was the one who had her let go."

"And Senga Hill baked the cupcakes, one of which knocked Isla out cold due to the addition of sleeping pill sprinkles . . ."

". . . which Senga admitted to having in her possession," I finished for him. "Things aren't looking good for the woman."

"She's a suspect, fer sure," Sean agreed, "but the evidence is insufficient tae charge her with the offense."

"We need iron-clad evidence," I said, remembering the training manual chapters I'd helped Sean with. Scottish procedures mirrored those in the States.

"Cast-iron," Sean echoed. "The evidence has to be supportable before incarcerating a subject. That's the challenge facin' us at the moment."

"What's next for you?" I asked Sean.

"I'm tae do a wee bit o' chatting up potential witnesses at the pub tonight."

"You might want to change clothes first," I advised him in case the stench coming off him had deadened his ability to smell himself.

After Sean went off muttering to himself about trash picking not being in his job description, I phoned the inspector before entering the pub. He didn't answer, so I left a message that I'd be in attendance at the gathering coming up in a few hours and hoped to touch base with him then.

Outside of the Kilt & Thistle, I paused to think about how much I liked this place. Scottish pubs are the heart and soul of every village in the Highlands. They are the glue that holds the community together. Births, deaths, marriages, every imaginable milestone—all are celebrated and honored within their sturdy walls. Pubs are havens from life's stresses and worries, refuges from blustery weather and stormy seas.

Friendships are renewed in these pubs, opportunities explored, humor and banter enjoyed, and for this romance novelist, characters and plots come alive in the recesses of this one in particular. The Kilt & Thistle brings out the best I have to offer.

I set up for a writing session at a rustic wooden table near the open hearth, in view of the door and directly in front of the bar, where at the moment a handful of patrons sat on stools watching rugby on a large flat-screen television.

"Are ye hungry?" Marg asked, arriving with the bill of fare.

"Yes, please. Oh, and Marg, I've been hearing a bit of talk circulating."

"Wha' a surprise," she said with a smile.

"I heard that Isla and her husband were having a row Friday night."

"Aye. That's the rumor."

"You didn't see an argument between them?"

"Me and the husband had all we could do tae keep up with business last Friday night. We had a full crowd and wouldn't ye know our waitress called in sick tae boot?"

"Dale might have seen or heard—"

"—only he didnae," she interrupted. "We both heard the rumor circulating and discussed it among ourselves. All we can vouch fer is that the two o' them were here as was the fund-raising group. Wish I could be more helpful."

"You do a great job," I said, hiding my disappointment.

"I'll be back shortly tae take yer order. Do ye want something tae drink in the meantime?"

"Water is fine," I said.

"I'll bring ye a glass."

I was starving, so I settled in with the menu before powering up my computer. I studied the list of traditional pub fare—including fish and chips; haggis; sausage rolls; Scotch eggs; mince and tatties, which was a Scottish favorite of minced beef and mashed potatoes; something called "cock a leekie" (described as chicken and leeks in a puff pastry); and steak pie, which was the dish I decided on. Not a light meal, but practically nothing was low-calorie here. I chalked it up to necessary research as I did every time I splurged.

After Marg returned with the water and took my order, I glanced around, not recognizing most of the customers, except Bill Morris, who rarely vacated his table in the corner. He was situated away from the walk-through traffic but close enough to the bar to catch the rugby match and pick up on conversations. That is, assuming Bill was sober and alert enough to focus.

While I waited for my food, I started up my computer and went searching for information on the local hospice. According to the Glenkillen Hospice website, the hospice received one-third of its funding through the NHS, the UK's publicly funded health-care system. The organization relied on other avenues of revenue for the remainder. The hospice was also supported through legacy gifts, willed to the organization through those who used its service in the latter stages of their lives. Volunteers also helped support the hospice in care services, fund-raising, and in various administrative duties.

Harry had been vague about the actual dollar amount taken, speaking only in terms of percentages, but news sources announcing this year's charity events placed current estimates of annual operating expenses at well over a million pounds, with these fund-raisers considered a key element in meeting those needs.

If Isla had been embezzling funds, and if Harry's twenty-percent estimate was close to accurate, and if I arbitrarily chose half of the required million as a conservative annual income marker, then I'd guesstimate that she could have made off with as much as one hundred thousand pounds this year so far. Not a sum to be taken lightly.

If Isla had been caught in the act, she could have gone to prison and—maybe even worse in her estimation, since she viewed herself as an upstanding member of the community—she would have been ostracized, and rightly so. Nobody likes a crook. Especially one who would steal from a facility that meets the emotional, spiritual, and pain management needs of the terminally ill and their family members.

She'd been self-righteous and angry when Harry had spoken with her, but she'd had the night to sleep on the idea. Why hadn't she taken Harry up on his offer of restitution outside of the public view? If I had been in her shoes, I would have gone to find Harry the next morning and agreed to his terms. Had that been her plan? Had she intended to meet Harry at the van and confess?

But if that was the case, Harry would have mentioned it to me earlier. Wouldn't he have?

My attention was diverted by a heated discussion going on amongst the rugby fans during a commercial break. They were loudly discussing secession from the United Kingdom, a hot topic in the Highlands and one that produced plenty of rants, especially after a pint or two. The most recent referendum had come and gone, but it had been a closer race than ever, and the subject of Scottish independence was one that perennially enflamed Scots' passions.

"The future should be in the hands o' the Scots!" one of them said.

"Aye, we'd have our own voice on the world stage," said another. "Not tae mention control o' the oil and gas in the North Sea."

"But Britain would withdraw the pound, and who would protect us from invasion?" This from a courageous individual with a different opinion than his rugby buddies.

"Stuff that!"

They went on this way, back and forth, until the game resumed. Then Bill piped up from his corner. The volume must have drowned out his suggestion because none of those watching acknowledged him, but I heard him say,

"The lot o' ye might as well haff let the Loch Ness Monster decide the vote fer all the sense ye're talking!"

I glanced over, surprised that he'd maintained a level of consciousness high enough to follow the conversation, let alone offer up an opinion of his own. Before he crawled back into his inebriated shell, our eyes met. His were barely focused. I supposed it was just another sign of how deeply the Scots felt on the topic of independence, that it could cut through even Bill's sodden brain.

Soon after that, Marg delivered the steak pie (which was delicious), and I forced myself to block out the rugby game and its spectators, and all the theories rolling around in my head regarding the murder, and take care of an important business decision while I ate.

It was time to send *Falling for You* to my editor at the publishing house.

But shouldn't I give it one more look-over first?

Rereading Ami's suggestion to let it go, I forced myself to do just that.

I composed an e-mail cover letter, attached the manuscript I'd worked so hard to create, and hit the send button. There, gone. Its future was out of my hands. Time to move on.

Several e-mail questions from Ami were calling for my attention from the in-box.

"Did you send off *Falling for You*?" one asked. "Have you started on book two?" another message inquired.

That was problematic. My writing had slowed considerably since I'd become involved in investigating a local murder. But what to tell my friend? The situation was complicated. Ami wouldn't mind that I was on a break from my work, but it would take the rest of the evening to explain to her my new role as special constable and the last few days of the investigation.

Her third question was easier to answer. "I hate to flip-flop on my original suggestion that you get going with a Highland romance of your own, but those scenes you created while abstaining were smoking hot. Are you bottling up all that juicy sexual tension of yours for the next book?"

"No time for that sort of thing," I replied without elaborating. Let her think I was writing rather than running around looking for a killer. "Although I did have the opportunity to go out on the North Sea with Leith Cameron and we spotted some amazing wildlife." That should give her something to ponder. I circumvented the nitty-gritty about other recent events and dove right into my thoughts about book two. No need to let on that most of those ideas were last week's brainstorm.

Actually, I'd given the next book in the Scottish Highlands Desire series quite a bit of thought early on, making notes as inspiration struck. It needed lots of conflict, something to set the two new main characters at cross purposes, and a situation that would bind them together.

Daniel Ross, brother of the ruggedly handsome hero from the first book, and Jessica Bailey, best friend of the heroine from *Falling for You*, needed to meet through some inciting incident, setting the tone for the action to come. I needed to create sizzles and sparks between them.

"Regarding book two," I went on. "What do you think of the title *Hooked on You*? I realize there's plenty of time to decide, but I have to call it something while I work on it." I sent the e-mail off and took a few bites of my steak pie. And I was surprised a few minutes later when her response came flying back through cyberspace. "I love it! So talk to me. Give me a teaser."

"I'm still having thoughts in progress," I wrote back evasively. "I'll have that teaser for you soon. Right now my ideas are a bit of a jumble."

If only real life were as simple as the lives of my characters. With all the real-life drama unfolding in Glenkillen, Daniel and Jessica and their quest for love were going to give me a needed respite once this case was solved.

Before I could think of anything else to add, I blinked back to the present and realized that the pub was beginning to fill up. The rugby match was over. Someone had thrown more logs on the fire, and now it roared and crackled, its warmth a welcome addition to the coziness of the pub. The pub's recently arrived customers weren't very familiar; I recognized some but none of them by name, other than the pub owners and Bill, who had several more empty pints in front of him.

I hit the send button to transmit the last e-mail to Ami and powered down the computer just as Vicki slid into a chair across from me.

"Perfect location," she said, beaming at me. "You couldn't have picked a better spot. Hope you don't mind that I invited a few others to share our table. We're a bit early as are some of the others. The family won't arrive until later. I thought we'd have a drink together before things get going."

Vicki was all dressed up in a black dress and sparkly dangling earrings and a matching necklace. And by her cat-who-got-the-cream smirk, I could hazard a guess— she'd invited Sean Stevens and Leith Cameron to join us.

Sure enough, within a few minutes of each other both of them appeared, pulled out chairs, and they ordered a round of ales and lagers. A pint or two was in order, especially after sending off my book and now surrounded by friends.

Sean had cleaned himself up. He'd changed out of his uniform into a pullover shirt and black trousers. His hair was slicked and groomed in a manner suggesting he had taken more care than usual. Almost as though this were a big date.

Leith wore a kilt with a blue dress shirt and a hot stomping pair of boots. What a handsome man! Those blue eyes. The sexy kilt. The way he wore his clothes and the relaxed manner in which he met the world. *Very* sexy.

"I can't stay long," he said, leaning in to share a private moment. "I'm picking up Fia fer the night. But I wanted tae pay my respects." His Scottish blues met mine. "And I wanted tae see how ye were fairing, too."

Caught off guard, I almost blushed. Then I collected myself and said, "I just sent the book off to my editor."

"Yer friend Ami approved, did she? I knew she would."

Our drinks arrived and the four of us saluted one another.

"I might have overstressed my point one day not too long ago," Leith said when we had a private moment again. Vicki and Sean were lost in a conversation of their own. "And should have rectified it during our boat ride, but my mind was favoring the moment. What I mean tae say is that I might have sounded like a heartless man, what with not letting the women turn my head."

Ah, yes. Leith's commitment to his daughter at the

expense of his own personal life. I certainly remembered that conversation.

"Not heartless at all," I replied. "The opposite, in fact. I think what you are doing for your daughter is totally selfless." Then, without hesitation, I told him about how my own father had abandoned our family. When I finished, he said, "I can't understand how a parent could do such a thing."

"Me either. But it was so long ago. He's probably dead by now."

"My parents are gone as well. The best we can do is live good lives while we're on this green earth and not look back with regrets."

I admired Leith's attitude. He didn't dwell on the dark side of humanity like Inspector Jamieson did. The two men were as different as day and night.

Leith drained his beer and leaned toward me once more. "Would ye consider spending time with me again later in the week? I could show ye a few fishing spots."

"Another boat ride?"

"Aye." I must have looked doubtful because he added, "We could wait tae decide, if ye aren't sure."

I gave him the biggest smile I had. "I'm only thinking we might want to wait and see if the weather is going to cooperate."

He returned my smile. "Aye, we can do that. So, what do ye say?"

Was he asking me out? A date? Or a neighborly gesture? *He's waiting for an answer. Don't overthink it!*

"I'd like that," I told him.

Just then, Bryan and Andrea Lindsey arrived.

Leith looked toward the door and said, "Okay, until then, Eden Elliott."

And with that, he rose and said his good-byes to Vicki and Sean. I watched him weave his way to the door, where he spoke with the grieving husband and his sister before disappearing into the night.

When my gaze returned to the table, Vicki shot me an inquiring look, as if to say, *What's up with you and Leith?*

I simply smiled in return.

CHAPTER 20

Dale had reserved space at the bar for Isla's family members. Bryan and Andrea were instantly surrounded by villagers showing their support and extending their sympathies. In spite of the somber occasion, the atmosphere was warm, the beer good, and the music that commenced a moment later wasn't overpowering.

I paused to appreciate the fiddler, piper, and harpist tucked in the corner, then picked up my laptop, slipped outside, and stowed it in the car. Since the evening was cooling off fast, I grabbed my fleece while I was out there, thinking I might take a short walk later before heading home for the night. With a clear sky and a slight chill it would be a beautiful night for a stroll.

Bryan was still surrounded as I made my way back to my table. I decided to wait until later to approach the grieving husband. Passing by Bill Morris, I sensed sudden movement, and something solid and unexpected popped up and hit me in the shin. I lost my balance and fell against him.

"You tripped me!" I said accusingly, as I indignantly righted myself.

"I didnae mean tae," he said, slurring his words.

"You did, too. You stuck your foot out!"

"Never mind that. I hear ye got yerself a position with the inspector and ye're prying intae the death of Isla Lindsey."

"'Prying' isn't the word I'd use. Investigating is more like it. Why?"

"She and her husband were havin' a right row, they was, the night before she was killed."

Another witness to the Lindsey argument. "Tell me."

"Herself was with a large party but when they broke up, she went tae the toilets, and then she met up with her husband, right there it was"—Bill motioned to the table next to his—"and they went at it like cats and dogs. I thought ye'd want tae know."

I'd had enough confirmation at this point to verify that the husband and wife had indeed had a serious disagreement. And even though Bill had been three sheets to the wind that night, and was again now, he was accurate. Plus, I suspected Bill heard and saw more than the rest of us thought he did, especially since regular patrons of the pub, used to Bill's inebriated condition, probably spoke freely in his presence thinking he was past comprehension. Bill Morris might turn out to be a fountain of valuable information.

"Have you mentioned this to the inspector?" I asked, although one more account wouldn't matter much. Charlotte and Oliver were more reliable witnesses when it came right down to it.

"Meself and Jamieson don't see eye tae eye. He looks down on me, he does. Thinks I'm a sot, if ye can believe that." Bill's eyes were bloodshot and his bulbous nose had red veins running through it. "But ye always treated me with respect. I don't mind helping ye."

With respect? I wouldn't have said that. Frankly, I mainly ignored Bill, since he was crude and rude even on his best days. But if he thought we were buddies I wasn't going to claim otherwise.

"The husband was spitting mad, if ye must know," Bill went on.

"Did you hear what the argument was about?" I asked, hoping he had. Charlotte had only been able to supply me with a general statement and Oliver said he hadn't overheard.

"Aye," he said. "A third party was involved. Somebody on the side, it was."

"And?" I prompted.

"And wha'? I just told ye there was cheating going on."

"You're certain?"

"It was admitted by the guilty party."

If Bryan had been unfaithful, he'd have no cause to be angry . . . so did that mean *Isla* was the one having an affair? Isla? Mean, bossypants Isla? I couldn't picture it.

"Are you absolutely positive you heard correctly?" I asked, my imagination taking leaps and bounds. *Remember the source. This is coming from the town drunk.* Yet he'd been aware of the conversation during the rugby game earlier, alert enough to comment.

Bill's eyes flickered and then closed. I didn't want to lose him. So I gave him a shake and his eyes popped open again.

"Are you telling me that Isla Lindsey was having an affair?"

He nodded his head at that. "That's wha' I've been trying tae tell ye. That sister o' his had words with him while the wife was in the loo, musta told him what his wife was up tae."

Andrea? I glanced toward the bar, where recent arrivals Oliver Wallace, Lily Young, and Harry Taggart were in the condolence line. Andrea was dabbing at her eyes with a tissue. "So you didn't actually hear?"

"Are ye going tae keep interruptin'?"

"Go on." If he closed his eyes again, I was going to clobber him.

"So the sister fills his ear and I can see he's gettin' hot around the collar. Then she takes off. Pretty soon here comes the wife, and I hear him ask her, 'Are ye cheatin' on me? Cuz I chust heard that ye were.' And herself, she gives him a smirk and says, 'Now, why would I go off and do a thing like that when ye provide fer me like I'm the queen o' England.' All sarcastic, she was, and he got a right temper at that."

So Andrea had instigated the fight? Interesting. "Did you hear who it was that Bryan accused Isla of cheating with?" I asked, wondering what sort of man would have anything to do with dreadful Isla.

"No, but I'm bettin' the bloke was Harry Taggart," Bill said, his head beginning to sag. "I saw the two o' them together right before and I heard that one's name bandied back and forth between herself and the husband a bit later.

What Harry saw in the likes o' her, I donnae have a Scooby." And his chin sank to his chest.

The excitement that had been building up inside me sank. Bill Morris had missed the boat on that one, since I knew Harry had been discussing serious embezzling business with Isla, not planning a rendezvous with her. He'd been throwing her a lifeline, albeit one that she'd refused to grab hold of.

Right?

Before I made it back to my table, I crossed paths with a couple just arriving, Kirstine and John Derry. I nodded in acknowledgment, fully intending to continue on. But Kirstine stepped in my path. I prepared for whatever trouble she intended to make.

To my astonishment, she apologized. Even more surprising, her contrite expression told me she meant it.

"I owe ye an apology fer my awful behavior," she said with sincerity. "I shouldn'ta hidden Vicki's kits, nor lied about posting them. I don't know what came over me."

"And I apologize for overreacting," I offered. "I shouldn't have sprayed you."

Kirstine glanced over to the table where Vicki and Sean were sitting and said, "That one's another I have tae make amends with." She nodded good-bye to me and moved on.

I stood there, still in utter surprise but feeling overwhelmed with relief, then spotted Inspector Jamieson off to the side in the shadows. I caught his eye and he motioned me over.

"You aren't having a pint?" I noted with a small tease. "You work constantly, don't you, Inspector?"

"I'm not here tae lolly, if that's what ye mean." He glanced in Sean's direction. "At least if he has tae be love-struck and forget his station and responsibilities, he isn't doing it while wearing the uniform." Jamieson didn't appear to be angry, though; in fact, his tone seemed almost kind and understanding. Or maybe he was relieved that Sean wasn't going to be underfoot tonight.

"What does it mean if someone says they don't have a Scooby?" I asked.

"No clue," he told me.

"You don't know, either?" I asked, surprised.

"No," he chuckled, "I haven't a Scooby means I haven't a clue."

Right then, patrons throughout the pub broke into song as the background music swelled with the familiar tune of *Auld Lang Syne*.

And surely ye'll be your pint-stowp!
And surely I'll be mine!
And we'll take a cup o' kindness yet,
Fer auld lang syne.

Inspector Jamieson and I sang along. He had a rich, deep voice with perfect pitch.

When it ended and the music had died down to a level more conducive to conversation, I told the inspector about my exchange with Bill, finishing with my own personal opinion. "He claims Isla was having an affair with Harry Taggart, but he obviously misread the situation. According to a conversation I had with Harry, he was actually confronting Isla about projections being off at the hospice. Bill saw Isla arguing with Bryan afterwards, and jumped to conclusions that she was having an affair with Harry."

"Bill's a drunk," the inspector agreed. "Ye can't put much stock in anything that comes outta his mouth."

"But if what he says is true," I said, playing devil's advocate, "Bryan Lindsey could have killed his wife for cheating on him."

"And why would Bryan murder his wife in such a public place when he coulda made it seem like an accident anytime he preferred?"

Which had been my original thought as well. "You must have questioned Bryan regarding that argument."

"In as gentle a manner as possible, considering. He's taking his wife's death hard, and hasn't been fit fer hard questions. His sister Andrea's been protecting him, but tomorrow she goes back tae her job and won't be hoverin' as she has."

"You didn't ask about him and Isla arguing that night?"

"He claims it was all a misunderstanding, something about mistaken identity, and that it amounted tae next tae nothing. I also broached the subject o' missing funds, not accusing his wife directly, but he doesn't seem tae know anything about that. Or so he said. I'll put those questions tae him again tomorrow."

"How much money is missing?"

"That's hard tae know, what with the possibility o' skimmin' cash right at the events. But the checks that were cashed amount tae just a bit shy o' fifty thousand pounds. The checks were written and cashed in small enough amounts tae ensure that the banker's suspicion wasn't roused."

"That's a lot of money to hide. Have you looked into their bank accounts?"

"Aye, and there's nothin' there tae show a crime's been committed."

If Isla stole the money, where had she stashed it?

"Harry's sister is in the process of sending back her kit," I told him, moving on to another subject.

"Did ye ask Andrea fer hers?"

I shook my head. "I was going to tonight, but now it doesn't seem like the right time or place."

"First thing tomorrow will be soon enough."

I'd been hoping he'd agree. This evening was a chance for people to say their good-byes to Isla, not a night to be interrogated.

"They should be remembering Isla in life," he went on, "not reliving her manner o' death. Let the husband grieve among his friends, family, and acquaintants. Tomorrow we'll go around again." Then the inspector added, "Sometimes, I'd gladly give this job tae another."

I could only imagine how difficult his job must be. There couldn't be much joy in it. Some satisfaction, maybe, when a case was solved, a criminal removed from the street. But the inspector's job was one of reaction, responding to unpleasant, horrible events that had already taken place. He rarely had an opportunity to prevent them.

After deciding to forego intruding on tonight's wake, we talked about Senga Hill, who hadn't made an appearance, at least not yet.

"She's on the short list," he told me from the privacy of our corner. "She coulda had it in fer Isla after she lost her volunteer position. Embezzlement of hospice funds could have nothing tae do with it."

He didn't sound convinced, though.

"Senga made the cupcakes and admitted to having sleeping pill samples that she claims she threw away," I said, recapping. None of this was new. "But since they are nowhere to be found, that could be a problem for her."

"I'll put more pressure on her, let her know she's a suspect," said Jamieson. "A confession would be asking fer a lot, though. If someone could place her near the van around the time o' the death, it would be the break we need. As it is, nobody working in the refreshment tent saw her disappear, not even fer a minute or two, until the very last cupcake was sold."

"Not even a bathroom break?" Something was nagging at the back of my mind.

He shrugged. "If she did, I haven't found a witness yet. I'll put that question tae her tomorrow, too, when I lay out the rest o' the facts. Hopefully, if she's the guilty party, she'll crack."

"What if she was Isla's partner?" I asked.

"Senga Hill and Isla Lindsey in cahoots?"

"Senga might have figured out Isla's scheme when she went through the books. Maybe after she was terminated, she caught on and decided to blackmail Isla."

"Anything is possible. Even something as unlikely as that. Problem is"—the inspector grinned—"we don't have a Scooby."

"Let's go outside," I suggested as the music swelled again, interfering with our conversation. He nodded, and we made our way to the bar, where Bryan and Andrea were still standing, but without the earlier line of locals. We offered our condolences and left the pub. I breathed a sigh of relief to be away from the crowd.

"Will there be speeches?" I asked, slipping into my fleece as we walked down the cobblestone street toward the harbor. Our strides were in synch as we enjoyed the chill of the night air and the clarity of the sky above.

"This isn't a proper wake," he said. "If it were, I'd say yes, but with an informal gathering"—the inspector shrugged—"'tis anybody's guess."

I walked beside him with my head down, something I do when I'm thinking hard (and also because I don't have a lifetime of experience on cobblestone like the villagers do—if I don't want a twisted ankle, watching my footing is mandatory until I improve on that skill).

Some subject we'd touched on tonight at the pub was bothering me, but for the life of me, I couldn't figure out what it was.

"Look up, Eden," the inspector said gently, startling me by using my given name, something he rarely did.

I lifted my head, and my eyes were instantly drawn to the sky over the North Sea, where ribbons of green and red swatches of color blanketed the stars like a curtain, undulating, waving, alive with motion.

"The northern lights!" I said with awe in my voice.

"Aye, aurora borealis. It's best observed on cold, clear nights in the winter months, but every now and then we have a display such as this in the autumn."

We stood observing in silence after that. For how long I wasn't sure, nor did I care. This was a magical moment, and I wanted it to last as long as possible. After some undetermined length of time had passed, the lights slowly faded away, leaving a deep blue, starred sky behind.

"That's something to put in yer book," the inspector said.

Yes, yes it was.

CHAPTER 21

First thing Tuesday morning, I bolted suddenly awake and sprang from my squeaky spring bed with the answer to what had been bothering me last night.

I called the inspector. It rang and rang, and I was about to hang up and call again, thinking I might have dialed the wrong number in my excitement, when he finally answered.

"I remembered something!" I said after identifying myself.

"What time is it?" he asked, sounding groggy.

I hadn't checked, hadn't given it a thought until now. "Um . . . five something."

"And ye have a proper reason fer phoning at this hour?"

"Yes!"

I heard a sigh, but ignored it and continued, "It came to me in the night. My brain was mulling it over and at some point it dredged up what was stuck. That's happened before, usually with some sticky spot in a plot issue that I can't resolve. This is the first time that I had an actual murder case epiphany, though."

"Now that it's unstuck, perhaps ye can get tae the point."

What was that in his voice? Annoyance? I didn't let it discourage me.

"We know that Isla's death occurred after one thirty," I said in a rush, "because she was seen then, right?"

"Aye. We've been over that already."

"And I know from the printed program that during the hour after that there wasn't a sheep dog trial going on, only John Derry giving a herding dog demonstration and Charlotte with her sheep shearing, so we haven't been able to eliminate any of the judges or the dog handlers. And now there's another person that we can't eliminate."

"That certainly will uncomplicate things," he said, showing plenty of early-morning sarcasm along with some impatience and frustration. I was dealing with an early-morning crank. "Let's go on tae make the list a mile long," he crabbed. "And wake me up tae do it."

"Are you going to listen or not?" I didn't want to hear his answer, so I didn't wait for it. "Senga Hill sold out of her cupcakes sometime during that time," I informed him rather smugly. When he didn't immediately react, I continued on. He hadn't had his coffee yet. I'd have to walk him to the obvious conclusion. "She'd saved one for me and when I went to get it, most of the cupcakes were gone. That was around noon. But shortly after, I know she ran out. Last night, you said that some of the other vendors had placed her in the refreshment tent until she sold all her cupcakes, which you assumed meant from the beginning of the trials until the end. But she sold out much sooner. You failed to ask those witnesses exactly *when* that happened."

There was a long silence on the other end while the inspector processed this new information. As I waited, I began to worry about how the inspector was going to accept a minion like me pointing out a mistake on his part. Could he handle his own oversight? I bet Sean never outguessed him, so he might not have any experience with admitting mistakes—to himself or to anyone else.

The silence stretched on. Either his wheels were turning, or he'd dozed off, or the boom was about to swing and lop off my head.

"Are you still there?" I asked after a length of time.

He cleared his throat and said, "Constable Elliott, I believe it's time I put the proverbial screws to a certain cupcake baker."

I was going to take that as a big pat on the back for a job well done. "Do you want backup?"

The inspector actually snorted. "Tae handle a pensioner? I'll give ye points fer a fine bit o' analysis, but I'm not so far advanced in age that I can't handle Senga Hill on my own."

"I'm here to help any way I can."

"Just find out which o' the kits is missing a skein o' yarn! How hard can it be? There are only two o' them left." This was a side of him I hadn't seen yet. One I was perfectly happy to bypass in the future.

"Aye, aye, sir. Will do."

After he gave me Andrea Lindsey's address and

directions to her home, which was fairly simple and straightforward since Glenkillen isn't exactly a huge metropolis, we disconnected.

After peeking outside and finding it overcast and chilly, I made a cup of instant coffee and a bowl of porridge, took a shower, dressed in jeans and a scoop-necked long-sleeved blue sweater, and impatiently waited around for the day to break and the rest of the world to wake up and get moving.

I even tried to get some work done on *Hooked on You* but ended up with a sheet of paper filled with doodles and a blank computer page.

Once it was a decent hour, I decided I couldn't stay indoors any longer. There were no lights on in the main house as I walked past, full of vigor, and wrapped in my fleece jacket with my credentials and pepper spray in the pockets, but Sean's red Renault was parked indiscreetly in front of the barn. The soon-to-be official police officer might be a bit of a bumbler, but he had a good heart and seemed to make Vicki happy. That's all that really counted.

I felt a slight twinge of something suspiciously like envy for what the two of them had found in each other. I told myself it was acid reflux and shook it off. Jealousy isn't a trait I admire in others or especially in myself. Still . . . did I want what they had? Or was it simply the lure of the Highlands and the romance of the place that had me pining for more? And what about Leith Cameron? Were we destined for something more than friendship?

Live for the moment, I scolded myself. *The future will be here soon enough.*

I hopped into the Peugeot, popped it into first gear while

working the clutch, and headed for Andrea's house, hoping to catch her before she left for her first day back at work at the Glenkillen Hospice since her sister-in-law died.

Andrea lived on Ardconnel Road in a traditional detached white villa elevated above the village with views of the harbor and bay. A stone wall and hedge ran along the front of the house, and as I parked, she appeared on the porch where she locked the door and bounded down the steps, turning toward Glenkillen at a brisk walk.

She hadn't seen me, so I hustled out of the car and called her name. She stopped in her tracks and turned.

"Eden Elliott," she said as she walked back to meet me. "What are ye doin' here at this early hour?"

"I wanted to catch you before you left for work. Looks like I made it just in time, too."

She smiled. "Well, here ye have me." Andrea was dressed in a powder blue nurse's uniform with sensible shoes and an artificial yellow flower pinned next to her embroidered name on the left breast pocket.

Before launching into my questions, I gazed at the villa for a moment. "You have a beautiful home," I said, admiring it.

"Thank ye. Bryan and I were raised in this house. Our parents passed on three years ago and the house was tae be sold, with the two of us sharing the proceeds. But Bryan is a generous man, and hasnae protested my remaining here. He's keepin' his interest in it fer a later date. It's been updated a bit, and I take good care o' it."

"I've been thinking about the two of you often since Isla's death. Bryan must be devastated. You and your brother seem very close." I already knew that Andrea had never married, and had heard that she was devoted to her career and, as was obvious, to her brother.

"Aye. We were born sixteen months apart, so we grew up together with many o' the same friends and same activities." She smiled sadly. "It's been difficult, but life goes on. My brother will recover from his loss in time. But what can I do for ye today? I cannae take long, I don't like to be late fer work."

"Only a minute or two. I'd hoped you could give me some insight. Anything you observed on Saturday that might have seemed unusual? What kind of mood was Isla in? Did she appear her usual self? Anything at all you can tell me that might lead to the person who did this."

Andrea thought for a moment then shook her head. "Isla was the same as she always is, and no, I didn't notice anything out o' the ordinary."

I didn't detect any hostility in Andrea's tone, any negative reaction toward her sister-in-law, even though I'd heard that Andrea was the one who'd told her brother about his wife's infidelity. And I wouldn't have been surprised if Andrea had had some hard feelings; I'd witnessed plenty of bullying from Isla. She hadn't been one to discriminate when it came to pushing people around—her family got the same treatment as the rest of us who found ourselves under her authority. Maybe even more.

Andrea couldn't possibly think much of the woman her brother had married, nor did she seem particularly shook up over Isla's death. She'd been much more concerned about Bryan and how he was handling it. Andrea might be a great caregiver, but she lacked much in the way of a backbone. That thought had crossed my mind during our very first planning meeting for the fund-raiser.

I hoped for a little dirt-dishing now. I tried a different tack.

"You were at the last organizational meeting Friday night at the Kilt & Thistle. I understand there was some talk of missing funds."

"Aye, 'tis true. Harry is calling fer a full audit. It's an unpleasant thought, that someone would do a thing like that."

I didn't tell Andrea that the audit had been completed and the results were in. Instead, I said, "Yes, well, if the audit shows a problem, I doubt that many of the employees had much opportunity. I'm sure the investigation will turn up the culprit fairly quickly."

"Ach, all of us had opportunities," Andrea said guilelessly. "We shared in collecting money throughout each event. Isla and Oliver usually made the rounds, but I did it myself on occasion. Lots of cash transactions and not much in the way o' accountability."

I wondered if Andrea thought the skimming amounted to no more than a few pounds taken during the events. It wasn't my place to inform her otherwise.

I brought up the more delicate subject of my conversation with Bill Morris. "Andrea," I began, "I also need to ask you what occurred after the fund-raising meeting on Friday night at the Kilt & Thistle. You were seen in conversation with your brother shortly before he had an argument with his wife."

Andrea's expression remained neutral. "I'm not aware o' any row."

From his account, Bill hadn't been able to hear what Andrea said to her brother, he'd only heard Isla and Bryan's raised voices shortly afterward. But Andrea couldn't have known whether or not her own voice had carried, so I did a little creative rewriting and said, "You were overheard telling your brother that his wife was cheating on him." Not exactly true, but close enough.

"Who said that?" A small crack appeared in her calm veneer.

"It doesn't matter. We know it's true." There. Using the plural form again, making it stronger and more official. "Who was the man?" I asked.

"I don't know. But when Lily Young told me that Isla had been unfaithful tae Bryan, I thought my brother deserved tae know."

Lily Young? I'd spoken with her at the farm yesterday and she hadn't even hinted at Isla's infidelity. "Who else knows about this?" I asked.

"Nobody else," Andrea said. "After Isla was killed, I . . . I . . . didn't want to cause any more pain for Bryan. He's been through enough. It was just as well that I didn't know who it was, because when I told Bryan what I'd learned, he reacted so strongly that, if I'd been able tae give him a name, there mighta been a double . . ."

She paused abruptly, realizing she'd said too much. I filled in the blank. "A double homicide?"

The crack in her composure widened, and Andrea visibly crumbled. "Isla was an awful person," she admitted. "She treated my brother as though he were a servant . . . no . . . not even with that much dignity . . . more like her personal slave."

"Infidelity is a strong motive," I told her.

"Bryan didn't kill Isla!"

"Did you?"

Andrea gasped. "No, I didn't touch her." Then, almost without pausing to consider, she said, "I only wanted to make him leave her, ye see! Isla was poison."

"Didn't you want to know who the man was? Didn't you try to find out? Didn't Lily know?"

"She refused tae say, but claimed she had pictures on her phone as proof. Then on Saturday, after Isla was murdered, Lily came tae me and said she'd made a mistake, that the man she thought was involved wasn't. She said she wasn't sure that anything went on at all. So it might have been nothing but gossip. And I've since convinced Bryan of that. He doesn't have tae go on thinking that his dead wife was unfaithful tae him."

"I need a name, Andrea," I pressed.

"Then ye'll have tae get it from Lily."

"Was it Harry Taggart?" I asked.

Andrea looked shocked. "Harry? He has a very good and trusting nature, and wouldn't be part o' something sordid such as that. Now, I best be off."

"We're almost finished, please, another minute. I hear Senga Hill worked with the books at one point."

"She did, but only fer a short time, and she left quickly under stressful conditions. If ye be thinking Senga had anything tae do with the missing funds, it's possible but I doubt it. She wasn't with the hospice very long before she was removed from the office, so she couldn't have been tampering with the collections."

I nodded, out of questions for the time being. "If you

think of anything else that might be useful," I said, "please feel free to contact me. Oh, and before you go, I'll need your yarn kit. I promise it will be returned after our investigation is completed." Meaning, once we have the killer in custody, and assuming your skein wasn't the murder weapon.

"Of course," Andrea said. She returned, climbed the steps, unlocked the door, and disappeared inside. I walked up to the top step and received her kit when she reappeared. As several of the other members had done, she'd already begun knitting the socks.

The only kit left was Harry's sister's. The skein of yarn from that kit must have been used to strangle Isla. I thought of Harry sitting at the table in my cottage, answering questions. He'd seemed so honest when he told me he'd sent the kit off with his sister. If her kit had been missing the skein, wouldn't his sister have noticed? As bad as it looked, there had to be a logical explanation.

"You're still looking fer missing yarn from one of the kits, then?" Andrea asked.

Reluctant to divulge that information (though obviously she was right since I was requesting that she relinquish hers), I nodded.

"How many still need tae be checked?" she wanted to know next.

I really wished she hadn't asked that question. "Several," I answered vaguely. "Next, I'm collecting the one Harry Taggart picked up for his sister."

Surprise registered briefly in Andrea's eyes and expression, and her body stiffened for a moment before she regained her composure and started down the steps. I followed closely.

"What's wrong?" I asked.

"Nothing."

"No, it was definitely something. What was it?"

We stopped at the bottom of the steps.

"I dinnae want to cause trouble fer anybody, especially my friends," she said.

"Keeping quiet when you should be speaking up would cause the most trouble," I told her, winging it. "So, tell me what it is."

"All right, but first, are ye absolutely sure about the yarn being fer Harry's sister?"

Something was off.

"Of course," I said. "He told me himself that she picked her kit up from him, and took it home with her to Glasgow. She's mailing it back to us now." A pit opened up in my stomach as Andrea looked like she'd rather be any place but here with me. "What's going on?"

"I don't like sayin' it."

"Saying what?"

"That Harry Taggart doesnae *haff* a sister."

CHAPTER 22

The Glenkillen Hospice impressed me. It was a large version of a home, with warm brickwork and well-tended, attractive gardens leading to the front door. As I waited impatiently in the parking lot for the inspector to arrive, memories of my mother's final days came rushing back to me. Especially the end-of-life support from our local hospice in Chicago—how skillfully the nurses assigned to her home care had helped manage her pain, and how they'd assisted me in coping. My mother had been fortunate: she'd been able to remain in her apartment. Some aren't so lucky. The terminally ill don't always have family members who are able or willing to tend to their needs. That's why having a place like this for them to receive treatment is so important.

I reaffirmed that I'd made the right decision when I decided not to renew the lease on the Chicago apartment

I'd shared with her toward the end. It was time to move on, leave the past and the darkness of those final days behind me.

I turned my thoughts to the case and Harry Taggart's nonexistent sister.

Why had he lied? Did he really think he'd get away with his deception? It certainly made him look guilty. Had he lied about the whole "Isla was stealing" story he spun for me? Could *Harry* have been the one who was skimming, and Isla the one who was about to rat him out? Had he killed her to keep her quiet?

I got out of the Peugeot when Inspector Jamieson pulled up and parked next to me.

"Ye can't let yer emotions take hold," he said when he unfolded from the seat and saw the expression on my face.

"Harry almost ran me down," I said, although the inspector had already been apprised of that fact when I'd called him after leaving Andrea. "I thought it was an accident at the time, but now . . ." I left the rest hanging.

"It might well haff been just that. Carelessness on Harry's part. When we go in, it would be best if ye keep yer personal opinions and thoughts tae yerself, and just observe. Ye cannae assume the man is our killer right yet."

"Of course," I snipped, annoyed that he felt it necessary to advise me on proper conduct. Wasn't that plain common sense? Although I *had* convicted Harry in my mind only a few minutes earlier.

"We'll wait a bit until ye pull yerself taegether," the inspector said.

That annoyed me even more, but I made an effort to

shake off any preconceived ideas about Harry's guilt. Or at least get them in check for the time being, no matter how damning the evidence against him.

Inside, the hospice had a pleasant, homey atmosphere, with plenty of natural light, radiating peace and tranquility. We walked past a large meet-and-greet area that opened up to a courtyard and passed by several other rooms, then the kitchen and dining room.

The inspector was acquainted with the layout. "Across the courtyard, in another wing," he informed me, "are private rooms occupied by those living out their end days."

I couldn't help worrying about what would happen to the hospice or its reputation if the head of the organization went to prison for murder. The thought made me sad.

The sight of Harry just made me mad.

I studied him across his desk as we appeared in the doorway to his office. He rose and offered us seats.

"We haff a problem," the inspector told him as soon as we were seated, foregoing any semblance of small talk and getting right to the point of our visit. "It seems that all the other yarn club member's skeins have been eliminated as havin' been instrumental in the death o' Isla Lindsey. Except the one ye sent off with yer sister."

I understood the inspector's reasoning. Hit Harry with a shocking statement coming out of left field and he won't have time to concoct alibis and excuses.

He was shocked, all right.

Harry blanched as white as one of the MacBride's hill sheep. Even his eyes went wild, like the sheep's do when they're cornered and frantically searching for a way out.

The inspector didn't appear to notice the change in

Harry's composure, or if he did, he hid it well. "Tell us aboot this sister o' yers," he continued.

Harry looked about to keel off his chair. "Wha'? Wha' about her?"

"The one you don't have," I piped up and said, not able to control myself any longer. Watching him sweat was only satisfying to a certain degree. After that, I wanted the truth.

The inspector shot me a warning with his eyes.

I shrugged a weak apology while a gurgling sound came from deep inside Harry's throat.

"I was going tae come forward," he managed to get out.

"Were ye now?" the inspector said. "And when were ye goin' tae do this?"

"It's . . . awkward."

"Awkward?" I exclaimed. "I can just imagine!"

"Now, Constable Elliott," said the inspector, resigned to playing the good cop, "we need tae give Harry a chance tae explain himself properly without jumpin' tae conclusions."

Taking the bad cop role was fine with me. Since I felt out of sorts anyway.

Except, watching Harry, I was suddenly having a hard time picturing him killing Isla. For one thing, he'd signed his imaginary sister up at least a month prior to the September distribution. He'd concocted this "sister" much earlier than Isla's murder had occurred. That meant major premeditation on Harry's part, which didn't explain why he would pick such a public crime scene.

Besides, he must have realized that his deception wouldn't hold up; it's not as if it would be difficult to prove that he didn't have a sister.

"I can explain," Harry said, taking a drink from a glass

of water on his desk, his hand shaking so violently that he spilled more than he drank. "I apologize fer deceiving ye. It's just that what started out as a little white fib turned into a whopper after Isla was murdered. And by then, I didn't know how to make it right."

"This is a fine time tae make it right," the inspector suggested.

Harry hung his head. "Ye see," he said, "the yarn kit was fer meself."

Harry was a closet knitter? Really? Did I look as surprised as I felt?

"Um . . ." was all that came out of my mouth.

"I don't dare knit in public," Harry said, quickly glancing up, "thinkin' my mates would never let me hear the end o' it."

I could understand his decision to hide his hobby. Maybe he wasn't as confident in his masculinity as he might be and so kept his knitting a secret. I could imagine bullies—like Isla—picking on this tall, thin man whose round shoulders gave him a slightly bent posture. Put knitting needles in his hands and he might very well be judged harshly by shallow, narrow-minded people.

Had I ever seen a man knitting? No, but I was open to the idea. Certain men might mock him, but I bet women would welcome Harry with open arms. Manly knitters. Hunh. I glanced sharply at the inspector, trying to gauge his reaction, but he was as unreadable as always.

"It was me da who taught me when I was a wee lad," Harry explained. "He was a sailor, and he'd picked it up while at sea. But at school a few o' the biggest bullies made fun o' me. Da said tae ignore them, but it's a painful thing tae be picked on at such an early age, and it scarred me."

The inspector maintained his neutral professional manner. "So ye say yer father was a sailor?" he said when Harry finished. "I'll be checking all the facts so ye best be telling the truth this time or we'll be hookin' ye up to a lie detector test and putting ye through the paces."

"It's true! I swear it. When I found out about the yarn club, I made up a sister so I wouldnae haff to go through the teasin'. How was I tae know that some o' that same type o' yarn would be used for murder? And now ye say 'tis me own yarn as well?"

Elbows on the desk, Harry buried his hands in his face. Either he was a skilled actor, or he really was terribly upset.

"Where's yer kit?" the inspector asked.

Harry shook his head, but didn't answer.

"Are ye refusing tae tell us?"

Harry stared down at the desk, silent.

An idea came to me, one that would test the truth of Harry's claim that he could knit. I rose and said, "I'll be right back." Then I rushed through the hospice and pushed through the entryway doors while I placed a call to Vicki.

"I need a little information on male knitters," I told her when she answered, outside now and almost to my car. "I'm in a hurry though. Do you know any?"

"Ohhh . . . I just love a man who knits," she said, practically gushing. "In California I knew so many! It was much more common there than here. There were men's groups with the best names—Bros and Rows, Knitty Gritty, and my personal favorite, Knit Like a Man." Then she laughed. "I remember what the male crocheters used to say—real men don't knit, they crochet. Give me one who does either, and I might fall in love."

"What about here in Scotland?" I unlocked the Peugeot, grabbed Andrea's yarn kit, and retraced my steps while listening to Vicki. "Any men's groups in the Highlands?"

"Not that I'm aware of, which is a shame. Knitting was once a male-dominated occupation in Scotland, did you know?" she said. "The sailors and sheepherders would knit sweaters and such in their spare time. It wasn't an uncommon sight. But now that you mention it, I don't think I've seen a single man knitting here."

That fit with what Harry had told us about his father. I thanked Vicki for the information and disconnected right as I walked into the office and deposited Andrea's yarn kit on Harry's desk, saying, "Show us your stuff, Harry. Add a row to this." Then I sat back down, feeling pretty pleased with myself.

Harry stared at the heap. "Now?"

The inspector waited without comment. So did I.

Harry picked up the needle with the looped stitches, looked at it, and said, "I'm left-handed. Whoever did this was right-handed."

Harry was left-handed? Interesting. The inspector, incidentally, was left-handed as well—that had been one of the first things I noticed about him. So was I, which was the main reason I'd struggled with learning to knit. I hadn't been able to find a left-handed teacher, and most of the ones I'd had just wanted me to learn right-handed, since, as they put it, "that would be easiest." Easiest for whom exactly? Not for me, that was for sure.

I removed the needles and undid the rows Andrea had already started.

"Now try," I said to Harry.

With that, he picked up the yarn and the needles and cast on (one of the few terms I remember from my failed lessons), then hooked a piece of yarn around his thumb and wove the needle deftly through a loop, tightening the new stitch onto the needle. I might not know the first thing about knitting, but I'd watched Vicki enough to confirm that Harry wasn't a novice knitter.

At least that much was true.

As he continued to work the row, I realized that— assuming we didn't have to send him to prison for murder— I had found myself a qualified knitting instructor. As another tidy row appeared, I had visions of gorgeous knits dancing in my head.

"Hang on a tic," Harry said, placing his handiwork on the desk. He pulled open one of his desk drawers and reached in. The inspector was on his feet before I could react.

"Careful, Harry," he warned, moving around the side of the desk.

"I'm only wantin' tae show ye my latest project." And with that, he withdrew a brown scarf that was almost finished.

"We believe you, Harry," I said, realizing I'd tensed up right along with the inspector when Harry had made the unexpected move. My voice had an edge to it. "You do know how to knit. That's obvious now."

"That's all fine and good, but the crucial thing at the moment is yer own yarn kit," the inspector told him, once Harry placed his handiwork back in the desk drawer.

Jamieson remained on his feet.

Harry went back to looking nervous and sweaty. I was willing to accept his reason for deceiving us with a trumped-up sister, but he shot back up on my personal suspect list when he said, "I don't have it."

"Why not?" I asked, thinking that was convenient.

Harry had that drowning look again—various shades of unnatural coloring, frightened eyes, gasping for air. "It's gone missing."

The inspector didn't look neutral any longer as he said, "Ye won't be getting out o' this that easily. Start explaining."

Harry had a pleading expression on his face. "I picked up the yarn kit from the welcome table and placed it on the seat in my truck. After that I didn't give it another thought. I was judging the trials, keeping busy with the run-off fer winner, and then Eden here and Oliver Wallace found Isla's body. Ye can't blame me fer not thinking about the yarn kit. It wasn't until the next day that I remembered it. When I went out tae the truck, it was gone."

I wasn't sure what to make of this new development. Perhaps if I wanted Harry to teach me to knit it would have to take place behind bars after all. "You told me your sister would mail it back? What was the point of lying about that? Wouldn't that have been the perfect time to come clean?"

"I didn't know wha' tae do."

"This doesnae look good, Harry," the inspector said.

"Ye have tae believe me."

"I'll have more questions fer ye later," the inspector said abruptly.

"I'm not arrested?" Harry asked, as surprised as I was that he was still free. "I didn't kill her, ye know. I had no reason tae kill her. Isla did a good job with the volunteers and sure, she could be overbearing at times, but she took care o' business as though it were her own."

Harry would have done himself a big favor by keeping quiet for the time being. He was off the hook for the moment and he should have taken advantage of it. Instead he gave the inspector more food for thought.

"Yet ye had words with her after the meeting," Jamieson said. "Over discrepancies and by then ye knew from the audit that she'd been embezzling from the hospice. That sounds like a possible reason tae me."

"But why would I murder her? All I wanted was the money returned. I was willing tae look the other way once that happened. No sense destroying the woman. She was misguided, was all."

All the while we'd been in Harry's office, I'd wanted to mention Bill's accusation, even though I was certain that the drunk had misread the meaning of the discussion between Harry and Isla. But Harry had been beside himself as it was, without that particular rumor raising its ugly head. Was I exceptionally sensitive to hurtful gossip and its lasting effect on others? Was that why I had been reluctant to broach it? Since the inspector hadn't, either, I had to assume that I'd made the right decision to let it go.

But I was learning quickly that Jamieson did things in his own way in his own time.

"The local blether circulating has Isla creepin' around on her husband," he said now. "Your name came up in the mix o' things."

Harry's mouth dropped open. When he composed himself, he said. "Ye cannae mean that! Our relationship was strictly business. Her husband is a good friend . . ." he sputtered out.

"Perhaps she was involved with someone else?" I offered.

"Herself?" Harry said. "Not likely."

"We'll be in touch." The inspector motioned to me that we were finished. "Harry, I expect ye won't be leavin' toon until this is cleared up tae my satisfaction."

I stood up and gathered Andrea's kit supplies.

Then we slipped out, leaving Harry with what would probably be a very long, agonizing day and a sleepless night.

As we walked to our cars, the inspector said matter-of-factly, "Harry didn't kill Isla Lindsey."

"I honestly hope not."

"He didn't." He said this with utter conviction.

"And how did you determine his innocence?" I asked, bewildered.

"Harry Taggart is left-handed. Whoever killed Isla was right-handed."

I thought about that as we paused by my car. Jamieson gave me the time to do so, waiting patiently to see if I would come to the same conclusion as he had based on one singular genetic characteristic. My mind passed over the cupcake and the sleeping pills. Nothing there that would exclude a lefty.

If the inspector was so certain that the murderer was right-handed, it had to have something to do with the yarn around Isla's neck. If that had anything to do with the declaration that Harry was innocent, I was at a disadvantage.

I hadn't been examining her throat that night. I'd only been handling the fallout.

My mind flicked back to the difficulty I'd had learning to tie my shoes. My mother had to find another left-handed adult to teach me. That's when I realized that we lefties make the first loop using our left hand rather than our right, and the entire bow is backward. The same would apply to a knot.

"I got it!" I told him, making the connection. "The yarn used to strangle her had been knotted in such a way as to confirm that the killer was right-handed."

"I dinnae even make the right-handed connection myself until Harry turned out tae be left-handed and then it clicked intae place."

I tried to imagine tying the yarn around her neck as a right-hander would. Impossible. And especially in the heat of a moment such as that one must have been. Harry couldn't have tied that knot any other way if his life depended on it.

The inspector seemed pleased with me, and I couldn't help feeling like I had earned some of his respect this day.

"Well, there ye go, Constable," he said, opening the door of his police car. "Well done. I'm off tae pester Senga Hill again."

Just to be thorough, once the inspector had driven off, I went back inside. Harry was *not* happy to see me.

"Here," I said to Harry, handing him the knitting needles and the yarn. "Give it a try with your right hand." If Harry was ambidextrous, if he was a switch-knitter, we needed to know.

"That won't work well," he told me.

"Try," I prodded him, wondering what percentage of the population could use both hands with equal skill. Very few, I imagined.

"I don't see the point," Harry balked.

"Humor me."

And so Harry gave it a whirl.

And it was as awkward as it would have been for me. It wasn't an act. He messed it up in exactly the same way that I would have.

CHAPTER 23

As I started the Peugeot and headed toward the MacBride farm, I went over the conversation with Harry Taggart in my head. Everything that he'd said and done made sense—maybe not exactly the best way he could have handled the situation, but it rang true. Harry had been embarrassed to go public with his hobby, and so had resorted to what he thought were little fibs that turned into big falsehoods after Isla's murder. Especially since he had to suspect that his missing yarn had been used as the murder weapon.

While I drove, I also considered again whether it was possible that Harry could have had enough wits about him, if he were the killer, to knot and bow the yarn as a right-hander would? Even after seeing the mess he'd made of right-handed knitting I had to admit to myself that it was not impossible, but highly unlikely. If I were asked to demonstrate a right-handed knot, I wouldn't know how to begin. And I suspected that a right-hander couldn't do a lefty tie, either, even with practice. And the inspector, left-handed himself, had clearly reached the same conclusion.

But there still was the information supplied by Bill Morris. What was I to make of that? I had to believe it happened since Oliver saw them arguing and Bill confirmed that by saying he'd overheard Bryan accuse his wife of adultery. Then Lily had attested to some kind of affair without naming the other man involved, later retracting her statement. So something had gone on. And that could have a whole lot to do with her murder.

A cuckolded husband could have killed a cheating wife.

Or a bitter ex-employee with a knack for baking could have killed for revenge.

In my opinion, Harry was off the hook. Not only would it have been a stretch for him to accomplish the deed, but he hadn't exactly had nerves of steel during the interrogation. Frankly, I didn't think he had the audacity required to have killed Isla with his own yarn, tie a knot in a manner against his left-handed nature, then coolly disappear into the crowd. He'd practically fallen apart under questioning. The inspector was correct. Harry wasn't our killer.

I found Vicki in the barn working with her beautifully dyed wool while her two Westies ran together in the field across the lane, steering clear of the alert sheep who watched their every move with unblinking intensity. The flock might be skittish around the border collies, but they were significantly larger than Coco and Pepper, and the Westies wisely respected that.

While observing the wool-drying process, I picked up Jasper and worked my hand along the barn cat's black fur while he purred in contentment.

Vicki had fashioned drying racks from wood slats and chicken wire and had draped the wool over it. At the moment, she was fluffing the fleece.

"Almost dry," she announced. "I can't wait to begin spinning the Merry Mitten yarn."

Vicki was back to her normal, happy self, so when she asked, "How's the investigation going?" I gave a little shrug of dismissal and said, "Nothing much to talk about." Which was true in a way. I wasn't going to talk about it.

"Kirstine apologized to me for hiding the kits," Vicki said next, which might have been one more reason why my friend was so content. "We're back on firm ground with each other."

"She spoke with me, too. Things are going to work out. And you did a wonderful job with the fleece."

"It's really turning out better than I expected," she said. "Thanks for giving me the push I needed." Vicki stretched with satisfaction. "After all this hard work, I think I'll take a nap."

"Expecting an exciting night?" I smiled. "Or recovering from one?"

"Aren't you the nosy one," she said with a wink, then headed for the house.

I released Jasper and sat down on a hay bale to think.

As much as I hated the thought, Senga Hill was still the most likely suspect at the moment. As it turned out, she had as much opportunity to steal Harry's kit and commit murder as anyone else. She also had a motive, since Isla had had her dismissed from her bookkeeping position at the hospice without sufficient cause.

I envisioned two possible scenarios.

In the first, I imagined Isla as the thief, herself, accusing Senga of stealing, threatening to sully Senga's name and future job prospects to get rid of her before Senga could stumble across her secret. And Senga subsequently lashing out.

In the second scenario, Senga *had* caught on to Isla, or maybe was becoming suspicious, and decided to blackmail her. But if Senga was cashing in by blackmailing Isla, why would she get rid of her source of revenue?

I was back to square one, theorizing without proof. Something had happened on Saturday to trigger her death. But what?

Jasper rubbed up against me as I called the inspector on my cell phone.

"Any luck with Senga?" I asked.

"She's tougher than she looks. She insists she had no part in the murder. Unless we can drum up a witness who can place her near Harry's truck or saw her near the van, we won't likely be charging her. We need tae keep digging."

Not through any more trash, I hoped.

"What about Bryan Lindsey? His wife might have been cheating on him. Even if she wasn't and he thought she was . . ."

The inspector interrupted. "Lily Young has backed down on her claim, and Bryan says it was just a misunderstanding with no basis in actual fact. His sister agrees. Unless ye have new information . . ."

Which I didn't.

"Eden, ye did yer job well and narrowed down the kits. Ye can go back tae yer writing noo if that suits ye."

I was expecting as much, and I really needed to, so why

was I so reluctant? "I guess I should," I said without any real conviction.

"Aye, I thought ye might."

"You'll call if you need me?"

"Aye. I will."

We rang off but before I got up, I spent a few more minutes on my own. I rubbed the barn cat around each ear and scratched the top of his head, enjoying the serenity of his purr and the quiet of the farm. Jasper had been stand-offish at the beginning. Now, he was becoming a real family member.

I decided it made sense for me to go to the pub to check my e-mail. As I strode toward the Peugeot with Jasper at my heels, Oliver's white van pulled up and parked next to my car. Jasper turned tail at the intrusion and disappeared inside the barn, leaving me staring at the side of Oliver's van. All the details of that horrible experience came rushing back when I saw that van. *My hand on the door handle, opening it, Isla's body falling out* . . .

"As ye can see, I'm behind the wheel once again," Oliver said after getting out of the driver's side. "I was determined tae sell it, but now that I'm driving her again, it's getting easier. I always loved this van and hate the thought of trading her in."

I nodded as though I understood, although I didn't understand one bit. If the vehicle I drove had been the scene of a murder, I wouldn't get back in it for all the money in the world. Those awful memories of finding her body would stay fresh in my mind for the rest of my life, without adding in that daily reminder. But that was me. Obviously Oliver was made of tougher stuff in that regard.

"And," he went on, "it's handy tae carry my boat supplies back and forth."

"You have a boat?" I asked. Mention of one brought Leith to mind and our ride on the sea. And the promise of another.

"Aye, a bonny wee thing. She's called *Slip Away*."

"I like that name."

Oliver smiled. "She's a right good boat, she is."

"What brings you out here today?" I asked him.

"Tae see how ye're getting on and tae let ye know that it was amazing how ye took control o' the situation on Saturday. And me as helpless as a newborn bairn."

"You weren't the only one having trouble," I pointed out. Despite his police uniform, Sean Stevens had been just as paralyzed with shock as Oliver, maybe even more so.

"It was the trauma o' having the dead body o' somebody I knew so well falling out like that. I wasn't prepared."

"Totally understandable. It was a shock to me, too, but I didn't know Isla nearly as long as the rest of you, so it wasn't quite as personal." Murder up close was personal enough no matter how you looked at it, but I was trying to make Oliver feel a little better. I went on. "Oliver, I'm glad you came by. I'd like to talk about that day and events leading up to it."

"Aye, if we must."

"You were at the Kilt & Thistle for that final planning meeting last Friday," I said. "Harry tells me he mentioned his concerns about possible financial discrepancies to the group. Did that come as a surprise to you?"

"Aye, it did. None o' us knew what tae say. Why would

anybody steal from the hospice? I've been involved in the planning and execution o' every one o' the events, and never got a whiff o' anything underhanded. I still cannae believe it and hope an audit will put that worry tae rest."

So, Oliver didn't know that the audit was over or that Isla had been revealed as a thief. Unless Harry chose to make it public, or it gained prominence in the investigation, I supposed nobody would ever know now. Perhaps that was just as well.

"Let's go back to the day of the trials on Saturday," I said, deciding to throw out one of my theories. "I'm pretty sure that Isla made arrangements to meet someone in your van."

Oliver's face registered surprise. "Wha'?"

"Either before Saturday or earlier that day."

"I highly doubt it."

I pressed on. "But she insisted that Sean Stevens park your van on the very far side of the lot. And when he put it on the side of his own car nearest to the traffic and shop, she made him move it to the other side."

"That isn't much proof," Oliver decided after a brief pause to consider.

"So I take it you don't know anything about her meeting anyone?"

"That is only speculation on yer part. I understand that the inspector has asked fer yer help, and that's well and good, but I hope ye don't intend tae run riot with wild ideas."

"Of course not." I felt the beginning of some bristling on my part. "Do you have a better explanation as to why she was murdered in your van?"

"Bryan Lindsey is the one who needs watching," Oliver said. "He's a hard drinker. I can attest tae that. Friday night he had a few drams too many by the time we concluded our meeting and was in fine form. That sister o' his likes tae stir him up. She was over at his table right after our meeting, putting ideas into his head. She caused quite the quarrel between her brother and his wife."

Which I'd already found out, but not through Oliver. "Why didn't you mention Andrea when you first told me about that situation?"

"I didn't want to shine a bad light on her then. But I've since thought it over and I think she could have caused a dangerous situation with her nonsense."

"Andrea Lindsey seems so harmless," I said mildly, although Andrea had admitted to me that she *had* been trying to sabotage her brother's marriage.

"If that's what ye want to think. But I saw Isla go tae freshen up after our meeting and Andrea run over tae Bryan's table. Then she took off and he had a face-off with Isla when she came and joined him."

"The rumor going around is that Isla had a lover," I said, just to see how he'd react. The truth was, I couldn't imagine Isla with any man on the face of the earth. I could sort of understand Isla and Bryan's marriage—they'd been together a long time, perhaps long enough for her to change from a decent woman to the hard person she'd become. But a new man on the side, with her dysfunctional personality?

No way!

Oliver apparently felt the same, because his reaction was to guffaw. "That's preposterous! And one more reason why I stay away from that sort o' talk. Isla Lindsey was as loyal a wife as could be."

I thought about some of her comments that day before she was killed—about Oliver being late as usual, and how he always left the keys in the ignition. More than casual acquaintances? "How close were you with Isla?"

"And what exactly are ye implying?" Oliver's fair features were darkening.

"I'm not implying anything! In a murder investigation questions sometimes are sensitive. Please don't take them personally."

He calmed himself with a deep breath. "A murder inside his own vehicle will do that tae a man, make him touchy. And ye hardly dodge around a subject, do ye?"

"Just routine questions," I told him, using the same line I'd heard the inspector employ when under scrutiny from a witness. "You knew her well?"

"To a degree. The lot o' us have worked closely all summer. Sure, she got on my nerves, but she did a bang-up job. I used tae stick it tae her in small ways just tae get some say in."

Yes, I recalled Oliver being a source of aggravation for Isla. Perhaps I was focusing too much on those small isolated occurrences, because I spoke without thinking the next question through. "Did you see Harry with the knitting club kit he picked up?" I asked.

"Noo, what's that got tae do with the price o' haggis?"

He had a point. Oliver didn't have inside information, didn't know that Harry's kit had been stolen or that the skein from it had been used to strangle Isla. Harry and his truck would be of no importance as far as he was concerned.

"We're just establishing everybody's whereabouts," I said, sounding lame, but unable to come up with a quick reason for asking that question.

"Good luck with that," he told me. "Spectators as far as the eye could see. All comin' and goin'. Most o' us can't even remember exactly where we were when or the order o' things. I hate tae be the one tae throw a spanner in the works, but unless some deranged dodder gives a voluntary confession, as I said," Oliver repeated, "good luck with that."

CHAPTER 24

I said good-bye to Oliver and was headed for Castle Street in Glenkillen when Sean Stevens rang me.

"The inspector and meself are on the way to Harry Taggart's office. Harry gave us permission tae fish aboot there and at his residence besides, regarding the kit he claims tae have lost. So we didn't need tae get a search warrant. We aren't goin' tae leave any stones unturned."

"That makes sense. Harry lied about a sister. What would prevent him from lying about the location of the yarn kit?"

"Aye. Just tae be on the safe side o' things."

"Let me know how it goes." In the meantime, my question to Oliver was still on my mind. "Do you know when Harry picked up his yarn kit?" I asked Sean.

"I'm the bloke who gave it tae him," he said, then after thinking it over, "I was standing at the welcoming tent, and it was right after Lily Young tried tae get a kit from

Vicki. Yerself was talking to the inspector. Or maybe ye had walked off with him by then."

I remembered the relief I'd felt when the inspector had whisked me away from the welcoming committee's bossy dictator. "I don't remember seeing Harry then," I added.

"He came along and picked it up shortly thereafter."

"Was he alone?"

"I think so . . . aye, he was . . . no wait . . . aye, he was alone, but then he walked up the lane with Oliver Wallace."

So, Oliver *had* seen Harry with his kit. Although this new insight amounted to next to nothing. Anybody, anytime before approximately one thirty when Isla was last seen alive could have lifted the kit from Harry's truck. Still . . . I should have pursued that line of questioning with Oliver while I had the opportunity. Perhaps he would have remembered something important.

We disconnected just in time for me to focus on a roundabout, pleased that entering them to the left instead of the right was becoming rote. I drove down Castle Street and nosed into the first available parking spot.

Here I was, back at my favorite writing cave and to my work as a romance author. But instead of looking forward to another trip into the make-believe world of Rosehearty, Scotland, I found myself firmly grounded in Glenkillen. I felt as though I had a lot of loose ends dangling regarding the murder I'd been investigating. The inspector was masterful at tying up loose ends, but they had made my head spin just keeping track of my own part in the investigation, let alone everyone else's. Still, although the inspector had given me an honorable discharge, I wanted to reenlist.

Instead of getting out of the car with my laptop in hand,

I suddenly thought of something, and picked up my mobile to call Senga Hill.

I identified myself when she answered and asked how things were with her.

"The inspector has been a wee bit unyielding," she told me. "He's convinced I killed Isla Lindsey, but I didn't!"

"I believe you, Senga," I told her, though I wasn't really sure I did. "But the best way for us to get him on the right track is for you to help me find out who did. Tell me, how did you manage to make two hundred cupcakes in that tiny kitchenette of yours?"

Senga's tone lightened at the prospect of discussing her favorite topic. "Ah, truth is I dinnae make them here. Lily Young and meself baked them at her house. Dinnae I tell ye that before? I thought I had."

She hadn't, but did it matter? I wasn't sure, but a private Q&A with Lily Young was long overdue. I'd ask Lily and see if it led anywhere.

"You told me you threw out that sleeping pill sample," I asked next, "but it wasn't in your trash."

"Aye, and the inspector was right bothered by that fact, he was. And I still can't believe that ye went through the rubbish!"

"Well, we both are concerned. Because I didn't find it."

"Tosh," she said.

"Tosh?"

"Nonsense," she explained. "And that's exactly what I said tae the inspector. Tosh! I threw it in there meself. Ye can ask Lily aboot that as well."

"Lily?"

"I just now remembered that I have somebody tae vouch

fer me. I think I'm losing my mind because o' all this turmoil. But there it is. Lily Young."

"Go on."

"She dropped me off after baking the cupcakes, and we were standing there blatherin' away. I was diggin' in my purse fer my house keys and that sample was right in front o' me, so I asked her if she wanted tae try them. She said no, so I tossed them in the rubbish."

Hunh! That was interesting. It would have been simple to pick them out from the top of the heap.

If only Senga had thought to mention this before I went Dumpster diving. It might have saved me some time. Or maybe not. I might not have connected the same series of dots that early in the investigation.

I thanked Senga and disconnected, feeling my heart beating to a faster rhythm.

My first impulse was to rush over to Lily Young's house and start grilling her, but I didn't have a clue (or a Scooby) where she lived. Senga Hill had been on my persons-of-interest list from early on. So had Harry Taggart, although both the inspector and I had decided that he was most likely innocent. But there was that little bit of doubt nipping at the back of my mind, telling me not to discount anybody quite yet. I had to assume that Lily Young could be as guilty as the others. What was one more suspect!

The inspector must have sensed something, too, because he was following up on Harry's kit right now.

Intuition kept tapping on my brain, shouting that I needed to continue to give the most attention to the inner circle, especially to my fellow welcoming committee members.

That included Oliver Wallace. His van had been the

crime scene. He was still on the list of suspects, although I didn't have any idea of a motive for him.

So was Andrea. Isla hadn't treated her brother well, and his sister had actively campaigned to split them up. Maybe she'd decided to improve the quality of his life in her own way.

Now there was Lily. She'd been publically vocal about her dislike for the dead woman. She'd spread infidelity rumors about her, whether true or false was still unclear, and she'd had access to those cupcakes at the source. Lily could even have made extras. And Senga said Lily had been right there at the moment Senga threw away sleeping pills that were the same kind used to incapacitate Isla.

I tapped lightly on the steering wheel, staring at the pub, deep in thought.

As I was about to call Inspector Jamieson to get Lily's address, I spotted the very woman I was seeking. Lily was entering the Kilt & Thistle. The thrill of the latest development almost caused me to burst into the pub and have at it. I talked myself down. Chances were slim to none that Lily would tell me what I wanted to know if I went at her the way I had with Kirstine. I'd have to figure out how to approach her just right.

Since Lily was vying for top of my suspect list at the moment (a position that changed with the wind, it seemed), instead of barging in, I entered quietly to see what she was up to. In all the times I'd written inside the pub, she hadn't been a regular customer. Other than special occasions, she didn't frequent the Kilt & Thistle, so why was she here today?

Lily wasn't in sight when I entered. I saw Dale squatting down behind the counter, shuffling through bottles on a lower shelf. It was midafternoon and the pub was nearly empty in the post-lunch, pre-happy-hour transition. A few patrons were talking quietly at tables. No one seemed to notice my entrance. Even Bill wasn't at his regular table. I slunk through the pub, peeking into one dark corner after another.

And finally found Lily standing beside my own favorite writing table, tucked as far out of the way as possible. Andrea Lindsey rose to greet her as I ducked out of sight, into a spot out of view but within hearing range.

"You shouldn't have brought Oliver intae this," I heard Andrea say. She sounded irritated. "That wasn't well thought out."

"I went off me head," Lily said with a bit of a whine. "I don't know what came over me. You didn't tell, did ye?"

"Eden Elliott came by my house and collected my kit." Andrea's tone was frosty. "And she wants a name." Were they discussing Isla and the mystery man? Was that person Oliver? I couldn't see those two together—she'd obviously annoyed him with her sniping, and he'd annoyed her right back. Had it all really been just a clever cover?

"Thank ye fer not telling her," Lily said. "It was all a big misunderstanding. I didn't see what I thought I saw and shouldn't have said a word tae ye."

"You sounded certain on Friday."

"No, no, ye have tae believe me."

"Oliver isn't interested in you, Lily. Quit covering fer him. Ye better call up the new constable and tell her about the mess ye made."

It felt strange hearing my name bandied back and forth without them knowing that I was within earshot. I had an epiphany of sorts, one that should have been obvious from the beginning. The welcoming committee had worked closely together. All but me, that is. I'd ducked out of my responsibilities as often as possible, giving Isla a wider berth than the others had. So it stood to reason that Oliver, Lily, and Andrea would get together after Isla's death and try to figure out who did it.

I could imagine their conversations perhaps getting heated at times, somebody saying something, someone else misunderstanding, taking some offhanded comment as an accusation. Tempers flaring. Fingers pointing.

Good! Let their emotions and suspicions rule them.

"Why shouldn't I go directly tae the inspector?" I heard Lily say. "Instead o' tae her?"

"Whatever suits ye best, but he's suspicious o' everybody. Ye might have better reception from Eden Elliott. She'll mebbe go easier on ye."

"I haven't done anything wrong!"

"Ye better call up the MacBride farm and inquire as tae the new constable's contact information."

"I have her number, but I don't think that's a good idea."

"Then why did ye ask fer my opinion?"

Just then, my cell phone rang, and I fumbled to silence it, annoyed with myself for not thinking of that earlier. I was sure the two women now were aware that someone was close by. I managed to stop the ringing, but Lily and Andrea's voices dropped to a whisper, well below eavesdropping range. I hustled outside to return the call, which had been from Jamieson.

"No sign o' that kit," the inspector said when he answered. "As expected. How's the writing going?"

"It's not. I have a few ends to tie up first."

There wasn't time to brief him on my conversation with Senga or tell him about the bits and pieces I'd just heard. So I said, "I'm just about to sit down with Lily Young and see what develops."

"It gets in yer blood, this work does," he said. "Those loose ends are hard tae tie up."

"I'll let you know how it goes."

"Kirstine Derry hasn't fully recovered from yer questioning," he pointed out. "There's a bit o' excitement in yer tone that reminds me o' that particularly tense situation. I expect no fisticuffs with this witness."

"Very funny."

He chuckled and disconnected.

Andrea passed me on my way back in, and we exchanged polite greetings. She continued on without any outward sign that I'd been a recent topic of conversation. My phone rang again. This time it was Lily on the other end, asking me to meet with her at the pub.

I agreed, mentioning that I was close by and could be there shortly.

"You wanted to speak with me?" I said when I slipped into a chair beside her a few minutes later.

"I need tae clear the air," she said, "about something I told Andrea Lindsey."

While I listened quietly, Lily told me her story, one that I couldn't help thinking might very well be as fictitious as the romance of *Falling for You*.

"Ye see, I was out at the harbor on Thursday, taking a stroll in the nice weather we'd been enjoyin', and I thought

I saw Isla Lindsey going out fer a boat ride with Oliver Wallace. I was a distance away, mind ye, so I wasn't completely certain it was herself." She paused and a blush rose on her cheeks. "I fancy him, if the truth be told."

That had been obvious, but I didn't want to embarrass her any further by pointing it out.

"I tried tae wait fer them tae come back, so I could make sure it really was the two o' them, but I hadn't made provisions fer that much sun, and it finally got the better o' me."

So that explained Lily's sunburn. She'd been on a stakeout at the harbor. "You had to give up the wait."

"Aye, but the idea of Oliver and Isla started festering inside me, and so I told Andrea, expecting that she'd tell Bryan. I wanted to make trouble fer Isla. It was a spiteful thing tae do, I admit it. After that, I began tae wonder. Had that been them after all? They'd been a good distance away. The more I tossed it aboot in my mind, the more I realized I'd been a bit hasty and perhaps I'd been mistaken. I decided tae ask Oliver."

"And what did he say?"

"That my head musta been full o' mince tae think a thing like that."

"Did he say who he'd been with?"

"A lady friend, is all, which dinnae make me any happier. So I had tae correct what I'd done by explaining tae Andrea what a dolt I'd been. Ye can ask Oliver. He'll vouch fer the fact that we spoke on the subject."

I groaned inwardly at the tangled web the former committee members were weaving. Hadn't Oliver, only a short while ago, made sure I knew about Andrea's actions at the

meeting and implied that there was more to her than met
the eye? Then Andrea had pointed me in Lily's direction?
Now Lily was hurrying me off after Oliver? I wondered
how Lily was going to handle what I was about to throw
at her next. Asking polite questions is the Scottish way.
But I'm an American. I can do polite with the best of them,
but I got better results when I threw something out there
and let it explode. I took a deep breath and went for it.

"Lily," I said. "You drugged Isla, didn't you?" I didn't
know if Lily had or not. It was a hunch and I had decided
to bet on it.

She couldn't have reacted with more shock than if I'd
physically slapped her. "Wha'? No! I don't know what ye
mean. Isla was drugged?"

I wasn't backing off yet. "You took the sleeping pills
that Senga had thrown away. You crushed up the pills and
sprinkled them on the cupcake frosting. Then you gave
that cupcake to Isla."

Lily stared at me, stricken. Had I been wrong? I was
just about to apologize for my brazen behavior—after all,
Lily had helped Senga bake hundreds of cupcakes for charity and here I was, looking for a criminal connection—
when Lily's entire body slumped in defeat. Tears welled
in her eyes and spilled over, running down her face.

Oh my goodness, I'd been right! The realization left me
feeling emotionally exhausted rather than elated. "Why?"
I asked her quietly.

She shook her head. "It was an awful mistake."

I took out my phone and called the inspector. "Lily
Young is the one who drugged Isla Lindsey," I told him

without preamble. "We're at the Kilt & Thistle at my usual table in the back."

"I'm on my way," he said, hanging up.

I kept quiet for a while after that, giving Lily time to think over her dilemma. It seemed like an eternity passed as we waited.

"I didn't kill her," Lily finally said. She hadn't denied drugging Isla with the cupcake, though, and it followed that she had killed her as well. It was easy to assume that Lily had murdered Isla for personal reasons, but I was still stuck on the issue of embezzlement. One of the theories I'd toyed with involved a partner. Or a blackmailer. The missing funds still hadn't been located. Could Lily have been in on it?

"Who was responsible for gathering cash proceeds that Saturday?" I asked, after we'd waited a reasonable amount of time and the inspector still hadn't made an appearance.

Lily, visibly relieved for a break from her transgression, didn't hesitate to cooperate. "As ye know, the welcome committee sold all the programs and such. Whoever was available would make the rounds tae the refreshment tent several times each day and collect from the vendors. Every couple hours, in fact. I did the collecting at the end o' the trials when Isla went missin'."

"So," I said to establish those who had authority to handle the cash. "You, Oliver, Andrea, and Isla. What about at past events?"

"Same procedure."

"Whoever was on the welcome committee?"

"The four o' us who were permanent members o' that

committee and had authorization tae collect. Yerself was-nae approved, as ye didnae come tae meetings, and Sean Stevens wasnae, either, since he only showed up tae help on the day of."

Lily was very straightforward with her answers. I wasn't getting any vibes that suggested she was hiding anything, or that my questions were getting too close to some hidden truth.

"And where did you put these funds after you collected them to safeguard for the rest of the event?"

"We handed them over tae Isla, except as I said this last time when I couldn't find her. She was in charge and she sure didn't let us forget it fer even a minute." Here Lily leaned in confidentially. "I dinnae like tae speak ill o' the dead, but we all were privy tae Harry's concerns, and if anybody was skimmin', it was Isla. If ye're looking fer her killer, ye'd best see aboot that."

If I wasn't learning anything else, I was learning this— Lily Young had it in for Isla. Even as an outsider, I'd sensed that from the minute those two went head-to-head. So it stood to reason that Lily would implicate Isla as the sticky-fingered bandit. She probably didn't realize how accurate her accusation was.

Right then, the inspector arrived.

"What took you so long?" I asked, rising and moving off to a short distance where the two of us could speak in private, but still keep an eye on Lily.

"Are ye scolding me?"

I guess I was. "I'm a little stressed is all," I told him. "It's not every day that I catch a criminal by myself."

"It's my auto that's the bother," he explained. "It's been

acting up and wouldn't start. I'll have tae call fer a tow. Noo, can ye explain a bit more o' this situation?"

"I could, but I'd prefer you get it from the horse's mouth."

With my prompting and Jamieson's prodding, we finally got Lily to admit that she had drugged Isla. "I didn't mean anythin' by it," she said. "I only wanted tae get rid o' her fer the afternoon and tae shut her trap fer a change."

"You planned it in advance."

"I guess it was on my mind fer a spell, gettin' her outta the way so I could take charge fer a bit. And after Senga threw away the sample, I came up with the idea, went back and got them. . . . I really disliked that woman!"

"Enough tae kill her, I expect," the inspector said.

But Lily wasn't taking the blame for Isla's death. She flat-out denied it, and as much as the inspector tried, he couldn't get her to confess to the murder.

Eventually, the inspector pulled me aside and said, "Good work, Constable Elliott. But at this point, I might have better results takin' her in tae the station fer further questioning. And with her statement regarding actions tae put Isla out o' commission, I'll be able tae hold her a spell. Noo all I need is a vehicle." He gave me a steady look. "Ye're back on the case, I'm suspecting."

"Yes."

"I thought as much."

"And if you need a ride, I'm sure Sean Stevens would be happy to chauffeur you around," I deadpanned.

"More o' that foolish talk and I'll have tae put ye on parking ticket duty."

"No you won't," I said in a tone the Scots would describe as cheeky. "You need me to help solve this case."

"Ye can wipe that smirk right off yer face," he said. "I've made arrangements with Sean tae use his car. Up until a moment ago it was unclear how he would get out and aboot. But now, he'll be the one riding with a partner, and can ye guess who that might be?"

My smile slid sideways.

CHAPTER 25

I stood on the cobblestone walkway watching the inspector drive off in Sean's red Renault with Lily Young beside him.

Sean Stevens slid into the passenger seat of my Peugeot. "Ye can do the driving, and I'll do the directing, Lesser Constable Elliott," Sean informed me as he closed the door.

I went around and got into the driver's seat. "Lesser?"

"We need tae make a distinguish between us, and since I have seniority, I thought Lesser would be appropriate until such a time as me own rank increases."

I considered the possibility of driving as close as possible to one of the many highland cliffs, reaching across Sean, opening his door, and shoving him out. But then Vicki would never speak to me again, and I valued her friendship. So that could only be a fantasy, one to escape into in trying times.

Like this one.

"We didn't find anything out o' the ordinary at Harry Taggart's office or his home or his automobile," Sean went on as he buckled up (the seat belt another complication in my fantasy to throw him out). "So fer now, we will assume that his story is true, and pursue the culprit who stole his kit. Where are we off tae?"

"The inspector just drove off in your car with Lily Young," I said, starting the engine, agitated at his cluelessness. "And we are supposed to follow."

"What are ye waiting fer, then?" Sean interrupted. "Snow on the mountain peaks?"

As I pulled away from the Kilt & Thistle my thoughts flitted back to the sheep dog trials on Saturday. We'd had amazingly sunny weather leading up to the event, and it had lasted right through Saturday. Several volunteers had been sunburnt as had many of the spectators. I'd learned that Lily got hers while staking out the harbor, waiting for a couple to return in hopes of confirming the identity of Oliver Wallace's guest. Isla had also had a bad case of sunburn. So had Oliver.

What if Oliver and Isla really *had* been out in the Moray Firth together? Not as lovers—I'd heard Isla snipping at Oliver too many times, showing her frustration with him for being late, or for disappearing when work was to be done, or . . . on and on. And he'd intentionally irritated her. I didn't believe for a moment that they were carrying on in a romantic relationship . . . but that didn't mean they weren't up to something else.

Did it even matter with the latest development? Lily Young had deliberately given Isla Lindsey a drug-laced cupcake, and she'd even admitted it. So it would have been easy for her to slip into the van and strangle the unconscious woman.

Case closed.

Or was it?

There was still the issue of stolen money. Lily hadn't shown any signs of stress when we discussed the money-collecting procedures during fund-raisers. She'd actually been forthcoming and helpful.

What about Oliver? He was one of the trusted inner circle, on the short list of those approved to collect cash at all the events. He might not be a killer, but he could be a crook. What if *he'd* been Isla's partner? That is, if she even had one. This was purely speculation on my part.

All kinds of scenarios were going through my mind as we left the center of the village behind us. I glanced at the harbor as we came directly parallel to the docks, thinking of Oliver's boat and Lily's suspicions. Maybe it would be worthwhile to walk around, see things from her point of view.

I slowed down, then made a snap decision and pulled over. "We need to make a short stop here," I told Sean.

"As ye stated, the inspector specifically ordered us tae follow him." He scanned the road ahead. I followed his eyes. The Renault wasn't in sight. "And ye didn't even try tae keep up. He's going tae be unhappy with us as it 'tis, without makin' things worse fer us. Ye can take a stroll afterwards on yer own time."

I climbed out.

"We haff tae follow orders!" Sean was becoming agitated. "And wha' do ye want at the harbor anyhoo?"

"Uh . . . I'm meeting Leith Cameron," I said. "But it will only take a few minutes."

"Can't the lovey-dovey wait?" Sean was out of the car, coming around, not at all happy with me.

"You go on," I told him, wondering how I'd get back. I supposed I could call Vicki for a ride. Or perhaps I'd really run into Leith. "Why don't you go on ahead and I'll catch up later?"

"This is not the way o' things."

Ah, but I had an ace up my sleeve. "Lily Young is the one who drugged Isla. She's admitted it."

That did it. Sean leapt in and planted himself behind the wheel before I finished speaking. "Why dinnae ye say so earlier? We've closed the case then!" he said, excited now.

"Hurry. You don't want to miss her confession."

Sean actually managed to squeal the tires on the old Peugeot as he took off after the inspector, trailing in his dust as usual. I watched him disappear from sight then turned toward the dock.

Off to my left, the beach was empty except for a few late-season strollers. Even though the sun beat down brightly and a warm breeze lifted a few strands of my hair, the waters of the North Sea had started to cool off in anticipation of the coming winter. No one was swimming.

Next to the beach, a row of canoes for hire had been pulled up onto the sandy shore and were being loaded onto the bed of a pickup truck, presumably on the way to storage until spring. Two sandpipers waded nearby.

As I walked onto the main wooden dock, swallows with

forked tails and pointed wings swooped gracefully overhead. A black-headed gull stood on one of the mooring
pilings.

Sailboat riggings sang on the breeze. These boats, too,
would soon be lifted onto cradles and stowed safely before
temperatures plummeted.

I walked the length of the main pier, looking for Oliver's boat. But all of these were the commercial fishing
boats and charters. *Bragging Rights* was in its slip, but its
owner was nowhere in sight. Today, Leith must be on the
River Spey, fly-fishing with customers who often hired
him to help them locate river salmon. It was a beautiful
afternoon for wading upstream.

I couldn't remember the name of Oliver's boat, but I felt
confident that I would recognize the name once I saw it.

Next, I walked along the dock to the left, closest to the
beach where the smaller craft were tucked into slips.
Slowly, enjoying the weather and the colorful harbor, I
checked the names of the boats. While many of them were
clever wordplays, and others were in Scottish Gaelic that I
couldn't translate, none rang a bell for me.

There was only one pier left. Oliver's boat had to be
docked there. I'd almost walked the entire length, admiring
the size of the cruisers, when a familiar boat name jumped
out at me. *Slip Away.* That was it!

Oliver's "wee" boat was hardly what I'd consider small,
but it sure was bonny. It was a luxury cruiser with multiple
levels including an upper sundeck. Stepping over thick
ropes securing his pleasure boat to the slip, I walked along
the planks beside it, calling out to Oliver. I noticed

immediately that his motor craft wasn't locked up. In fact, it appeared that someone had been here recently. So when he didn't answer, I stepped on board.

A toolbox was open in the cockpit and the hatch leading below deck was open. I stopped at the steps and called down to Oliver, again without a response.

I slowly descended to find a galley, a bedroom to rival any fine hotel's luxury suite, and a bathroom with a full shower. The closet contained a rack of menswear. As I poked around, I thought about possible hiding places for large sums of cash. There were all kinds of nooks and crannies. Everywhere I turned, I encountered more hidden storage spaces. While I listened for signs of Oliver's return, I couldn't resist opening this and that, reasoning that this might be my only chance. If I had stashed cash on a boat like this, where would it be?

That was a perplexing question. One that I decided I better save for another day. All signs pointed to someone's imminent return, and that someone would be Oliver and he shouldn't find me down here snooping, especially if he was up to something.

The question was, what?

Lily had practically confessed to Isla's murder. Or had she?

Isla had been killed in Oliver's van. He had been seen with Harry right after he picked up his yarn kit. *And* he'd had access to collected charity funds.

I couldn't shake the feeling that Oliver had secrets. They might not involve murder, but embezzlement was a serious crime. I hadn't intended to go this far alone. My quickly hatched plan had been to wander around by the pier and try to put a few puzzle pieces together. The man could be dangerous. Instinct kicked in. I needed to get out of here.

As I hurried toward the stairs leading to the deck, I gave the rooms one last scan. I'd discovered plenty of equipment that was completely unfamiliar to me. But no safe for valuables. And no money.

Once above, I turned my gaze briefly to the open sea, pausing to admire the view instead of minding the dock. Too late, I heard footsteps behind me. Turning quickly, I saw Oliver. He was on board, and he had his hands filled with ropes, the same ones I'd noticed earlier that had been holding his cruiser securely in its slip.

"Eden Elliott," he said, his eyes flashing with smoldering anger as he threw the lines in a pile. "So nice tae have you aboard. I'm guessing ye haven't seen one o' our sunsets from the sea yet. Ye're long overdue fer a boat ride."

The implication wasn't subtle. This would be my one and only.

I moved toward the pier, but he blocked my path. "Ye need tae go below until we're safely out o' the harbor," he said.

I frantically looked for assistance but there wasn't anybody in the immediate vicinity. All the tourists were gone. Summer was over. It was a workday. There were all kinds of reasons why no one was around. Regardless, I opened my mouth to belt out a cry for help.

Before I knew what was happening, Oliver had shoved me toward the stairs. I tried to catch my balance, but he picked me up, took a few steps to the hatch, and attempted to throw me down. I reached out, grabbing and securing a hold just in time to save myself from a fall, and stumbled down, managing to make it below without a crippling injury. Within the space of a few seconds, I was locked below.

I heard the engine start up.

A few minutes later, we were moving.

CHAPTER 26

The first thing I did was dig out my cell phone to call the inspector. No signal. The boat had picked up speed, and thanks to a zillion-horsepower engine, I'd already lost cell coverage.

The next thing I did was look for a weapon. My pepper spray! I'd forgotten about it. It was my go-to protection but I wanted a backup in case the spray failed me.

There were knives in the galley kitchen. My first impulse was to choose the biggest and sharpest, but stealth might be more important to my future than showmanship, so I tucked a medium-size knife inside my waistband, hoping the blade was sharp enough to do damage. I tried not to imagine having to use it, or whether I could if the time came.

Next, I rummaged around searching for life jackets and finally found them in a berth. I put one on. It had a whistle dangling from a cord that would come in handy, if I managed to keep the vest on when I went overboard.

I was pretty sure I was going to end up in the water. And I really hoped that this life preserver lived up to its name. *And* that the sea was teeming with available boaters just waiting to rescue a damsel in distress.

Unless . . .

Unless, Oliver intended to strangle me and then dump my body.

Next my rogue mind stopped and dwelled on a shark attack. Dead or alive, the thought of being eaten scared me silly.

I considered the likelihood of a timely rescue. Since I'd lied to Sean about meeting Leith, I couldn't expect any help there.

So I had my pepper spray, a life preserver, and a knife tucked into the band of my underwear. What else could a girl possibly wish for?

To wake up from this nightmare, for starters.

Now that I was as prepared as I could be, I staved off paralyzing fear by considering Oliver and the reason I was about to feed the fishes. Of course it involved Isla Lindsey— either her murder, the missing money, or both. Even in death the woman was causing trouble for those of us left behind. If there was another life after this one, I was going to find her and get my payback.

Eventually the engine died. Or idled. Or something. Whatever the case, it wasn't as loud as before, so I assumed we'd reached our final destination. I thought I might be sick. My stomach was roiling, and I was pretty sure it wasn't due to seasickness. I talked myself out of crumpling into a helpless mess, focusing on survival instead.

The hatch above me opened up, and my heart flew into

my throat. Blue sky shone through, until it was blocked by Oliver coming into view. Would he come down to finish me off? I white-knuckled the pepper spray canister. The knife tucked away gave me a small bit of reassurance.

"Up with ye, nice and easy," he said, giving me a few moments of reprieve.

A new dilemma arose. Do as ordered? Or take my chances here below? Make him come and get me? I still had choices, as few as they were.

"I don't think so," I told him.

He crouched and peered down, and I noticed that he wore a life vest, too. He was framed in the hatchway, though too far away for me to hit him with the pepper spray. "Be a lamb," he practically cooed.

As in lamb to the slaughter? I didn't think so.

"I'll consider coming up," I bargained, stalling for time, "if you tell me why I'm down here in the first place."

"Because," he answered easily, "I dinnae invite ye on board."

True enough, but not the real reason.

"Were you having an affair with Isla Lindsey?" I demanded.

"What?" Oliver began to laugh. "With that stupid biddy? That cow Lily Young saw us going out together on this fine cruiser and jumped tae the wrong conclusion. That one's fond o' me, ye know."

So Lily hadn't been mistaken about one thing—she'd seen them together on this boat.

"You stole money from the hospice," I guessed next. I took a step closer to the hatchway, nervously calculating my chances with the pepper spray.

He watched me with intensity and distrust as he said, "It wasn't me. Isla was the thief. I caught her back in the spring, writing checks tae herself, so I watched and found out she was skimming cash from the events as well."

"Why would she do that? She didn't have a financial problem, did she?"

"Isla was a nasty woman, thinkin' she was entitled, sayin' she was underpaid fer the responsibility she undertook. She did it tae get even."

"What about her husband? Did he know?"

"Bryan? There's a bloke with his head in the sand. Besides, the money was safely stowed away where his prying eyes couldn't find it."

Another few steps, while I tried to remember how far the pepper spray would shoot. When I'd used it on Kirstine, I hadn't had to worry about distance. She was right in my face at the time.

"You knew, yet you didn't turn her in. You wanted a cut." I tried to sound impressed, hoping to feed his ego and keep him talking.

"She wasn't a bit happy aboot that, and tried tae get out o' it, but I held her feet tae the fire." Oliver smirked and went on, "Last week she overheard her boss on the phone, talking with an auditor. That put a bit of fear intae her. By Saturday morning she was sayin' if they caught her she wasn't going down alone. Her mistake. 'Meet me at two o'clock,' she said, like she was the big boss. 'I'm not in this alone, and I'll say as much. We have tae figure this out together.'" Oliver shook his head as if in disbelief. "She was nervy, all right. I can say that much fer her."

My delusional mind wanted to believe that I was safer

if I didn't mention the murder. The rational side knew it was way too late to walk away alive. I didn't have anything to lose that Oliver didn't plan on taking away regardless.

"So you stole Harry's yarn kit and used the yarn to strangle her," I finally blurted out. "What about Lily's part? What about the cupcake? Were you two in it together?"

Oliver looked confused. "What cupcake? Ye're blathering, woman."

So Lily had acted on her own. I took another step closer. "The one that contained sleeping pills. The one Isla ate."

Oliver, still wary, looked thoughtful then enlightened. "So that's why she was such a wet rag, just lying aboot when I got in the van tae take care o' that business."

I was close enough, but I was shaking and not sure I could aim properly. But I had to. And I also had to make sure I didn't get so near that he could grab me.

"So wha' about coming up, love?" he asked, his voice silky.

"I don't think so."

His face reddened then. "Ye're about tae go fer a swim whether ye like it or not."

I chose that moment to lunge forward, whipping my hand out, nearly hitting the button on the spray can. But Oliver had anticipated some kind of action on my part and he ducked out of sight.

Without considering the consequences of my actions, I hurried up the steps onto the deck. He was forward of the cockpit now. I swung the spray can toward him but hesitated. Not only was he too far away, the blowback from the spray might affect me as much or worse.

Oliver seemed to be enjoying himself. "Ye are feisty,"

he said, laughing, "but that silly little can o' spray won't save ye."

I backed up closer to the wheel, not taking my eyes from Oliver. Behind him, the shoreline was barely visible in the distance.

I wedged in behind the steering wheel, realizing with something close to despair that I didn't know how to operate a boat. But I had to try. I glanced down at the instruments and gadgets, and my spirit dove into that deep blue sea I'd been avoiding. I could hardly manage a manual car—how was I going to hold off Oliver *and* learn to drive his boat at the same time?

While I worried, he stayed where he was, as alert as a wolf about to attack a helpless sheep.

"Stay where you are!" I shouted, holding the canister at the ready.

"And how long do ye expect this little standoff tae last?" he asked.

That was a good question. Eventually Oliver would rush me. I might have time to use my spray, but that might only slow him down. He had a lot of weight on me. And his arms under the sport shirt he wore were buff. I hadn't noticed that before. He'd overpower me, and nobody would ever find my body.

I chanced another glance down at the instruments, at the key dangling in the ignition, and gave my chances of pulling this off a moment of discouraging consideration. The odds were against me.

Suddenly I heard static and spotted a marine radio lying right in front of me. Voices over the waves, someone talking about docking at the harbor. I'd seen marine radios before, but I'd never used one. Could I figure out how to operate it?

When I picked it up, Oliver made his move. He came in low, guarding his head like a bull charging. He was too fast, too close to risk taking me down with the spray.

I didn't know what to do.

So, radio in hand, I jumped overboard.

I had everything I needed—a radio to call for help, a life jacket to keep me afloat, and most dear to me, my life. I braced myself. The water was colder than I had imagined it could be.

I didn't even know if the radio was waterproof. But it had to be, right? Sure enough, as the life jacket deflected the force of my landing, the radio crackled to life. I fiddled with the dials, one eye on Oliver's position. Even if this were the States, I wouldn't know what channel to use.

I kicked off my shoes as the boat roared to life.

Swimming came naturally to me. I'd been on a competitive team in high school, had worked as a lifeguard in the summers, and generally swam like a fish. Although I'd never been chased by a mega-horsepower cruiser before. Not to mention that the vest would slow me down significantly. I wanted to keep it as a flotation device, but it was a serious handicap, one I couldn't afford.

I struggled out of the vest, reluctantly let go of it, and began swimming for the distant speck of a shoreline. I didn't get far before Oliver brought the boat around. He headed directly for me.

As the boat approached, I took a deep breath of precious

air and dove under. The underbelly of the cruiser flew past, shockingly near. I resurfaced and treaded water while fumbling with the radio.

Oliver was coming around again. I pressed the buttons and started calling into it for help. I didn't know if anyone could hear me, but I kept going, giving my name, and Oliver's name, shouting into it that I was overboard a good distance from Glenkillen—and then switched to straight out yelling into it, "Help! Help! Oliver Wallace is trying to kill me!"

The boat rushed at me again, and again I prepared to dive. But I could feel myself tiring. I now regretted ditching the life vest, but I hadn't had a choice.

I dove again, staying under until my lungs were about to burst, watching *Slip Away* finish another pass. Then I popped up and continued swimming toward shore. To my increasing horror, it wasn't any closer.

I readied to take another dive on the next run, refusing to acknowledge my weary limbs. But instead of throttling up, Oliver cut the power and came up slowly drifting alongside me. The boat bobbed on the waves.

"I can do this all day," I told him, even though we both knew it was a lie. "I used the radio to call in. Someone will be looking for me soon. They know you're trying to kill me."

I treaded water, holding the radio up where Oliver had a good view of it, while really hoping I wasn't bluffing. But if anyone had heard, how long would it take them to find me?

Oliver didn't know what to do. I could tell he was torn. Should he do me in? Or not? Had my distress call gone through? Or hadn't it? Would I be able to continue to evade him? A dilemma.

"Come around the back," he said, evil lurking in his eyes. "Come on, then. I'll help ye back on board and we can talk this out."

I paddled around to the back of the boat where there was a ladder to make climbing on board easier. He was there to meet me, extending an arm, offering a hand. I gave him my right hand and felt the strength contained in his grasp as he pulled and my body popped out of the chilly sea.

And as I swung up, I rounded with as much force as I could, swinging my dominant left hand. And I stabbed him directly in the thigh.

He stumbled back, his face registering shock as I pulled the knife clear, feeling it rip through his flesh. Attacking him like that was one of the most difficult things I'd ever done.

My original idea had been to target his torso, but the life jacket he wore was an obstacle, and I couldn't risk failing on my first attempt. It would have been my last.

And if it was to be my life or Oliver's, I planned to fight until the bitter end.

He fell then, grabbing his thigh, tucking it against his body and screaming. I scrambled on board and ran past his prone body to take control of the steering wheel. The engine was idling and miracle of miracles, I figured out how to get it into forward gear. I kept one eye on Oliver only a few yards away and gave a firm command to stay where he was if he didn't want more of the same.

With the knife in my hand still dripping with his blood, I turned toward shore.

Where I ended up ramming right into the end of one of the piers.

That drew plenty of attention. Several experienced boaters came hurrying down what was left of the dock.

Soon after, thankfully, I was relieved of my post at the helm.

CHAPTER 27

A week later, Sean's going-away party was held at the Kilt & Thistle. The pub was full of all the local residents who wanted to wish him good luck at police college. Vicki stood at his side as he greeted and preened. She glowed with good health and spirits. My friend was going to miss Sean, but she'd be busy with her Merry Mitten project, and that would help the time pass until he returned.

All of us were relieved when Isla Lindsey's murder investigation had been wrapped up before Sean's departure, as he'd threatened to postpone his training if the case was still ongoing when he was due to leave.

Once the inspector had located and recovered close to one hundred twenty thousand pounds locked up in an access panel under *Slip Away*'s pilot berth, Oliver Wallace sang like a canary. The only place Oliver would slip away to at this point was lockup. Not only did he face murder charges for the death of Isla, but attempted murder as well for what he'd tried to do to me. I was looking forward to testifying on my behalf.

Oliver's past came out. He'd been the black sheep of his family, squandering his own money in unwise, ill-timed investments before marrying into wealth. When the marriage was over, Oliver had had a comfortable bank account once more but again managed to lose his proverbial shirt (which would have included his beloved cruiser) to the bank. Then the opportunity to manipulate Isla presented itself, and he took full advantage of her. Some of the funds stolen from the hospice had been used to stave off creditors, but everyone had been grateful for the return of most of it. Unfortunately, it was at the expense of Isla Lindsey's life.

Lily Young had her own legal problems. She'd been charged with endangerment and obstruction for her part. "And tae think I was protecting him from suspicion and never once thought he had a hand in the poor woman's death!" Lily had told us under further questioning. "All I got out o' it was a bad sunburn."

So she was in big trouble, all because of a man, and one who wasn't worth a second glance, let alone losing her freedom over. Some of us have to learn everything the hard way.

The pub continued to fill up with well-wishers. Charlotte Penn arrived, as did Senga Hill, whose good name had been restored along with a position at the hospice managing the accounts. Harry Taggart came soon after, and I had no qualms about asking him for help.

"I'll be happy tae teach ye tae knit," he told me when I explained my predicament. "An' I'm considerin' coming out in public with my own knitting projects. Vicki tells me the women will be all over me. I hadnae considered *that* before!"

Bryan Lindsey and his sister Andrea made an appearance. They didn't stay long, but took time to thank each of us for our role in catching Isla's killer. Word had gotten out about Isla's part in embezzling from the hospice. Bryan and Andrea were embarrassed and ashamed of her actions. The locals did their best to put them at ease, but it would take time. It even came out that the brother and sister had secretly suspected each other, and both were relieved when the real culprit was in custody.

Even Kirstine and John Derry came to see Sean off. Vicki hadn't expected them. Neither had I. It was an encouraging show of support.

"And what would we do without Bill Morris sitting in his regular spot?" Vicki said to me. "It wouldn't feel right in the pub without him."

I glanced over. Bill was three sheets to the wind, as usual.

Vicki frowned then announced, "Almost everyone who counts is here. But I thought the inspector would come round. He must have been held up." Her face lit up. "Ah, there's our Leith."

Following her line of sight, I saw Leith approaching. He shook Sean's hand, wished him well, greeted Vicki, then turned to me.

"The pier will be salvageable," Leith told me, grinning. "We worked on it today. Thank ye kindly fer avoiding my boat."

"You're welcome." I returned his grin.

"Ye're about as good with a boat as ye are with a car."

"For your information, I haven't totaled any cars," I said, thinking, *Not yet, anyway*.

Leith still had a big smile, enjoying himself. Self-assured as always. "Ye sure do have a temper. Wallace found that out quick enough."

"Only when my life is threatened."

"And ye're resourceful."

"Thank you."

"I was thinkin' tomorrow would be a fine day fer another boat ride. I know ye just had a scare on the water, but ye need tae get back out there."

"Like falling off a horse? You have to get right back on?" What was it about this Scotsman that always put a smile on my face?

"Aye," he replied. "Get right back on."

"I'd like that," I told him.

"Ye can be my first mate," he went on.

We both laughed at that. I was definitely *not* crew material. Kelly would be more helpful than I could possibly be.

Shortly before the festivities began, I'd tucked away in the back of the pub with my laptop and responded to several e-mails that had arrived in my in-box. Ami and I had been in constant contact recently as I related the finer details of the murder investigation, and the final scene between Oliver and myself on the high seas.

That had been the cause for plenty of concern from my friend back in Chicago. But I had survived unscathed, and after enough reassurance, Ami had settled down.

"I'm as technology challenged as ever," I'd written at the end of my narration. "The radio S.O.S. never went through, so it was a good thing I didn't rely on outside help arriving in time."

"Scottish intrigue!" she wrote back. "What a story!! Speaking of stories, do you think you will be able to finish a rough draft of *Hooked on You* by the end of December? Once you get back to Chicago, I'd be happy to go over it with you. Is that doable, what with all the extracurricular activities you've taken on?"

Yes, I could easily whip up a first draft by the end of the year. I had almost three months to work on it. I intended to stay focused, work hard, and still find time to have a little fun.

Because my real life in the Highlands would be over before I knew it.

And I wasn't looking forward to that.

As I stood beside Vicki, I glanced around the room, appreciating the new friends I'd acquired in my time in the Scottish Highlands. I wouldn't trade this experience for anything. And I had Ami Pederson to thank for these past months. I owed her a boatload of gratitude.

Almost at the very end when things were wrapping up, after Leith and most of the others had gone, the inspector finally made an appearance.

"Work got me tangled up," he told me, after first wishing his special constable the best of luck. "But I'm glad tae find ye still here. I still have visions o' what might have happened tae ye if ye hadn't kept yer wits about ye."

"Slamming into the dock was pretty witless," I told him.

"Ye handled yerself fine, in my opinion."

"Thanks." That was high praise coming from the inspector. "The only thing I'm still struggling with in this whole unpleasant business is Isla's reason for stealing. It was so senseless."

"She must o' started small, then got bólder, thinkin' she couldn't be caught, all the while justifyin' her actions by tellin' herself that her service was worth the extra. I've seen it before in my line o' work."

I nodded, realizing how much I had to learn about people and their motives.

"On a pleasanter note," he said next, "I thought ye might like tae see some o' the Highland sights while the weather still permits it. The leaves turning on the trees will make fer a pretty drive. How would ye like tae take a trip over to Loch Ness? We might spot Nessie before she goes deep intae her winter place."

"So, it's a she?"

"Aye. A male wouldn't be nearly as wily an' mysterious." His intelligent eyes sparkled.

"I'd like that," I told him.

What in the world was I getting myself into in the Scottish Highlands?

I wasn't sure, but I liked it.

WELL-CRAFTED MYSTERIES FROM BERKLEY PRIME CRIME

- **Earlene Fowler** Don't miss these Agatha Award–winning quilting mysteries featuring Benni Harper.

- **Monica Ferris** These *USA Today* bestselling Needle-craft Mysteries include free knitting patterns.

- **Laura Childs** Her Scrapbooking Mysteries offer tips to satisfy the most die-hard crafters.

- **Maggie Sefton** These popular Knitting Mysteries come with knitting patterns and recipes.

- **Lucy Lawrence** These brilliant Decoupage Mysteries involve cutouts, glue, and varnish.

- **Elizabeth Lynn Casey** The Southern Sewing Circle Mysteries are filled with friends, southern charm—and murder.